LACE 'EM UP
BY ELISE FABER

Newsletter sign-up

Dear Diane,

It's hard to believe you're gone. More than hard; it's devastating. Lars says time will ease the band of pressure that cuts across my chest when I think of you. But no amount of time will make me miss you any less. I suppose the passing years will only result in an acceptance of reality.

I lost my best friend.

Just the other day, I picked up the phone to tell you about the twins' mess at school. It involved crazy glue (stolen from the teacher's supply closet) and googly eyes! Needless to say, Jakob was NOT happy. He's been so serious and severe the last few years; it's a good thing he has the twins to make him crack a smile now and then.

Anyway, I picked up the phone to tell you, and then I remembered. Oh, the waves of anguish are unbearable and relentless whenever I remember. My therapist says that's normal. In fact, it was her idea that I write to you. She said it could be cathartic. Healing.

Little does she know we'd uncork a bottle of wine and spill our guts, no doubt dissolving in laughter, whenever one of us needed to heal a heartache. Your bad breakup with Joe. My sadness when Jakob divorced. Your mother's passing. Leif nearly being expelled from university. We've seen each other through all the ups and downs.

It's difficult for me to move forward and start a new chapter without you.

But I bought this diary. And now, I'm sitting here, at the kitchen table, writing to you.

The house is quiet. Lars left early for practice. And the kids... They're all grown up. After years of pinching their cheeks and reminding them that mother knows best, they're out into the world. Blazing trails and finding their footing.

That's another reason I can't accept you're gone. You, Diane, with your flashing blue eyes, loud, boisterous laughter, and penchant for mischief—how can you be gone? I contacted your niece and nephews after your funeral. They were kind and gracious. But they don't remember you the way I do. I'm not sure anyone does. And that sits heavy on my chest, keeping me up at night.

What's a life without love? Without friendship? Without family?

Lars and I are coming up on thirty-five years of marriage. I know how fortunate I am to have married the love of my life and then stayed married for thirty-five wonderful years. I'm blessed to have birthed six healthy, beautiful children who all pursued their passions and are making their way in the world.

And yet, I can't help but wonder—are they fulfilled?

None of them are close to family. None of them have

found or kept love. They're...adrift. Just like you were before I forced you to join my family. "An honorary Bang," you laughed. But I saw the happiness it brought you. It was the same happiness I felt.

King's in his thirties and hasn't had a serious relationship since college. Jakob is a single parent struggling with raising children on his own. Jensen and Annie are still thick as thieves but on opposite ends of the country. Leif avoids commitment like the plague. And Tanner's living his best life, partying like it's his job.

When will they settle down? Find the type of happiness I've known for over half my life? I don't mean to sound old-fashioned—although I can admit that I am in many ways, but I want more grandbabies. And to know that my children are fulfilled. Happy. In love.

I want them to find what Lars and I share. Love, respect, commitment. Trust.

I want them to have everything I wished for you, Diane. And perhaps the most challenging part of letting you go is knowing you didn't have the great big love you desired.

It's true what they say: life is too short.

Which is why I have an idea. A plan, really, although I haven't told Lars yet. I think the kids—all of them—need help. A mother's touch, so to speak, since I obviously know best. And, with Lars coaching the junior league, he's either at the rink or traveling with the team. Most of the time, I'm on my own. It's lonely without you to come by for a cup of tea or meet for lunch. Depressingly so.

My therapist thinks a change of scenery will help. She thinks I should shake up my routine.

And so... What if I visit them? The kids. I can help

them. Cook their favorite meals. Look after the boys so Jakob can go on a date or two. Give them the nudges they need or, in some cases, the well-placed shoves. It will be an adventure, Diane! For all of us.

I just need to run it by Lars, but...soon, I'll write to you from King's place in Oakland. Isn't that grand? I'll be living my best life in the sunshine well before the first snowstorm hits Minnesota. If you were here, I know that would delight you!

I miss you, my friend. I'll write more soon.
Love, Stella

This letter starts Mama Bang's matchmaking journey across the US and Canada. Lace 'em Up is book one in the Bang Brothers Hockey series and it follows King, the oldest brother, and his prickly princess of a heroine, Rory! While the Bang Brothers Hockey books interconnect, you can enjoy King and Rory's story as a standalone. Lace 'em Up also fits into the Eagles Hockey world and is book 2 in that series. Happy hot hockey reading! <3

ONE

Kingston

It's the flash of white on the side of the road that draws my focus.

That glimpse of brightness stands out from the black pavement, damp from the afternoon rain.

It contrasts with the green shooting off in every direction on either side of the winding road—the dry, brown rolling hills of summer transformed into something that's lush and beautiful and sandwiching me in peaceful oblivion.

Except for that bright white.

Trash maybe—bags or a mattress dumped by some asshole.

Or maybe an animal of some sort?

A dog or a horse or a cow?

It wouldn't be too much of a surprise, not amongst these small, local farms and isolated plots of land that aren't found in other parts of the Bay Area. Fences give way, barbed wire breaks, and...

The white object moves again.

Animals get out.

I slow down because, strictly speaking, I'm in violation of my contract by riding my bike. Taking it out like this—well within the speed limit, on a deserted road, the sun going down behind me and the wind in my hair, on my face—is barely cleared for *off*-season use.

In early November? When the season is just barely underway and an injury would be catastrophic for my game?

If anyone finds out, I'm dead.

It's just...

Too good of a day.

I need this—one last time—before I put my bike up until the following summer.

That white moves again, and I slow down further. No crashes. No injuries. Nothing to fuck up my life and career and future—

Except...slowing down means that I have plenty of time to see.

That the white isn't a plastic bag caught in a bush, waving in the winds.

And it's not a cow or a horse or a dog.

It's a person.

A *woman* in a huge, poofy white dress.

And a veil that glitters with crystals in the setting sun.

A woman with long blond curls hanging down her back—

A woman...

Whose face I recognize.

I hit the brakes hard—too fucking hard considering the slick road—and nearly skid out. It takes far too much effort to control my bike, to wrestle it back upright, to calmly stop and put the transmission into park when I manage to do so.

I flick down the kickstand, slide one foot off to rest onto

the pavement. Then I'm lifting my other leg over the seat, rounding my back tire, and hurrying over to the bride-to-be.

"Rory," I say, skidding to a stop and reaching for her. "Are you—?"

But I don't finish the question because the moment my palms touch her shoulders, she's flinching back...

And stumbling over the hem of her dress, falling backward into the little gully on the side of the road.

Water—from the same rain that left the pavement slick—splashes, soaking into the fabric of her dress, the long blond curls cascading along her spine, and up onto—

Her face.

"What. The. Fuck?" I snarl as red hazes across my vision.

Most of her face is done up in makeup—what my sister Annie would call The Works. Lashes and glittery eye shadow, her brows on fleek, pink shit on her cheeks, lips filled in with a bright red color that makes her mouth look all too kissable.

That's beautifully done.

Making Aurora somehow look even more gorgeous than she is normally—and, for the record, this woman could have her head in a goddamned paper sack and she would still be breathtaking.

But it's not her makeup that has rage snarling through my veins, tearing like lightning through my middle.

It's what's showing beneath the smudged edges of her foundation, what's being revealed ever more clearly as water from the puddle drips down her face.

A bright red mark on her jaw.

A fucking *handprint* on her throat—complete with the impression of four fingers on one side and a thumb on the other.

And a bruise forming across her fucking cheekbone.

I bend over—slow and steady so as not to scare her, but inexorably because I'm not going to stop moving, not going to leave her there, wet and cold and fucking terrified on the side of the road even if we don't get along, even if she despises me, even if every interaction ends in a fight.

I slip my arms beneath her back and scoop her up into my arms.

She cries out in pain.

"Sorry, princess," I murmur, shifting her even more carefully, holding her even closer as I scale the embankment and carry her over to my bike, settling her onto the seat.

Climbing on in front of her.

Bring her arms forward, wrapping them around my middle, holding them in place.

She's shaking, and I don't miss that tears are soaking into my back.

"Who?" I whisper before I start up the engine.

"Phillip."

I turn the key.

I'm going to fucking *kill* her fiancé.

No.

Her *ex*-fiancé.

TWO

Aurora

My throat hurts.

And my jaw.

And my cheek.

And my ribs.

And my...

Well, there's not much of me that doesn't hurt right now.

Ass and hip from falling.

My torso and ribs and neck and face from—

I shudder then gasp when the pain radiates through me—and through all of those still-forming bruises—as the memory of Phillip's rage-filled face bursts back into the forefront of my consciousness—

I'd seen him angry before.

I'd seen him angry many times over the years...that number growing increasingly more frequent over the last months.

As our wedding neared.

I'd thought it was the stress of the planning, the money, the seating charts and handmade favors and his mom wanting to make every decision.

But I hadn't seen anger like *that*.

Never like that.

Never paired with hands that hurt and a foot that kicked and words that sliced deeper than ever before—

"Easy," Kingston says, his arm tightening around mine, pressing it into his hard stomach as he slows at a signal and the wind whipping around us eases. I realize that I'm trembling. That I'm doing it so hard that likely the only reason I'm still on the seat of his motorcycle is because his big body is keeping me there.

"I-I-I'm o-o-okay," I say through teeth chattering so hard that I nearly bite off my tongue.

He doesn't call me on the obvious lie, just slowly starts forward again. "We're almost there."

I don't ask where *there* is.

I don't care, not when the hurts are growing and the helmet Kingston gently settled on my head is pressing in on my temples and making them ache. Not with the wind tangling the hair beneath it, ruining the perfect fall of curls for which I sat still for hours so the stylist could get them just right. Not with my makeup ruined and my dress stained and torn.

From the tears and the puddle and Phillip—

Enough.

I shudder again, but Kingston doesn't say anything this time, likely because I wouldn't be able to hear him over the road noise—the growling sound of the bike's engine, the wind whipping by us, the other cars, the tires finding purchase on the asphalt beneath us.

Then the cacophony is quieting again.

King turns a corner and drives along a long two-lane road that crawls up the side of a canyon—back and forth, back and forth—until we reach a round-a-bout at the precipice and take a right.

Thick redwoods and oak trees, large lots set back from the street.

Porches and circular driveways.

One that King pulls into, driving by the front of the house and around the corner toward a small garage that's separate from the main one.

A pause.

Then the door rumbles open.

And we're inside the small, enclosed space.

My heart hiccups, but I don't have time to panic because Kingston is shutting off the bike's engine, slowly climbing off, arm steadying me before he removes my helmet.

I wince even though he's careful, my hair catching in the buckle.

"Sorry," he murmurs as he extracts the helmet from my hair, his touch beyond gentle as he untangles a curl from the strap.

Despite all that gentle, it takes every bit of the strength I have left to hold back my grimace as that light touch sets my scalp on fire.

"Sorry," he says again, but then the helmet's free and he's setting it to the side before reaching for me again.

I flinch.

I can't help it.

"Your feet are bleeding, princess," he murmurs. "I can't let you walk inside like that."

I glance down, almost surprised to find that he's right, that I've lost the blue sparkly pumps somewhere—the *some-*

thing blue of my wedding outfit. My feet are scraped and cut and blood is dripping on the floor.

Another shudder that sends a bolt of pain through me.

"I'm going to carry you inside," King says as though talking to a wounded animal.

And I suppose I feel like I am one right now.

I'd fought for something, fought hard and to the brutal end...

Only to find out I'd never had it in the first place.

That it wasn't what I'd thought it was.

That I was right back to that same shit—an unwanted annoyance who's unlovable and—

"Okay?"

I blink, realize that King's still talking.

And pairing it with action.

I hold steady this time as he carefully reaches forward, wraps his arms around me, and lifts me effortlessly, as though I'm no heavier than a box of tissues. And then I'm up in his arms, cradled against his chest as he walks out of the garage. A pause and the door rumbles down behind us before he walks toward the other garage, punching in a code at a different door, sending it rolling up, moving inside as soon as it's cleared his six-foot-plus frame.

Dim light penetrates the windows on the far side of the space, a bulb in the opener overhead helps guide our way to the door leading into the house.

Ten long strides across.

One. Two steps up.

Another pause and press of the button to close the garage door behind us.

And yes, I know I'm fixating on the little details, the mundane shit, the step by step by *step* so I don't freak out—

Phillip.

The sound of his fist meeting my flesh.

I'd heard it before I felt it.

I shudder again, but I fight it, try to stop it in its tracks, and that's likely why it's so much worse, why the pain is a blazing wave that threatens to incinerate me.

I distantly feel that we're moving again, that lights are flicking on and we're climbing up a flight of stairs.

I should be more aware. Should climb them myself. Should tuck this away and move on.

But...I hurt.

Not just my body. But my mind and heart and soul.

They *hurt*.

"Breathe, princess," King murmurs, the bed depressing as he climbs on with me in his arms, holding me against his chest, one hand gently rubbing my back in slow, even circles. "Just breathe."

Which is when I realize I'm crying.

Deep shuddering sobs that make my ribs cry out in protest.

Messy tears that stream down my face, drip off my jaw.

But King doesn't hurry me, just keeps stroking my back, holding me close until the tears stop, until exhaustion saps my mind. I want to give in to the fatigue, want to slide into sleep and pretend this didn't happen.

But...

"I should go," I whisper.

His big body turns into a statue beneath me, arms tightening around me, though not enough to hurt. "What the fuck?"

I push against his chest. "I should go."

"You're not going anywhere," he mutters. "You're fucking bleeding and shivering and covered in bruises. You're not going *anywhere.*"

"I'm fine," I snap, shoving at his chest.

Unfortunately, as is often the case with one Kingston Bang, my annoyance with this big, stubborn man has me forgetting myself.

I forget that my ribs hate life right now as I push against him hard.

He doesn't move.

Not one goddamned inch.

But *I* do as pain radiates up my arms, my side and—

"What the fuck?" he mutters, sitting up from the headboard in a rush, capturing me carefully, rolling me off him—just as carefully. And then he's sliding a hand behind me, unzipping my dress in a motion that's too fucking smooth and speaks of too many women, all of whom I *shouldn't* be jealous of, considering I'd been planning on getting married to another man this evening (but women who I'm jealous of for some dumbass reason anyway).

King peels open my dress, draws it down my arms.

Off my chest.

I gasp, but he's not looking at my breasts barely contained in a lace bra.

He's stopped with the taffeta and chiffon with embroidered flowers bunched around my waist.

And then his eyes jerk back to mine, deep blue pools blazing with fire.

"I'm going to fucking kill him."

THREE

Kingston

There are fucking bootprints on her ribs.

Boot. Prints.

Fucking *plural*.

The abrasion on her cheek is infuriating. The bruise on her jaw rage-spiraling.

The goddamned imprint of a man's hand on her throat had my control splintering to mere threads when I first saw her on the side of the road.

But...this?

I carefully climb off the bed, back away from her. Putting some distance between us because fury is coursing through my veins, splintering through my nerves. I whirl around and slam my fist into the wall, denting the Sheetrock and sending up a little puff of dust.

Pain bursts up my arm, but it's not enough to cool my anger.

Not enough to make up for the pain this woman went through.

I rear back, start to allow it to fly forward again, wanting the hurt, wanting—

"No," she says, snagging my wrist, halting me. "Don't," she whispers.

I could break her hold in a second.

But...I don't.

Not when there are bruises on her body and tear tracks on her cheeks and she's holding her dress up around her middle.

She's fucking beautiful.

And broken.

I exhale quietly, temper my anger, then gently order, "Back in bed."

She holds my gaze, eyes firm. "No more punching things," she whispers. A breath. "You need your hands to play hockey."

This is not a lie.

So, I nod—letting her know I hear her—before I turn her back toward my bed, guide her to sit down on the side of it. "Off those feet," I order. "I'll get you some dry clothes to change into."

Her chin juts down. "Thanks."

But she sounds like she's cutting glass, and though it probably shouldn't—considering the circumstances—it makes me smile.

This is the Rory I know.

The one who calls me on my shit and is prickly when I'm nearby and...frankly, it's probably the only thing that can settle me at this moment.

Rory's nice...to everyone but me.

Rory loves animals. Rory loves her friends. Rory sees

right through the smiling, joking, casual demeanor I put up between me and the rest of the world.

Which means it's likely she sees the man I am deep inside.

(A scary proposition).

But also...no wonder she's prickly.

Because that shit *is* scary.

It's much easier to be King Bang—the bachelor hockey player who goes through women like pairs of socks, to be the King of *Banging*.

Once upon a time, I tried to be something different.

Something *more*.

And that shit...

Well, it made me realize that I'll only ever be King Bang, so I might as well wear the mantle, carry the scepter, and do it with aplomb.

Something that rubs this woman the wrong way.

Probably because she's as real as they come, and I always know where I stand with her. No patience for false masks and bullshits.

So...no patience for me.

Which is fine.

I have no interest in a woman like her.

A fucking lie—even though I cling to it like it's gospel.

Mostly because I *can't* have interest in a woman like her —not just a woman who's—who *was*—in a relationship...

But a woman a man keeps forever.

Inhaling, I move to my closet, yank a tee and pair of sweats out of the drawers, and bring them back to her. "Careful now," I murmur, helping her shift her dress the rest of the way off, taking it from her and leaving the clothes beside her. "You need help getting those on?"

Please say no.

Because this woman may not like me, but...she's fucking beautiful, and the lingerie she's got on should be a fucking sin.

"No," she snaps. "I'm not a fucking invalid."

"No, Mrs. Pricklestein," I mutter. "You're not an invalid. You're just bruised to hell and back."

"What did you call me?" she snaps.

Snaps.

Something else she only does with me.

She puts herself out there to protect others, *has* done it over and over again, for both human and not.

Looking out for her best friend, Chrissy, when things got dicey with my teammate, Rome, and the relationship they were building.

Watching out for animals of all shapes and sizes—most recently in the form of a litter of corgi puppies and other dogs and cats she helped rescue from a hoarder house. I've watched her carry a spider outside and volunteer for hours at Chrissy's rescue, helping with the other woman's spay and release program. Hell, I've heard Chrissy go on about all the time Rory puts in with her *own* pet adoption group.

I've watched Rory when I was supposed to be focusing on hockey as she helped a crying and lost kiddo at the rink.

I've seen her lead a group of giggling and tipsy ladies from a bachelorette party at the winery when the normal—and extremely pregnant—tour guide was feeling light-headed and I was...

Picking up wine.

And not drawn to Oak Ridge Vineyards because I know this woman has an office there.

More lies.

And—

"Kingston!"

More snapping, but luckily, this time, it snaps me out of my own head. "What?" I mutter.

"What the hell did you just call me?"

"Mrs. Pricklestein," I tell her, snagging the T-shirt and pulling it over her head because I can't stand there, seeing her in that white lace stretched taut over her breasts, the hints of hard, pink nipples beneath, I can't stand there while catching a glimpse of a plump pussy between her bare thighs and not do something stupid. "Though, I guess it should be Miss Pricklestein since you're not married—"

I stop, clamp my teeth together so quickly that pain radiates along my jaw.

Stupid.

Fucking *stupid*.

She's sitting here bruised and battered, her dress a crumpled mess next to her, and I'm reminding her that her wedding hadn't happened.

Because her fiancé beat the shit out of her.

"Prickle Princess," I blurt as a wave of sadness crosses her face. Wanting her mad, wanting her to feel anything other than hurt, emotionally or physically, and if that takes her being pissed at me, then I'll gladly make her pissed at me.

Not that it takes much.

Because she clamps down onto the bait.

"What. The. *Hell*. Did—"

I touch her cheek—the unbruised one. "Prickle Princess," I say again. "Because you're a goddamned cactus, always throwing barbs my way." I lift my hand away from her skin, lest I continue to touch her. "Now sit the fuck down, watch some TV"—I shove the remote at her—"so I can call the police."

"What?" All of the pissiness leaves her face, panic taking its place. "You can't— I—"

"Breathe," I order. "I *can* call the police, and I'm going to," I tell her softly. "But I'm going to call Chrissy first," I add as I see her alarm peak.

That settles her, eyes sliding closed, body relaxing marginally, enough for me to coax her back onto my pillows, those curls splaying on the navy case, making my dick twitch again.

Disgusting pig.

King Bang.

You're not a good man.

Right. I'm not.

I exhale long and slow and silent—

Then I tug the blanket up from the foot of the bed, carefully covering her.

And then I'm moving out of the room, the tightness between my shoulders easing as I hear the TV turn on, the sound of the streaming program load up. A glance back tells me that she's not really watching it.

But that's fine.

She's not panicking.

She's not crying.

She's safe and staring off into space, and...

Well, I'm going to find a way to fix this.

And I have the feeling it's going to involve murder.

FOUR

Rory

"He's dead," Jean-Michel says, hovering near the bed, face a mask of fury.

There's something extremely *not* fun about having your boss at your bedside while you convalesce, but it bypasses uncomfortable and turns into worry when your boss is a man like Jean-Michel Dubois.

Jean-Michel is the owner of the NHL team that Kingston and Rome—standing behind him, both nodding their agreement, their expressions filled with rage that sends ice collecting on my vertebrae—play for, along with the winery that stretches over the hills in the distance that I work at.

Jean-Michel is smart and ruthless and powerful—an actual billionaire—and...he has a protective streak a mile wide.

Something that's going around this room in spades, considering that Chrissy looks ready to go to battle on my behalf, and the pair of hockey players next to her are prepared to put their fighting skills to work. Even Zeus—the corgi pup that King adopted a few weeks back—appears ready to take up a tiny sword and join in.

The only one who's calm is the doctor that Jean-Michel called in.

She carefully shooed everyone out while she took photographs of my injuries and then *doctored* my feet which, unfortunately, fared the worst of all my injuries, my heels long gone in my sprint from the winery. The soles are cut— quite deeply in places—and filled with thorns and dirt and rocks. I hadn't even felt them, not after...

Be brave and kind.

I exhale carefully, my father's voice in my head.

Kind isn't super applicable right now—aside from being nice to the people in front of me (and perhaps trying not to let King push my buttons).

But brave is.

I'll be okay.

I've been through...

Enough to know that I'll get through this too.

Even if my freshly cleaned up and glued back together in a few places feet are starting to ache, the pain killer the doctor gave me wearing off...

So. Much. Fun.

I grind my teeth together, wince against the pain that shoots through my bruised jaw, hating that it causes all of the people in the room to look newly ready to commit murder.

Though, still not Dr. Halston.

She just lightly touches my shoulder and places a basket of items on the nightstand. "Put this"—she holds up a glass container, unscrews the top and shows me the same balm she smeared over the bruises on my face and throat and ribs—"on once more tonight and then twice a day until you feel better. There should be plenty of this"—she holds up a couple of rolls of the wrap she used to bind my torso so I can breathe with only a minimal amount of pain—"for you to rewrap each time, but if you run out, just let Mr. Dubois know and I'll drop some by." She holds up a bottle. "Antibiotics. Finish the full course." Another. "For your pain. Don't be a hero," she murmurs, probably seeing my face.

And my intention to skip the heavy narcotics and use something less scary than a substance that'll land me on *Criminal Minds*.

King takes a step forward. "I'll make sure she takes it."

I narrow my eyes at him.

She gives me a knowing look then pushes upright. "My card is in there as well. Call me if you need anything, or if you feel worse."

"Thank you," I murmur, and genuinely mean it. I can't imagine having to go to the hospital, having to deal with cold, antiseptic walls and a ton of strangers and—

Well, this is better.

"I'll check in with you in a couple of days." A nod toward my feet. "Stay off those for at least the next twenty-four hours."

"My dogs," I whisper. I made arrangements with my network of fosters for the wedding, for our honeymoon, arrangements that I'll keep. But I'll need to check on them, make sure they're safe, that Phillip didn't—

"I've got it."

My head whips toward King. He can't even begin to know how to do that, but one look at the determined expression on his face means I don't bother arguing.

I'll figure it out.

Okay.

More likely, he and Chrissy and Rome will figure it out in spite of what I try to do.

I bite back a sigh. "I'll need to get my stuff out of the house too."

"I'll take care of that too," King says softly.

Dangerously.

Stubbornly.

A tone that earns a nod of approval from Dr. Halston as she moves toward Jean-Michel. "It sounds like you all have everything under control," she says. "Let me know if you need me to make a statement to the authorities."

He nods curtly. "I'll walk you out."

"Me too," Kingston mutters.

Rome nods and follows them, and, echoing in from the hall, I hear the good doctor say, "I'll forward you the pictures."

I shiver.

Not wanting to see those photographs.

Ever.

Not wanting to know what I look—or looked—like before Dr. Halston cleaned me up—like. Not wanting to have the image of what Phillip was capable of burned into my mind, not ever, but certainly not when I was bearing the marks of his rage on my skin.

Chrissy moves slowly to the bed, perching on the side like she's worried the wrong jostle of the mattress will send me into debilitating pain.

And I guess that's answer enough for how I look.

Because I sure as shit won't be able to forget Chrissy's expression or the careful way she adjusts her weight.

I force my lips up into a smile, know that it's fake as shit, but also that it's one of the few things that's going to hold me together right now. "Sorry to ruin the party."

Chrissy, a survivor through and through and my best friend, doesn't miss a beat, lips curving as she quips, "I hated the bridesmaid dress anyway."

I release a short laugh that has my ribs protesting. "You picked it out."

"I know." She winks and then any false lightness she'd been allowing me fades. Sighing, she takes my hand, linking our fingers together. "I'm so sorry, babe."

I sigh then wince. Because too deep, too fast, too much hurt. "I…" My eyes sting. "I don't understand. I don't know what happened, how he could do that to me."

A gentle squeeze. "Can I ask a question and have you give me an honest answer?"

That has me going still—or more still, anyway. But my insides don't settle—worry curls in my gut, threatens to climb up the back of my throat. But…this is Chrissy. My friend. My partner in crime. My ride or die.

Only, I'd thought that Phillip was that too.

I sigh again, eyes sliding closed, tears threatening.

"It can wait," she whispers, fingers tightening around mine. "You should just rest, and Rome and I will deal with the venue and—"

My lids peel back.

The venue. The caterer. The cake. The *guests*.

"Oh my God," I whisper, that worry turning to panic, all of the planning details I'd fretted over for months exploding in my mind.

So much work.

And all of it to waste.

Chrissy grimaces. "Stupid," she mutters, more to herself than me. "I shouldn't have said anything." She pats my hand, starts to stand. "Rome and I've got this. I promise."

"But—"

"You heard the doctor about your feet," she says, tone fierce. "You're going to stay here safe and sound and recovering, and let us deal with that bastard who—" A muscle in her jaw flexes hard, taking her words with it for a long moment. "I'll make sure the vendors are sorted and the guests know the wedding's off, but I'm bringing the cake back. That was fucking delicious when we did the tasting and no way is that bastard going to get a mouthful of it."

Somehow...I smile.

Then sober.

Because...she's doing too much.

"Chrissy—"

"No," she says, voice going even firmer. "You know that if our roles were reversed, you'd be saying the same damn thing."

"I—"

Her eyes fix on mine, rage burning in the blue depths. "When I saw the mess in the bridal room..." A breath. "When you were just gone..." Another. "I was so fucking worried about you." Her throat works, eyes glassy now, but my friend is fierce as ever when she says, "I'm glad you're okay, but I'm not going to pull my dad and all his resources"— and the billionaire businessman and professional sports team owner has a multitude of them—"back from this. No. *Fucking*. Way."

"Honey—"

"No," she says vehemently, "I know that you don't see yourself the way I do, don't grasp how fucking wonderful you are—"

My lungs inflate in a rush, sending pain through my torso in a hot wave.

"—but you are," she says. "Fucking *wonderful*. And you deserve better than Phillip."

Damn, I love this woman.

"And further that, *no one* deserves what happened to you. *Fucking no one.*" She touches my cheek. "But least of all you, babe."

I cover her hand with my own. "Thank you," I whisper, feeling the words settle deep inside, knowing they're logically the truth, but also knowing that beneath all of that, so freaking buried that most of the time I forget it's there, those words will just...slide off.

Become meaningless.

Never heal the gulf within.

I ignore that truth and hold my friend's eyes, summon a smile that's not fake this time because I love this woman, know that I'm so damned lucky to have her in my life.

"I was just going to say—"

Her brows lift, and I know that she's preparing to shut me down if I insist on handling it myself.

I don't.

Because...I don't think I can.

So, I just keep talking.

"—to get the groom's cake too."

FIVE

King

Laughter echoes down the hall and I feel some of the tension leave my body.

Sliding from violent, murderous rage down to…

Murderous rage.

Baby steps.

Jean-Michel stills then nods with an approving smile on his face. "That's my Chrissy."

I get it.

Jean-Michel's daughter has the same inner light that Rory has.

It's like a fucking drug. I want more of it, even though she so rarely deigns to shine it in my direction.

A sigh and slight shake of his head, any softness fading from Jean-Michel's face. "I'll take care of the asshole. You and Chrissy deal with the rest of the wedding shit"—a nod to Rome—"You"—to me, eyes sparking with fury—"you make sure she doesn't so much as move an inch until she's fully recovered."

I nod. "That's exactly my plan."

"Good," he mutters and reaches for the doorknob. "I'll send over someone to watch her during the game tomorrow."

Right.

Hockey.

My job.

Something that seems very far away at the moment.

"Thanks."

He doesn't acknowledge that, just locks eyes with Rome for a second and then is wrenching the knob, pulling it open and disappearing out into the fading sun.

The door slams shut.

"How are you doing?" Rome asks a long moment later.

"After finding a woman we all care about beaten on the side of the road?" I growl, ignoring the way his brows shoot up in surprise. "Not great."

He studies me closely. "Yeah, I get that." A beat. "Want to talk about it?"

"No," I mutter.

His big chest inflates on a breath. "Rights," he says.

Then he nods, turns, and walks back down the hall, retrieving Chrissy to go deal with the remnants of a wedding that ended in disaster.

Leaving me with a woman who I rescued but who can't stand me.

A woman whose strength I'm in awe of, whose beauty draws me in...

Who I can never have.

I exhale, flick the lock on the front door, then move back toward my bedroom.

And the moment I cross the threshold, I find that I've already broken my promise to Jean-Michel.

"What the fuck are you doing?" I snap, quickly moving to Rory's side as she hobbles across the room.

Her eyes flash to mine, hot and angry. "None of your fucking business."

"Okay, Miss Prickle Pants," I growl, taking her arm and drawing her to a halt. "I know your fucking ears work."

She glares at me.

"Which means," I snap, "that I know you heard when the doctor said to stay off those feet for at least the next twenty-four hours."

"I heard her," she says icily. "I just—"

"What?" I press when she breaks off, eyes sliding to the side, cheeks turning the slightest bit pink.

"Never mind," she mutters, tugging at my hold.

"No," I say, "tell me. *Tell* me what was so important that you're trying to undo the work the doctor did."

She exhales.

Winces.

And God, I'm an asshole.

But I don't even get to sit in that for a second before I feel even *more* like an asshole.

Because then she says, "I have to go to the bathroom."

Fucking hell.

"Ror—"

She shakes her head and guilt jabs at me repeatedly, but that's the least of what I deserve.

"I—"

"No," she whispers, pulling at my hold.

I release her, but don't back away as she takes a step forward. Which is why I don't miss the grimace that crosses her face.

Christ.

I move without thinking, scooping her up as carefully as the priceless, breakable object she is.

"King!"

But I don't pay attention to her furious tone, to the way she's gone stiff. I just start forward, carrying her into the bathroom, setting her on her feet near the toilet.

Then I hesitate...

Her mouth opens and closes, opens and closes. Then she seems to notice that I'm still standing there.

"What?" she growls.

I wave a hand at her. "Did you need some help with...?"

I trail off before I say something stupid like panties.

Or stupider like—

Something stupider.

Because what am I offering to do?

Strip her naked and fuck her senseless?

That would be pleasurable for both of us. Just...not right now.

"No," she snaps, glaring at me. "I *need* you to go."

Right.

I spin on my heel, take off out of the bathroom, freeing Zeus from his crate (where he's being a perfect, patient pup, waiting quietly for the chaos to settle).

And then I plunk him on the bed.

And I wait. For the toilet to flush and the sink to turn on and the sound of footsteps to come toward the door.

I open it.

She sighs.

"Deal with it, Prickle Princess," I mutter, moving toward her and scooping her up again, trying not to recognize that a part of me hidden deep inside is already used to the feel of her in my arms.

I carry her to the bed.

Get her settled under the blankets, smiling as Zeus settles carefully into her side.

Such a good pup.

Not a surprise since he came to me via Rory's rescue.

And then I crawl in next to her—

"What the fuck are you doing?" she demands.

I click on the TV.

"I promised Jean-Michel that I wouldn't let you move so much as an inch. Now"—I look at her, hitch my head toward the TV—"what trash TV show are we watching?"

Her glare should be setting me on fire.

I ignore it.

Okay, fine, some part of me is reveling in it.

But, still, I don't speak. Just wait.

Wait until she huffs out a breath that has her wincing and turning her glare toward the TV. "*The Incredible Dr. Pol,*" she finally mutters.

"Excuse me?"

Those words don't make sense, especially when they're not some combination of *90 Day Fiancé* like the shows my mom and sister watch, or *The Bachelor,* or some *Housewives* franchise.

"It's a show about a vet," she mutters, sticking out her hand, palm open, fingers twitching as she silently demands the remote. "I'll put it on."

My brows lift, but since this is an activity that means that she'll be remaining in bed, I pass over the remote, watch as she navigates through the streaming services and puts on a show.

That is entertaining and heartbreaking and has a ton of animals—of all shapes and sizes—on it.

Which means it's totally up her alley.

Which means...

I don't complain when one episode turns into another, and my eyelids grow heavy.

Because I glance to the side and see that hers are drooping even more than mine are.

And then I fall asleep to the sight of a barn full of happy cows on the screen.

SOMETHING wet and warm wakes me after what feels like five minutes.

I peel back my lids, see that Zeus has made it his duty to pull me out of sleep.

"Ugh," I grunt when his tongue slides into my mouth. "And that's entirely too much togetherness for this early in the morning," I mutter.

Because it *is* morning.

I can see the sunshine sliding through the windows, sending slanted beams of light across the rug in front of my bed.

My...*empty* bed.

Or at least the space beside me is empty.

Is devoid of a certain woman who's not supposed to be moving one goddamned inch.

I push up from the bed, look into the bathroom, peek through even though the open door already clues me into it being empty.

Which it is.

"Fuck," I mutter then systematically search the rest of the house, Zeus at my side.

But even the fluffy version of the King of the Gods can't produce Rory.

And I have the feeling I know exactly where she is.

And if I'm right...

I'm going to kill *her*.

SIX

Rory

"Be brave and kind," I murmur as I get out of the rideshare, my socked feet aching as I stride slowly up to the front door.

Socks I stole from King's dresser.

As he slept through Dr. Pol delivering a bevy of infant cows that were breech, and thus saving more than a handful of mama cows.

A crime against humanity that.

Missing out on one of the greatest shows in television history—

Either that or the drugs Dr. Halston gave me drove me to delusions.

Maybe both.

Probably, though, I should have taken one of those pills before I snuck from King's house in the early hours of dawn, creeping as quietly as a woman with sliced up feet and bruised ribs and a throat that hurt to speak, let alone to snark, could creep.

Luckily, Kingston was *out*.

He hadn't so much as moved as I slipped from the bed and hobbled into the bathroom, hadn't twitched when I opened the closet door and riffled through his drawers for a pair of sweats that wouldn't trip me as I did more of that hobbling, along with socks and a pair of boxer briefs I was able to swap for my sexy wedding lingerie, which was beautiful but wholly uncomfortable—especially after an escape from a church and a hike through a thick grove of oak trees and a safari along a wet, rain-covered roadway.

Oh, and a cool, refreshing dip into the lovely roadside pool of dirty water.

Where I probably picked up a nematode or something.

Great.

But another problem for another day.

And nematodes are creatures too—

Said no one ever.

But...

I'm delaying.

Because I want to do anything but complete the walk up to the front porch, anything but punch my code into the keypad and walk into the house I created with Phillip.

The house that was a big fucking lie.

"Be brave and kind," I whisper again, more out of habit than intending to actually be kind.

Phillip is a giant asshole who doesn't deserve kindness.

Or forgiveness.

Or...

Well, anything except for someone to do to him what he did to me.

Someone bigger and stronger and more powerful than him.

So he'd understand exactly how he made me feel.

The dick.

I inhale. Exhale.

Put the petty aside. Hug the wounded little girl inside me who'd been hurt too often.

And force myself to keep the promise I made to my dad, myself.

Be brave and kind.

Even if, right now, I'm just settling for being brave.

Because it feels like a big thing to just turn the handle and push into the house, to walk by the wall of pictures I hung there, carefully measuring and remeasuring so that not one was a single millimeter off, so that—

Phillip wouldn't be upset that everything wasn't just perfect.

I freeze mid-bend, preparing to remove my shoes, when I remember I don't have any on.

Because my Cinderella-esque pumps, covered with so many blueish crystals that they gave the impression of a glass slipper, were lost somewhere during my escape.

I swallow hard, brave a bit harder to come by.

Then I walk by the wall of pictures, move toward the stairs, start climbing them slowly and carefully and...painfully.

Shoes. Clothes. My computer and makeup and the box from my dad. My papers and purse—not the tiny one that Chrissy had promised to retrieve for me from the church with just my ID and an emergency bride kit, but the larger bag that has my life in it.

The first thing I see is my suitcase parked on the far wall right next to Phillip's, packed and ready to take on our honeymoon to Hawaii.

The sight makes me...

Sad. Angry.

Broken.

I sigh and hobble over to it, grabbing the handle, dragging it near the door. I hit the closet, grab a duffle and shove more clothes in—but comfortable ones, not the stylish ones that are filling my suitcase. These ones are of the comfortable-I-just-broke-up-with-my-fiancé-because-he's-an-abusive-asshole variety.

Loungewear is a requirement for this situation.

Not dresses and blouses and lingerie.

I exhale, putting a hand against my ribs when they protest, then finish shoving as much as I can into the duffle, along with my makeup and a couple of pairs of comfortable shoes.

Now for my papers.

I leave the bag by my suitcase, hating how much of a struggle it is to heft it and carry it over, and then hobble down the hall and into my office, snagging my backpack and computer and cords and the file with all of my important documents.

Social security card. Passport. Birth certificate. Car insurance.

All of those go in alongside my computer and cords and then I'm hobbling back to my bedroom, and...my heart is suddenly in my throat.

Because I don't like to look at what I'm going to retrieve next.

Because it's pretty much the most important belonging I own.

Because it contains the only memories I have of my parents.

And if it's not there, if Phillip somehow remembered how important it is to me and came back to the house and—

Well, if it's not safe and whole then I think he's lost any chance of kindness altogether.

I move to the side of the bed, to the little door that encloses the bottom of my nightstand, grasp the shiny metal knob, and pull it.

Then exhale sharply when relief floods through me.

The box is there.

I slide it out, careful to keep it perfectly level, to not unduly jostle the precious contents.

And then, so damned slowly, I open the lid.

More relief. Another breath making my ribs protest.

But it's there. The picture of my parents, smiling and happy. The photograph of baby me in my mother's arms, her expression tired but incandescent. The only picture I have of the two of us.

I carefully put it back inside, blinking back the burn of tears as I flip to the last picture, the one of me on my dad's shoulders, hair in pigtails, grinning like a tiny lunatic.

He's smiling, but it's not like the first picture.

His happiness tempered by grief.

By loss.

I sigh softly, carefully tuck his picture where it belongs—right next to the one of my mom—and touch the bracelet I stashed inside years ago. Because Phillip said it was childish and I didn't want to fight. Because it was too precious to keep putting him off about it.

But I didn't realize how naked my wrist had felt since the moment I took it off.

No more.

Be brave and kind.

My dad's words, spoken to me over and over again.

Be brave, like him. Be kind, like the mother I don't

remember, the mother I *can't* remember because she died mere hours after my birth.

I lay the bracelet flat, fumble with the clip for a moment before I manage to get it secured, and then I lift my arm, smiling at the cheap plastic and wood and metal charms that my dad brought me back from each of his business trips.

I have an Eiffel Tower, Big Ben, a koala, the Colosseum, a boat, and even the Golden Gate (though we'd picked that one out together on one of our visits across the bay and into San Francisco). And...I have a charm my dad's assistant found in his briefcase, after he'd had that heart attack while on his final business trip.

This one shaped like a kangaroo.

I smile and touch the little trinket, sending the kangaroo hopping on the link that hangs from my wrist.

My dad wasn't perfect.

But I never doubted he loved me.

Not like—

I freeze, fingers clenching on the edge of the box, as the hairs on my nape prickle.

Slowly—oh so slowly—I turn my head, and glance back over my shoulder.

I see Phillip standing in the doorway...

And the fury on his face is absolutely terrifying.

SEVEN

King

I don't bother knocking as I run up to the front door of Rory's place—just wrap my fingers around the doorknob and twist it, shoving the wooden panel inward so hard that it slams into the wall with a loud *thud*.

Because there's a car in the driveway.

And it's not fucking mine, not fucking Rory's.

Which means—

I hear her cry out and my already increasing speed grows faster.

I'm up the stairs in a flash, pounding down the hall, looking through the open doors as I go.

Searching for her.

Finding her.

Crouched in the corner, wearing my tee and sweats, her sock-covered feet tucked beneath her as that fucker—

I see red.

Because that fucker has his hands on her.

She cries out again and the red in my vision goes black. I barely recognize that I'm moving, reaching for the fucker, gripping his shoulder hard enough that *he* cries out. I jerk him back, send him flying across the room, skidding along the floor, crashing into the wall.

Rory's got tears streaking down her cheeks and she's clutching her hand to her chest, but I don't see any obvious injuries to her—any new ones anyway.

"Stay there," I order, turning around and intending to deal with the motherfucker that's her ex.

Only...he's not there.

There's a dent in the Sheetrock where the fucker hit it.

But there's no sign of Phillip.

Fucking hell.

I glance back at Rory. "Stay there, princess, yeah?"

She gives a shaky nod and I move through the bedroom, checking the space for any sign of the asshole, and when I don't find any, I cross into the hall, clearing each of the rooms as I move along it and down the stairs. I'm on full alert for the bastard to jump out at any point, to try to sneak attack me like the coward he is.

The front door is open, but I don't trust it as I systematically search through the space, checking closets and each room.

But there's no sign of the fucker, and when I finally look through that open front door, I see why.

Phillip's car is gone.

I exhale, grind my teeth together, and carefully close the door, secure the lock.

And then I'm climbing the stairs again, crossing that hall, moving into the bedroom.

Finding Rory, still on the floor, still with her arm curled against her chest.

But it's not, I realize now, because it's hurt—or I don't think so anyway. Because she's holding something close, protecting it against her body.

"Ror?" I ask carefully, moving slowly toward her, crouching down to meet her eyes.

"I'm fine," she whispers.

"Did he hurt you?"

A shake of her head. "No," she whispers then adds before I can press her about the cry of distress I heard when I came into the house, "He didn't get the chance to before you were here. He just"—her eyes flick down—"tried to take it." A beat. "Take them."

I follow her gaze, see that she's clutching a little box like it's her most precious belonging. It's battered and the corners worn, the paint chipped, the little brass hinges on the side I can see tarnished.

"Take what?" I ask.

"My box," she whispered. "And my bracelet." She holds up her wrist, showing me a cheap-looking bracelet with painted wooden charms hanging from it. "It's all I have left of him. My dad—" Her throat works. "He'd buy me a new charm for it every time he had to take a business trip. Until..." Her voice cracks.

I hold my breath.

Brace.

"...until he didn't come back."

Fuck.

I want to tuck her close, hold her tight, let her cry as she gives me the full story.

But now's not the time.

So, I touch her cheek, drawing her focus. "You kept them both safe, princess," I murmur. "Good job."

Her nod is shaky, her whispered, "Thanks," equally so.

And then silence falls.

And…I don't know what to say, how to make this better.

How to fix this.

You're not your father.

I clench my teeth together then exhale silently. "Can we get out of here?" I ask. "Or do you need to keep packing?"

Packing she was *supposed* to wait for me to do.

But even though that has a sharp rebuke sitting on my tongue, I don't allow it to escape.

Not the right time.

Especially as she nods again and says, "I'm going to Chrissy's."

Like hell she is.

Risk that bastard going after her somewhere I can't protect her? Fuck that.

But I don't say that out loud and I don't allow the logic that Chrissy's place—set up with panic buttons and a killer alarm system—would probably be safer than mine.

Phillip's been there before.

He hasn't been to my place.

That's enough for now.

The rest—the utter possessiveness that's boiling in my belly at the thought of her somewhere else—I push down.

I can't think about that right now.

I just…need her safe.

"That all you need?" I ask, nodding to the backpack propped next to the duffle and suitcase.

"Yeah," she whispers. "I just need my box. And my bracelet."

"Okay, princess," I murmur. "I'll load the car. You okay to sit there for another minute or two?"

She bobs out a nod, and I hate that she flinches when I stretch my hand out.

But something settles in me when my thumb brushes lightly over her skin, her eyes slide closed, and she whispers, "Yeah."

Right.

I pull my hand back, straighten, and snag the bags.

Less than a minute later, I'm back for her, scooping her up, careful with that box she's holding on to for dear life. I track the wince that crosses her face, adding it to the list of shit this asshole needs to make up for.

And then we're moving down the hall, out the front door, down the driveway.

"Buckle up," I order softly, drawing the belt across her middle, holding it steady until she grabs the metal clip.

I hear the soft *click* as I fold out of the car. I close the metal panel then hustle up to the front door, pulling it shut and starting to reach for the lock when I remember.

The animals.

"Shit," I mutter, thinking about the room that Chrissy has in her house for her rescues—and how it's full more often than not.

Crap.

What kind of menagerie am I going to have to Tetris into the back of my car?

Back down the driveway, to her door, cracking it open. "Where are your dogs?"

Her eyes come to mine.

Then slide away and my stomach sinks like a fucking anchor heading straight for the ocean floor.

"Where, princess?" I murmur.

"All adopted."

"No," I say. "I mean *your* dogs, baby."

Her throat works. "Adopted," she whispers, glancing back

at me. "After Teddy died, I didn't take any more perma-nently. Phillip—" A shake of her head.

Fuck.

"They're all adopted," she whispers. "The final one went last week and my fosters have the rest. I need to check in with them. But they'll be good for a bit. I already made the arrangements for the honey—"

She inhales sharply, exhales long and slow.

I touch her cheek, a gentle brush along that silken skin, a touch that could make me feel some things, could really make me feel *something*.

If I let it.

Which I don't.

But still I press, "Why don't you have any dogs at your place?"

Her eyes drift away, but then I watch her straighten her shoulders, lift her chin. Those deep pools of emerald come back to mine. "Phillip didn't like them."

The fucking man was marrying a woman whose passion was animal rescue...

And he didn't like animals.

What the actual fuck had he been thinking?

What the actual fuck had *she*?

But I don't ask either question, just nod and maneuver out of the car, round the hood.

And then I get into the driver's seat and take her home.

To my place.

Because that's where I can keep her safe.

EIGHT

"You could have stayed at my place, you know," Chrissy murmurs from next to me on the guest bed.

The only argument I've won with King to date.

That I'm staying in the guest room.

And he's sleeping in his own bed.

Because...

Waking next to him this morning had been—

Right in all the wrong ways.

"I know," I say, "and I might take you up on that. But, King's right. Phillip's been to your place, knows that Rome lives next door." I sigh and my ribs protest a little. "I know your dad has his security working on tracking him down"—doubly so after last night—"so I also know it won't be long, but..."

"You'll just stay put here until that's done," Chrissy says. She lightly bumps her leg against mine. "That makes sense."

I bump her back, just as carefully, pleased when my ribs barely complain.

My throat, on the other hand. I still sound like a vampy old Hollywood actress.

I run my fingers through Zeus's soft fur, the pup having been glued to my side since King carried me back into the house. And, not that I would admit it to anyone, but he was my favorite corgi of the litter that we rescued from a hoarder house not long ago. Adorable, sweet, and lazy for the breed, more cuddler than herder, but with a high ball drive.

Perfect for a busy man with a demanding career. No endless hikes or stimulation needed, just some basic daily exercise and spending the rest of the day following King around.

Plus, he and his sis, Athena, get plenty of playdates together because Rome was also suckered into buying a house in Corgi Town (a.k.a. adopting one of the mischievous pups).

Who could resist their tiny legs and floofy bodies?

A sociopath, that's who.

My mouth kicks up, wounds inside me settling the slightest bit.

Because animals don't judge you or break your heart.

Because...I'll get through this.

Because...I've gotten through worse.

"All of which means that now we get to veg and eat this delicious cake"—she holds up the groom's cake that we're making a serious dent in—"and watch the Eagles take on the Grizzlies." Chrissy picks up the remote and starts clicking through the guide of the streaming service.

It's almost game time, I realize, as she selects the channel and brings up the feed.

"I can't believe you've turned into a hockey fan," I grumble.

Her mouth kicks up. "Just because you can't stand sports in general but hockey in particular..." She slants a gaze my way. "Why is that, anyway?"

Because a certain sexy *King*-like player is on the team.

And because I was in a relationship and couldn't think about any man the way my mind wants to when it comes to King.

Dangerous. Tempting. With the potential to wound deeply and permanently, and—

Plus, his reputation precedes him.

A playboy through and through.

Only...

He's not like that.

I haven't known him long, but I've seen enough to know that—volunteering to help with Chrissy's rescue, devoted to Zeus, working hard with the team, having my back.

Not a drama or controversy or...

Woman in sight.

And he saved me from the side of the road and protected me from Phillip.

And offered up his place for me to stay as long as I want.

So, really I know he's not a bad guy—even if it would be more convenient if he was.

I sigh and lean my head onto her shoulder. "I didn't thank you for helping me with dealing with all the vendors and guests and stuff."

"You did." She rests the side of her head against mine for a second, and I know she's smiling. "And nice try with the change in subject." She lifts up, kisses my cheek. "But I'll let it slide considering the last twenty-four hours you've had."

Relief slides through me and I relax back against the pillows, watching as a couple of men in suits hold microphones up to their faces and blather on about lineups and injuries, all while the players skate around behind them in a mess of organized chaos of sticks and shots and pucks and stretching.

I watch for King on the screen, feeling that familiar blip in my chest when the camera cuts to him talking to Rome, both of them appearing supremely serious.

Chrissy sighs.

"What?"

She turns to me only when the camera cuts back to the announcers, lips turning up at the edges. "My man is hot."

Amusement in my belly. "Have I told you how much I love you?"

Gentle in her pretty blue eyes. "Well, the good news is that it's as much as I love you."

I snort, but I settle. "Look at us being all sappy."

"I know," she teases. "Who even are we?"

I laugh.

But I'm thankful when the puck drops and Chrissy's focus becomes more about the game.

Because I love my friend, I'm thankful for King's kindness and Jean-Michel and Rome's concern, but...I'm worried about what's going to happen next.

Big feelings.

So many feelings.

And amongst those, I'm not heartbroken.

Which makes me wonder...

If I'm not sad about my relationship ending, if perhaps I'm feeling relieved that I don't actually have to go through with it, that maybe for the first time in a long time, I can take a full breath because Phillip isn't going to be my husband...

If I'm not any of those things...

Then who the fuck am I?

"I'M PERFECTLY capable of working at a desk," I say the next day, after having wrestled my way into work clothes and slapped on enough concealer and foundation to cover the bruises on my face and throat.

Terrible, having to swap sweats for this shit.

But a necessary evil.

My heels, though?

I'm not sure I can muster the strength to actually shove my feet into them.

Yes, my feet feel a lot better.

Just—I study my pumps—not in these shoes.

But I've spent almost two full days in bed and King just got the call that Jean-Michel's security team located Phillip.

At our house.

Sitting in front of the fucking TV like nothing has changed.

Like he hadn't done what he had and—

Well, I need to work.

I need to get away from my thoughts.

And...

Away from a certain stubborn hockey player who's leaning against the open door of his guest bedroom.

"I know you're perfectly capable," he says. "The question is why you feel like you need to."

Because I *need* to get out of this house?

And away from my thoughts?

And far, far away from this man?

"You have the time off," he continues. "Why don't you take it?"

Because if I have to sit alone with my thoughts, with this man any longer I'll go insane?

Maybe because of *that*?

None of which I say aloud. Instead, I just glare at him. "I can't help with my fosters right now"—can't walk dogs or heft bags of kibble or clean out hoarder houses, so the least I can do is my work for Jean-Michel, especially since he was instrumental in apprehending my abusive ex and all—"so I might as well make myself useful." I lift a brow. "Is that okay with you, your highness?"

"Back to Prickle Princess I see," he mutters.

I glare.

Then move toward the door.

He steps in front of me.

"What?" I snap.

"Just work here," he says. "I have a desk, a quiet space. You can do what you need to do without getting interrupted."

"I don't mind interruptions," I tell him, shifting to the side to move by him.

He doesn't retreat, doesn't give me an inch, and I feel my lungs tighten as our bodies brush.

Feel that flicker deep inside that always comes when we touch.

It doesn't seem to affect him, expression recalcitrant when he says, "How about you can stay safe in the house while you do what you need to do?"

"I *am* safe," I remind him. "Considering you're the one who told me that Phillip's been arrested."

He scowls.

And...I've had enough.

I shove by him, start moving down the hall, my shoes in hand.

I'll put them on for the walk to my desk and nothing more.

There. Good plan.

"Fine," he snaps, following me. "How about the fact that if you *do* go in, you'll get me in trouble with Jean-Michel?"

NINE

King

I get her with that one.

Finally.

And relief is heady as she slides to a stop, turns to stare at me over her shoulder, that beautiful face covered in makeup.

Covered because of the bruises beneath.

I grind my back teeth together, fight against the urge to punch something.

I've done enough of that, the hole in the wall in my bedroom, the sore knuckles I'm sporting from the fight I got into last night more than enough reminder of that.

But it's her snapped out, *"Fine,"* that actually pulls me back from the edge.

Then she lifts her brows.

"What is it?" I mutter.

She tosses her hair, gives a frustrated exhale. "Where's this office of yours?"

"Oh." I shake myself. "Right."

I move by her, snagging those stupid ass heels she has in her hands as I go.

"Hey!"

But I don't stop, just chuck them down the stairs in the vague direction of my shoe rack.

"*Hey!*"

And I keep walking, turning the corner around the stairs, starting down the hall. "I'll grab them later."

She huffs out a sigh but doesn't stop following me.

I'm aware of every step, every breath, every quiet hissed out murmur of pain.

And then I open the door and I'm aware of...

So. Much. More.

The soft curves of her body, the rounded bow of her mouth, the long, thick curl of her lashes, the smell of her hair.

"*Oh,*" she gasps, slowly stepping by me and moving into the room. "*Wow.*"

Floor-to-ceiling shelves fill three walls of the space and the fourth is a full wall of windows surrounding a centered French door. Dark cabinets. Light pouring in through all of those windows.

I turn as she does, seeing the huge desk that takes up most of the space. A desk I love because I never feel cramped or crowded. I allow my gaze to run over the shelves filled with books and pictures of my family—a lot of the latter because there are a lot of Bang siblings in the world. Me, the oldest. Then Jakob, Jensen, Leif, Tanner, and I can't forget Annie, our only sister and the woman who keeps us all on our toes nearly as much as our mom does.

And my mom...

I hold back a sigh.

God, I love that woman, love that I always know she has my back and would kill herself to be there for all of us.

But my mother is recently retired and with an empty nest...she has far too much time on her hands to meddle in my life.

Trying to match me off.

Not knowing—or maybe knowing but not particularly *caring* that I don't want that.

The happy ending. The love-filled relationship. The soulmate connection she has with my dad.

That I *can't* have it.

You're not your father.

"You even have a reading chair," Rory whispers, jarring me out of my thoughts, seeing that she's completed her revolution of taking in the space and is now looking at me.

I shrug. "I like to read."

"I didn't know hockey players had it in them to be scholarly."

Wow.

I open my mouth, but I don't get the chance to retort.

Because she's exhaling through her nose, shaking her head, and holding my eyes.

"I'm sorry," she says, tone genuinely contrite. "That was bitchy and uncalled for." A sigh. "I'm not usually mean."

My mouth hitches up. "Except with me."

Pink on her cheeks, barely visible with all that makeup. "I'm sorry," she says. "*Really.*"

I touch that faint spread of pink. "It's okay, Princess Pricklesticks," I say lightly.

"Still," she mutters. "I'm a jerk."

"Like I said, Princess of the Prickle, it's fine." And then I find myself adding when she rolls her eyes, the words just tumbling off my tongue, "Especially, considering how fucking beautiful you are when you're annoyed with me."

She inhales sharply.

Then winces and clamps a hand to her ribs.

"Damn," I mutter, carefully wrapping an arm around her shoulders. "Sorry, princess. Come on and sit down." I guide her over to the desk. "I'll grab your computer." I pull the chair back, press her down into it. "Do you need anything else?"

She mutely shakes her head.

And I get the fuck out of the room before I say anything else stupid.

I DON'T LEAVE the house until I peek in and see that she's firmly entrenched, not wanting to risk having to track her down again and piss off Jean-Michel for moving more than that inch.

So, it's only when I find her full on in the groove that I leave for the rink.

Practice time.

I actually like it—something that might be a surprise to most people. The monotonous drills, going through the same shit over and over again until it's just right, until it's muscle memory and happens with game speed without thinking.

It's routine.

It's comfortable.

It's planned and structured and good for me.

I may not be the best player, may not have the natural talent my dad did when he was playing, the same abilities as my brothers, the same beautiful instincts Annie had when she was competing for a gold medal, jumping and spinning in a way that I'll never be able to—with grace and power and speed.

I'm big, but not the biggest of my siblings.

I'm strong, but not the strongest either.

Not the funniest or the most laidback or the most talented of the Bang athletes.

But...I can work hard.

And I like that practice allows me to do that.

"So."

I turn, see that Pat—resident asshole on the Eagles, and unfortunately, there's usually always one...but with *this* team, there's plenty, so really Pat is the *president* of the assholes.

Do not engage.

I turn away, pick up the puck, start running through a series of stickhandling exercises. Toe to heel of the blade, up into the air, twisting to the side, then back down onto the ice and moving it around me, tracing a mental diamond on the ice, hitting some spots, dodging around imaginary obstacles, through my feet, back to front, side to side—

Pat swings his stick at mine and—

Crack.

My stick snaps in two, stinging pain radiating up my palms, my forearms.

See? Asshole.

Slashing—and breaking—my stick for some goddamned reason that only makes sense in Asshole Land.

Plus, I just retaped the blade, and it was a damned good tape job.

And yeah, we go through a lot of sticks every season, and the team pays for them and the rest of my equipment, but...

What the fuck?

I grind my teeth together, rotate on my skates just enough to meet his smirking eyes. "Did you need something?" I mutter, bending to grab the half of my stick that's resting on the ice.

He waggles his brows. "Did you fuck her yet?"

I still, my gloved fingers wrapped tightly around the

halves of my stick, wanting to turn around and send it like a spear straight into this asshole's stomach.

Thankfully, I have more control—or more teeth to grind.

So, I just straighten, skate to the bench, stepping off the ice and dumping the broken pieces into a trash can before murmuring a "Thanks" to the equipment guy—who's ready and prepared as always—when he passes a fresh stick over to me.

Taped. Waxed. Prepped.

But not the one I wanted to use.

Not my lucky stick with the perfect tape job.

And it's because of the smirking bastard still standing on the ice, now blocking my entrance back to it.

"Is being an asshole in your genes?" I ask, stopping for a squirt of water. "Or just a skill you've honed over the years?"

Pat's a good hockey player.

But he's lazy.

And, as mentioned previously, an asshole.

However, he's not particularly smart, and I watch his dumb brow furrow, likely as he tries to process the words—had he ever heard the word *hone* before? It takes long enough that I'm able to nudge him back, to move by him, to skate back toward my little square of the ice and stickhandling practice. Drills are done, as well as the scrimmage, and we have the rink for some free time for the next half hour.

Rome's not far, so I bypass my spot, move over to him.

Strength in numbers.

Or maybe if I'm busy, the asshole will get a clue and leave me alone.

That's not to be.

Because Pat's either worked out what *honed* means or he's trying to run for reelection of the asshole presidency.

"I *asked*," he says, coming over and smacking the backs of

my legs with his stick. Hard. Because…asshole. "If you've fucked her yet."

"I heard you," I snap. "And I'm not discussing a woman whose fiancé beat the shit out of her with you."

Something crosses his face and, for a second, I think he's going to be an actual human being.

But then, as quickly as it came on, that flash of humanity disappears and he's back to sneering. "Yeah." He smirks lasciviously. "You fucked her."

Thought about fucking her?

Damn right I have.

But would I prey on a woman who's been through what she's been through?

Fuck no.

And that he would so much as insinuate that?

Well, I want to say that I know he's just trying to piss me off and that I ignore him and go back to what I need to get done.

Unfortunately, I've been tabling my temper ever since I saw Rory on the side of the road with that bruise on her cheek and the handprint on her throat.

Rome's eyes widen. "King, just take a breath and—"

I whirl on Pat, see he's sporting that dumb ass smirk, and—

I punch it right off his even dumber face.

TEN

Rory

King comes home from practice angry and sporting a black eye.

Which means I give him a wide berth after telling him I made him some food and it's on a covered plate in the oven.

He doesn't snap at me, isn't mean, doesn't take out what had clearly been a shit day on me.

He just murmurs, "Thanks" and disappears upstairs.

A few moments later I hear water running.

Kingston Bang in the shower.

Kingston Bang naked and soapy and—

My stomach tightens, a bolt of desire winding through my belly.

Retreating from the thoughts, the temptations, I stick to my work in the office, not coming out until I'm fighting to keep my eyes open and exhaustion clings to every one of my cells. I'm still recovering, but this need for an afternoon nap is ridiculous.

I've barely gotten through my backlog of emails.

Sighing, I make a pit stop in the kitchen, get myself a glass of water. But then my curiosity gets the better of me and I can't stop myself from peeking in the oven. Strictly for safety purposes. I need to make sure that it's off. Can't have the house burning down around us.

But really, I want to see if he's eaten.

If he hasn't...

Well, I don't know what I'll do.

Take it upstairs and return some of his pushy by force-feeding it to him?

He's a big man and has a demanding job and was at the rink early that morning. He needs fuel.

Unfortunately, I find myself strangely disappointed.

The oven is empty.

And the plate is sitting in the sink.

I move to the trash, glance inside.

No food dumped there.

And that...well, it's stupid, but it eases something inside my chest. Phillip—

I don't want to think about Phillip, but I can't help it. Because I know I would have found the food uneaten in the trash. Because it wouldn't have mattered if I hadn't done anything to make his day bad.

That food would have been in the trash.

I quietly close the lid, nibble at my bottom lip.

I should go take a nap.

I should go to sleep and when I wake up, start getting back to normal. Find an apartment because—after everything —I can't go back to Phillip's and my place (really, Phillip's, since I moved in with him). I need to move on, to find a way to start over.

Find a way to begin again.

Again.

I sigh.

But instead of going to the guest room, I move to the fridge, pull out the bowl of cookie dough I made earlier when I was feeling energetic and spritely and...

Then had run out of steam.

I'd made a half-hearted attempt at covering it with plastic wrap, but now I pull that off, move to the oven and turn it back on.

King has a well-stocked kitchen for a bachelor, and I open the drawer beneath the oven, extract a pair of cookie sheets.

One of which I load up with my Everything dough.

M&Ms, peanut butter chips, bits of marshmallow, crunched-up graham crackers, sprinkles—basically everything and the kitchen sink.

A.k.a. every sugar-filled, calorie-laden deliciousness.

And hot, gooey, straight-out-of-the-oven Everything cookies are the perfect remedy for a shitty day.

Something that proves Chrissy knows me too well because she'd brought the supplies yesterday, knew that at some point in the near future, I'd need the power of Everything cookies.

My heart squeezes.

I'm lucky—despite everything, I'm lucky.

"Lucky," I whisper, holding that thought close as I slide the tray into the oven and set the timer.

Then I snag the other baking sheet and fill it with balls of dough, and when the timer goes, I remove the golden-brown cookies from the oven, swapping it for the tray loaded with the unbaked ones. And then I repeat the process—roll, bake, remove, put on the rack to cool—until all of the dough is used up and the kitchen is filled with the delicious smell of Everything cookies.

Do I sample?

Hell yes, I do.

But do I also load a plate with five huge, hot cookies when I pull that final baking sheet out?

Yup.

Leaving the others to cool, I snag the plate and ignore the fact that my heart is beating fast enough to make me dizzy.

He had a bad day.

He helped me when he didn't have to.

I can do this one small thing for him.

I just...well, I hope he—

"What are you doing?"

I spin so fast that the cookies nearly slide off the plate, seeing King standing in the doorway, face unreadable, big body still and eyes locked on me.

"I—" I swallow hard. "Baking cookies?"

Only it's more question than statement.

And I watch his face soften. "You're baking cookies?"

"You had a bad day," I murmur. "And I made Everything dough earlier, so I thought..." I shrug, continue inanely, "Well, Everything cookies make everything better."

His head tilts to the side, eyes still on mine, and I freeze, heart in my throat.

Why does this suddenly feel like a big deal?

"What are Everything cookies?" he asks.

My pulse speeds, mind spinning.

Then I hear my dad's voice again, and it settles me.

Be brave and kind.

I blow out a silent breath and smile at him. "They're my specialty," I say, offering up the plate. "Want to try one?"

He's still and focused, but then his mouth turns up at the corners, just slightly, as he reaches forward and takes a cookie from the plate I'm offering. It's huge—because cookies should be delicious and huge and not something that people skimp calories on—but it looks tiny in his hand.

Big and strong and fierce.

But...I'm not scared of him.

Maybe I should be, especially after Phillip.

But...I'm not.

"Fuck," he snaps and I jump, skitter back a step.

Or maybe I am.

"Woman," he says, wiping the crumbs from the corners of his lips, his gaze going disapproving, "this is just plain mean."

My brows shoot up. "Um—"

He takes the plate, holds it against his chest. "These are mine," he says. "They're going to make me absolutely sick with sugar and crap, but they're all mine."

I blink.

"My precious," he says in a Gollum voice.

I blink again.

"Okay fine," he says, "I'll share *one* with you."

I blink a third time.

And then, because the begrudging expression on his face is so freaking adorable, I find myself laughing. "Gee, thanks," I mutter.

He winks but passes the plate back over. "Thanks, princess," he says softly. "That was nice of you."

"These are actually"—I return the plate—"for you." I tilt my head toward the container I'd filled with the rest of the cookies. "And those are too." I shrug. "I know it's not much, but sugary, not-good-for-you cookies have excellent healing properties."

He studies me closely.

Too closely.

"What about you?" he eventually asks. "Were you able to partake in those same healing properties?"

Something warm bubbles in my belly. I inhale, nod.

But he doesn't press me further, just says, "Good." Then goes to the fridge, pulls out the carton of milk, and pours himself a glass. "Do you want—?" He holds it up.

"No," I whisper.

A nod before he puts it back, closes the door. "Work go okay?"

It's small talk.

But it feels like more.

Probably because we're not arguing for once.

But also maybe...because it *is* more.

"Yeah," I say after a moment, answering his question about work. "Lots of emails and then I worked a bit on the planning for our fundraising gala."

He takes a bite, decimating half of the cookie with that one action. "The one for Chrissy's charity?" he asks around it.

"Yes," I say. "Though it's also going to benefit my dogs."

Blue eyes softening further. "I'm glad." He juts a chin toward the hall, and I turn to see a sleepy-eyed Zeus laying like a little potato in the opening. "I wouldn't have him if not for the work you do."

My heart squeezes. "He's a good boy."

"The goodest." A wink before he moves to the doggy cookie jar, and I watch the sleep clear from the pup's golden-brown eyes, see the razor-sharp focus snap into place as King pops open the top of the container, reaches inside.

Click-click. Click-click.

Zeus is in front of him in a flash.

"It's the last one, bud," King says, holding out the treat.

Zeus takes it like the *goodest* boy he is—gently. Then he spends the next few seconds chomping noisily, leaving a trail of crumbs in his wake that he deliberately licks up. But even though the little-legged fluffer is adorable and normally I could watch him just be a dog for hours, I find my gaze drawn to King. He's gone to a cabinet near the hall that leads to the garage, pulls a binder off the open shelf there, and sets it on the counter. A flick opens the cover and then he's flipping to a page—

"What's that?" I ask.

He snags a pen from the little cup on that same shelf. "What's what?"

I tilt my head in the direction of the binder. "That."

"My Life Planner." Said matter-of-factly.

Both like this is common...and like I should know what a Life Planner is.

My brows shoot up, nearly to my hairline. "*Your* Life Planner?"

He lifts and drops one big shoulder in an approximation of a shrug as his eyes scan the page. "Yup."

"Your *Life Planner?*" I don't know what that is, just that the name makes it seems intense and far too much work.

"Yup," he says, jotting something down in it.

"I don't understand."

His gaze flicks to mine. "It's a binder I use to keep track of everything I need to keep track of—shopping and road trips, appointments and shit that needs to be done on the house."

"Oh."

This big, giant hockey player with the hard body and black eye from practice and beard that's thick and rough that I want running over my naked skin, has a binder he uses to *plan his life?*

I just—

"How? Why?"

"What?" His tone is light, eyes dancing, obviously enjoying my shock. "Do Prickle Princesses not organize their own lives?" A tap to his chin. "Oh no, of course they don't. They have servants for that—tiny, fluffy servants who are magically trained to complete the most common of household tasks."

I narrow my eyes at him. "Really?"

He grins. "And, let me guess." Another tap. "Ms. Pricklestein doesn't believe in organization without the aid of her fluffy servants either?" He smirks. "Or maybe you use your spikes to prompt them into action when they move too slow?"

"Okay," I mutter. "This is getting ridiculous."

"What about Spiny Sweetie? Does she organize? Or Barbarella? She has to plan at least something. No? Maybe Your Thorny Highness does?"

I groan.

"No?" he asks. "None of them like to plan ahead either?"

"That is far too much talk of pokey things," I tell him. "Plus, I have enough deadlines with my design work and the rescue. I don't need to hold myself to firm targets in my own life."

"That's an excellent point," he says lightly then hops up on the counter, nudging the binder toward me. "But I don't make deadlines for myself. See?" He taps a finger on the page. "It's just to keep track of all the moving parts." A beat, his lips curving. "Like when the dog treat jar gets low."

Now that's smart.

I have to give him that much.

His expression is confident bordering on cocky. "I see that my Princess of the Pointiness understands my logic."

Oy.

This man pushes my buttons like no other.

And yet...I'm enjoying myself.

Dumb. So fucking dumb.

"King," I say, sighing heavily even as amusement coils in

my belly. I turn the binder toward me, start to study what's on the page—a note for dog treats in the pet section of his grocery list. "I'm going to need you to stop with the prickly references."

"So, switch over to scientifically proper cactus references then?" His lips twitch. "I'll call you Queen of the Night. *Ooooo*." He wiggles his fingers.

I choke on my laughter—goddamn he's funny.

And annoying.

And...not what I thought he was.

Which makes me feel even more like a jerk for judging him...and for being the aforementioned prickly.

Something I swear he clocks because he looks far too proud of himself.

I sigh again.

But I'm still biting back laughter.

I ignore the amusement threatening to escape—and his spirit fingers—as I flip through the pages of his binder, clocking a meal plan and grocery list, a cleaning and chore schedule, exercise and training plans (for both himself *and* Zeus). Contact lists—his local vet and several emergency clinics, his own doctors, a nutritionist and skating coach and physical therapist.

The man is organized, almost to a frightening extent.

And I love that he owns it.

That he's not embarrassed.

Though, I suppose I should have picked up on those organization skills when I was pilfering his pantry's contents for Everything cookie ingredients and saw the little clipboard with a pen attached hanging on the wall just inside the door. It held a pad of paper beneath the metal clamp, a scrawled out list of items written on it.

"I'll give you *Queen of the Night*," I mutter instead of

letting him know he's won the conversational battle—at least so far. Then I flip the page and freeze at the sight of a color-coordinated calendar that's so prettily organized, it makes my graphic designer heart thud with joy.

It's so pretty it takes me a minute to process all that's on it.

Games and practices. Vet appointments for Zeus. Skating sessions for King. Travel schedules with the team. And—

"You have a schedule for when you call and text your family?"

ELEVEN

Her smile is fucking breathtaking.

Even though she's giving me shit, the sass dancing in those emerald eyes.

I want to kiss her.

She's bright and happy and beautiful.

A siren calling me to shore.

And, for a moment, I don't care that a shipwreck is imminent.

I just—

"You seriously have a schedule to contact your siblings?" she asks, jerking me out of my thoughts—thank fuck.

"I have a lot of siblings," I hedge.

Grinning, she runs a finger down the page, reciting from my notes, "Jakob text every Tuesday. Jensen on Thursdays. Leif on Wednesdays. Annie on Monday, Friday, and Sundays. Tanner on Saturdays." Her eyes flick up, green depths dancing with mirth. "Poor Annie—" I sigh. "Does she get a moment of space with five overbearing brothers?"

"I resent that," I tell her, even as my heart starts thudding. Why did I show her this shit? It's dumb—ridiculous that I need a schedule. Why can't I be a normal sibling who just—

"Calls for Annie on the first and twenty-second, for Leif on the fifth and twenty-eighth, Jakob the seventh and twenty-first, Jensen the third and nineteenth, and Tanner on the sixth and twenty-seventh." Her mouth quirks. "What happens if they call you and mess up the schedule?"

I shrug. "I'm flexible."

Plus, I have erasable pens and can adjust the schedule as needed.

"Sure you are," she says lightly. "Because this"—she waves a hand at my binder—"screams flexible."

I open my mouth to reply—not that I know what I can say in response.

Pandora's Box has been opened.

She's seen behind the veil.

There's no saving me, not now.

"I'm impressed though," she says before I get a chance to reply, to attempt to dig myself out of this hole. "Two days per sibling—" Another mischievous glance. "At least Annie is spared extra phone calls from her protective older brother."

God, she's pretty.

"Annie," I say, reaching a hand toward my binder, "can put any of us in our place any time of the day."

That makes Rory smile.

Not a surprise, I suppose, considering that this is a case of like recognizing like—a strong woman recognizing strength.

"Now, as for Mom," she says, tapping a finger on the paper. "I see that you call her every—"

"Right," I say, snagging the binder, closing it up and setting it to the side. "I think you've seen enough, princess."

"You call her once a week?" Rory asks.

"Yeah," I mutter. "I love my mom. She's the original GOAT—raising six kids virtually by herself for half the year when my dad was playing and then coaching, all while working a full-time job."

Rory's face changes. "What does she do for work?"

I shove the binder back onto the shelf. "She's recently retired, but she was an elementary school teacher."

"Surrounded by kids at home and at work." She smiles, and it's soft this time rather than filled with mischief. "Your mom must be pretty special."

I nod. "She is definitely that. Truthfully?" I pause and Rory nods. "She's amazing. And just as busy now as she was when she was working—volunteering her time, visiting her kids." I grin. "I wouldn't be surprised if she has her own schedule that we're not privy to."

"You had to get it somewhere."

You're not your father.

I freeze, grind my back teeth together, hating those words, the woman that implanted them into my head.

"You all play hockey, right?"

Thankful for the distraction from the bullshit in my head, I grab on to the conversation gambit. "All of us play except for Annie. She's a skating coach now for a team in New York, but before that, she was a competitive figure skater."

"Did she go far?" Rory asks.

"All the way to a silver medal at the Winter Games."

Admiration on her face, in her voice. That nice I've seen so often directed at other people making a reappearance. "That's amazing."

I lean back against the counter. "She is."

A pause, her expression considering. "And what's your dad doing while your mom is doing all that traveling and volunteering?"

"He's still coaching."

"And they're both in Minnesota?"

I blink. "How'd you know?"

"Those long O sounds?" She grins. "Next thing I know, you'll be saying *you betcha.*"

I jokingly narrow my eyes. "You really want to go down that road, Prickle Princess?"

Her brows lift dangerously. "I thought I told you to cool it with the cactus talk."

"Are you threatening me, Tiny Spikey Queen?"

"Yes."

She's fierce, those green eyes sparking now, and I can't help the laughter that bursts out of me at this ridiculous conversation—something that distracts me enough that I don't really process what she's doing, what she's moving toward.

My binder.

I jerk forward. "What—?"

She holds up my planner threateningly. "You really want to go down this road, Sir Organizer Color-Coding McGee?"

"Excuse me?"

She lifts her brows, then opens the binder, rings down, fingers wrapping around the bottom and top hoop, like she's preparing to—

"Stop," I order, all amusement fading.

"Oh, so you *don't* want to play this game after all, Mr. Spreadsheet?"

"Ror—" I begin, moving toward her.

"Uh-uh-uh," she tuts, shaking my binder—my life—threateningly. "I wouldn't if I were you."

I freeze. "Princess—"

"Don't you mean *Prickly Princess?*"

"I—"

But I don't get to finish what I was going to say because—

She gasps and I watch in horror as the binder slips from her hold, the flash of horror on her face, clinging to her voice. "Shit!"

She dives for it.

So do I.

Our bodies collide.

She gasps.

I grunt as her elbow hits my ribs, but I react fast enough to ensure that I don't crush her, rolling so that I land first and my body breaks her fall.

The binder bounces off my shin, skittering away, the sickening sound of papers flying making my stomach twist.

"Oh my God," Rory whispers, pushing off my body in a rush, making me grunt at the contact. "Oh my God," she says again. "I'm so sorry. I was just messing around." She clambers over to my planner on her knees, hands darting out this way and that. "I didn't mean to ruin it. I-I—"

It's the break in her voice that finally unsticks me enough to push up from the floor, to move over to her, snagging her hand when she reaches for one of the papers scattered around. "Princess, it's fi—"

"I ruined it," she says and I don't miss that her eyes are glassy with tears, that regret is painted into the lines of her face. "I fucking ruined it and—"

I take her hand. "Ror—"

Her eyes lock onto mine. "I'm so sorry."

"Princess—"

"Really. I—" She swallows hard and looks away. "You've been so nice to me. This whole time you've been nice to me, and I've been a total bitch because I assumed you were what social media and the blogs say you are, and I believed the reputation—"

I touch her cheek. "Everyone does."

"That's not you," she says. "The playboy"—she lifts her hands, makes air quotes—"*King* Bang. You're not what they say you are—"

"I'm not a fuckboy, no," I say.

But the rest of it—

You'll never be half the man your father is.

My eyes close and this time I'm the one looking away, those words a razor-sharp slice of memories.

"King—"

Right.

I know that tone—soft and gentle and sweet.

And I don't want to think about it now, don't want to think about a woman being soft and gentle and sweet...and in love with me.

And then...*not*.

"The pages are numbered," I blurt.

She rocks slightly, brows drawing together. "What?"

"It's not a big deal that the pages fell out," I whisper. "They're numbered."

Still. So still. Then she seems to process my words. "Oh," she says, glancing at the bottom corner of the page in her hand, where there is indeed a number. "Right." She reaches for the binder, starts organizing the sheets then glances up at me. "But I'm still sorry."

I shrug. "It's fine."

"I—"

But I ignore her, just grab a handful of papers, start organizing them and pass the stack over.

She takes them, but doesn't move for a long moment, long enough that I look up and meet her gaze again. "I don't make plans," she tells me quietly. "Because they always go to hell."

I'm frozen, the glimpse of heartbreak in her eyes slicing nearly as deep as the memories in my mind had. I open my mouth and ask, some perverse piece of me needing to know, "What do you mean?"

She's silent for a long moment.

Then sighs.

"Well, obviously you know about the cancelled wedding."

Fucking asshole Phillip. "Yeah," I bite out.

She touches my hand. "I'm okay."

Maybe.

But I still want to murder the asshole.

"But before that—" She presses her mouth flat, releases it on an exhale. "For my whole life I've had to be flexible, had to adapt."

"What do you mean?"

A hesitation and then—

"My mom died giving birth to me."

Shit.

I turn my hand over, gently capture hers. "I'm sorry, princess."

She exhales. "It's hard to miss what I never knew." A shake of her head. "Okay, that's not precisely right. I did miss it, miss what I never knew. But my dad was great—"

She stops.

Probably because I went stiff at the word *was.*

"He died when I was twelve," she says, giving a shrug

that belies the serious words. "Then it was just my stepmom and stepsisters and...me."

Why do I feel like there's much more to the story than that?

But even as I open my mouth to ask, she's finishing with the binder, popping to her feet, and slipping it back onto the shelf.

I'm finding my feet too. "Princess—"

"I really am sorry about your binder," she whispers, gaze sliding away. "I was just—"

I touch her cheek, turn her back to face me. "I'm telling you the truth, baby. I'm not upset."

Her eyes close—just for a second—and then she's nodding.

"Thank you for the cookies," I murmur, knowing I should drop my hand, should back up and let her head off to do whatever she wants to for the rest of the evening.

"It was nothing," she whispers. "Not after everything you—"

Her throat bobs.

And my heart aches.

I cup her jaw. "You didn't deserve for him to do that to you."

Her inhale is sharp. "King—"

"And I'm sorry about your parents."

Glimmering green orbs of light.

Plump, pink, kissable lips.

"And I want you to stay here for as long as you need." I stroke my thumb over her cheek. "It's nice to have someone else in the house." My mouth quirks. "After growing up with the Bang crazy, it gets a little quiet with just me and Zeus."

"Thank you," she whispers. "Though I'm not entirely sure you mean that."

My brows lift.

"Did you forget the rant you gave us all about your mom the last time we were at Rome and Chrissy's?"

My mom, who as we've established, I love to the fucking moon and back.

But who also drives me fucking insane.

Mostly because she seems to have made it her mission to marry me and my siblings all off as quickly as possible.

"I haven't forgotten," I grumble. "She's coming to town next week, so I'm sure you'll have plenty of time to revel in the tornado that is Mama Bang."

Her lips twitch. "Mama Bang?"

I lift a shoulder, drop it. "Nicknames are rampant in hockey," I tell her sagely. "And it's all too easy for those around us to lack creativity when it comes to having a last name like Bang."

She giggles. "In fairness, it's quite a name."

"Technically, it's *Bäng*," I say, pronouncing it with its proper Nordic phonetics. "But no one seems to remember that detail."

"No"—her mouth is curving—"I can't say they do."

"And, anyway, I love my mom—as I've made clear—I just wish that she would stop with the matchmaking." I shake my head, exhale as all of those bad dates flash to the forefront of my mind. "It's already cost me a watch *and* a laptop...and that's not including my time dealing with the drama the women she picked unleashed on my life."

She winces. "That sounds like a lot."

"That's my mom," I say and shrug again. "She gets an idea in her mind and then just...puts her head down and grinds through."

Rory's lips twitch. "Like a certain hockey player I know."

"Prickle—"

She leaps forward, covers my mouth with her hand. "We've been getting along so well," she says like she's imparting state secrets. "Can we just leave the prickle insults alone?"

She's close enough that I can see her eyes have specks of peridot amongst the emerald, that she has a small scar on her chin, that the tiny stud shaped like a flower she wears in her nose is missing a crystal in one of the petals.

And I don't think.

I press my lips to her palm.

She gasps, hand falling away from my mouth, the charms on the bracelet from her dad tinkling.

I go still—watching, assessing, searching for any sign of unease on her face.

But there's no fear in her eyes.

There's...attraction.

Need.

"King," she murmurs, her body drifting toward mine.

I settle a hand on her hip, draw her toward me until our bodies are pressed together. I inhale the soft floral scent of her deep enough in my lungs to scent the hint of Everything cookies in her hair, on her skin.

Soft curves.

A palm settling on my chest, just over my heart as she rises on tiptoe.

I bend down, mouth coming to hers—

Just as the doorbell rings.

Sending Zeus barking and skidding down the hall.

I curse softly, but she smiles and backs away. "I'll get it."

"No," I murmur, taking her hand, drawing her to a halt. "You stay here and..." I trace my thumb over that plump bottom lip. "Hold that thought."

She inhales, eyes wary for a moment. Then they clear, determination entering their depths, and she nods.

I step back, turn for the hall and the front door and Zeus barking on this side of it.

I scoop him up, turn the handle, and—

"Surprise!" my mother says, launching herself into my arms. "I'm early!"

TWELVE

"My baby boy!" I hear. "I've missed you so much."

I freeze, heart sinking.

It's not Rome or Chrissy or Jean-Michel—all of whom have popped in over the last days to check on me. I'd been looking forward to the interruption, to them breaking the tension—

The *need*.

I'm less than a week out from not getting married.

And I almost kissed another man.

Or...well, I *had* kissed him because our bodies had been plastered together, our lips had touched, and—

My mouth is still tingling.

Hand shaking as I slowly lift it, I press it to my mouth, trying to capture the sparks of sensation still coursing through my skin.

A brush of lips and...

I'm shattered into a million pieces.

I've never felt anything like it—something so intense that all of the air left my lungs, every nerve was firing with sensation. I was—or maybe *am*—desperate for his touch and lips and—

Cock.

I shudder, push that aside.

Because...

The voices are coming closer.

"I could use a cup of coffee," I hear the woman—presumably the aforementioned Mama Bang (what with all the *baby boy* talk)—say. "My flight was delayed and I almost missed my connection and—"

"Mom," I hear King say. "I actually need to talk to you about—"

A petite woman with hair as dark as King's turns the corner into the kitchen and skids to a stop, eyes going wide. "Oh."

King's right behind her, wearing the beleaguered expression of a son who knows there's no point in fighting it.

"*Oh,*" Mama Bang says again, clamping a hand to her chest, mouth opening and closing. "I—" She turns to King, voice dropping. "I didn't realize you weren't alone."

"Clearly," he says dryly. "Hence, you showing up early and unannounced on my porch?"

She swats at him. "Hush now," she tells him, positively bouncing with emotion. "And introduce me to your girlfriend."

I choke.

"Mom—"

But Mama Bang doesn't give him the chance to explain. She just strides across the kitchen, hair bouncing, hand extended.

I think it's for me to shake, so I lift my own. "Hi," I say. "I'm Rory—"

Only our palms don't get the chance to meet.

Because...

Her arms are wrapping around me instead.

I still, heart pounding.

This...is strange.

I never really realized it before—that there are different kinds of hugs. I *should* have because I know there's a difference between a lover's embrace and a friend's comfort.

But *this* is so unlike anything I've ever experienced.

It's not the bear hugs I used to get from my father.

It's not what Phillip and I had long before everything went bad.

It's not what Chrissy and I gave each other when life seemed determined to kick us in the teeth.

It's not...

Like King's hold from just moments before.

It's...a mother's touch.

Warm and firm, confident and sweet, wrapping me up in a soft floral scent, holding me close as she says, "We're all family here." Her arms tighten for a moment before she pulls back enough to smile up at me—*up* because she's tiny, even though I'm not tall in any sense of the word. "I'm Stella," she says, eyes delving into mine. "It's so nice to meet you Rory."

"Mom," King begins, moving toward us. "Want to release Rory for a second so I can explain—"

Mama Bang's—er *Stella's*—purse starts ringing.

"Oh"—she smiles apologetically—"I'm sorry but that's the twins. Jakob—King's brother—"

I nod, letting her know I've got that much.

"—said they would call me when they got home. Will you

excuse me for a minute? I can't miss talking to my grandbabies."

"Of course," I tell her.

"Thank you, honey," she says softly, giving my arm a squeeze before she starts riffling through her purse, pulling out her cell. She swipes across the screen as she reaches the hallway, lifts it to her ear and says, "Hey, baby. I'm glad you called. I just met King's new girlfriend—"

My mouth falls open.

King groans from next to me.

"I—" Slowly, I swivel to look at him. "Did she say—?"

"Yup," he mutters. "Twice." He sighs again then turns toward me, takes my hand. "Don't worry, I'll straighten her out."

A thought pops into my head—a way to pay him back for being so nice, for holding me when I cried, for rescuing me from the side of the road and from Phillip's house. A way to thank him for letting me use his guest room and office, a way to make up for being so grumpy and judgy with him and well...nearly destroying his Life Planner.

Something better than Everything cookies.

Something better because his mom's obsessed with playing matchmaker.

"You don't have to," I blurt.

He rocks back on his heels, shakes his head. "What?"

"You don't have to straighten her out—"

His brows shoot up, nearly to his hairline.

"We can pretend to—" I swallow hard, trying to not take in the obvious shock in his eyes. If I look too hard I might see that he's disgusted or upset or furious. "I know she's been matchmaking hard, and you said the dates she set you up with haven't gone well, and..." I swallow again. "I'm already here and it might take the pressure off you for a little bit." I bite my bottom lip then force a smile. "Save your new laptop even if I do threaten your Life Planner."

That has him unsticking, the shock sliding from his face. "That's really sweet of you to offer," he says, shaking his head. "But I can't possibly ask you to—"

"You're not asking," I say. "I'm offering." I shrug. "Just think of it as a thank you for your help."

His expression and tone are extremely gentle. "I don't need a thank you for helping you, princess."

My heart flutters at the earnest words. "I know." I push past the butterflies in my belly. "But..." I sigh, hold his eyes. "I'd really like to feel like I can do something helpful for a change."

His big chest rises and falls on a breath. "Something more helpful than rescuing countless animals?"

Be brave and kind.

"Will you let me help you with this?" I ask. *Be kind.* "Just for a little while to take the pressure off? I know I'm not—" My eyes skate to the side. *Be brave.* "—I know I'm not the type of girl you normally date and—"

His expression changes from bemused to furious in an instant.

"You are fucking *beautiful*," he says fiercely. "So fucking beautiful that any man would be lucky enough to date you, let alone me."

Let alone *him?*

This gorgeous professional athlete with the kind heart and love for his family and willingness to adopt a puppy and a planner that includes a list to pick up more treats for the pooch had told me—

Let alone me?

I open my mouth to demand an explanation for *that* insanity—

"Oh my God," Stella says. "You two are so sweet."

We jump and turn toward her, King's arm coming around my shoulders, steadying me when I misstep, drawing me back against his big, strong body.

Now's my chance.

Be brave and kind.

Inhaling, I summon that courage and reach up, touching his cheek. "I'll just go up and make sure the guest room is ready for your mom, okay honey?" His fingers tighten. "And give you two a chance to catch up."

His bright blue eyes hold mine for a long moment before he sighs quietly and tucks a strand of hair behind my ear. "Thank you, princess," he murmurs.

Then he presses a kiss to my forehead and moves over to his mom.

"You have to try these cookies," I hear as I slip from the room and hurry up the stairs to the guest room, heart pounding the entire way.

Be brave.

Be kind.

And...

Please don't let this bite me in the ass.

THIRTEEN

King

"A black eye," my mom comments archly later that evening as we sit around the kitchen island, devouring the plates full of steaming pasta and chicken in front of us courtesy of Rory, who'd changed the sheets in the guest room, moved her things into my bedroom, and then came down and started dinner.

Like a girlfriend would.

Christ.

Now, I'm staring at my plate, still spinning from the turn of events.

Rory seems unaffected, though, playing the part of my girlfriend with surprising ease.

I guess not *surprising*.

My mom is good at making anyone comfortable, and Rory is a nice person with a big heart. It's no surprise that they hit it off. Probably because my mom raved about her cookies, but also because my mom ultimately wants me to be happy, so she would give any woman in my life the benefit of the doubt before forming her own opinion.

Not that her opinion took long to form.

Case in point?

"I love her," my mom whispers in my ear, all but bouncing in her seat.

I glance up at Rory, who's carefully folding her napkin, and know it would be far too easy to love this woman.

And...I'm tap-dancing in dangerous territory now.

"How was your nap?" I ask, trying to divert her. And myself.

Not a shock.

It doesn't work.

For either of us.

My gaze is drawn back across the table.

Her grin is wide.

And knowing.

Christ.

I go for diversion again. "Mom?"

Her brows come up.

"I asked how your nap was?"

She studies me, and I brace, waiting for her to say something else about Rory.

She doesn't. "Fine."

But my relief only lasts a second.

Because then she's back to the shiner I'm sporting from practice.

"Why the black eye?" Her eyes pin me in place. "I know it wasn't from your last game."

Always with her finger on the pulse.

Always watching each of our games.

I sigh, know it's pointless to try to keep the truth from her. "I lost my temper and punched Pat."

Those brows rise higher. "King," she begins, "how often have I said that violence isn't the—"

"I bet he deserved it," Rory mutters.

I freeze with my fork halfway to my mouth, reeling from the whiplash of disapproval to pleased, Mom to Rory.

"Explain," my mom demands.

"Pat is a total jerk," Rory says, bailing me out. "He's been actively trying to cause drama with the team."

My mom's eyes widen.

"He's always got a snarky comment, loves to degrade women, and doesn't care about bringing the team together. In fact, he's doing everything he can to destroy it."

If she only knew.

It's that...and so much fucking more.

I can barely stand to be on the ice with him, let alone to have to be in the locker room or on a plane with the asshole.

The shit he says about Chrissy, what he insinuated about Rory, how he talks about women and treats his teammates and—

He's scum.

And I get to play eighty-two fucking games with him.

Just the thought has my blood boiling again.

"So what?" my mom asks. "You took issue with something he said?"

My gaze flicks to Rory and then back to my mom, and I know she gets it with that one look. Gets that he said something about Rory and I lost my cool and...she might not appreciate me starting—and then finishing—a fight with my teammate, but she *gets* it.

Because she always taught me to stand up to bullies.

Because she knows that I would never stand for my woman to *be* bullied.

"Yeah," I mutter. "I did take issue with it."

My mom scoops up a forkful of pasta, brings it to her mouth then chews and swallows. "Well," she says, tone casual—far too fucking casual when it's paired with the gleam of satisfaction in her eyes. "I'm glad that you stood up for yourself." A beat. "And everyone else." Her mouth quirks. "Does he have a black eye as well?"

"No."

"Oh," she says and I don't miss the disappointment in her tone.

My lips twitch. See? She can't stand bullies. "He has two."

Nodding approvingly, my mom pats me on the shoulder. "That's my boy."

Rory laughs softly but then does me another solid and turns the topic of conversation away from my black eye and my asshole teammate. "I've heard about your apple pie from no less than three Eagles players," she says softly. "Is there any way I can tempt you into teaching me the recipe?"

My mom grins. "Will you trade it for your Everything cookie recipe?"

Rory nods. "Absolutely."

My mom extends her hand over the island for Rory to shake. "It's a deal."

"It's a deal," Rory agrees.

I look between my mom and Rory, warmth pulsing in my belly and my heart as they seal their agreement with a handshake.

Sitting here like this, like we're a real family...

Well, it feels normal.

Feels like the most normal thing I've ever done. As though I've done this same thing for years and years and years.

And I can pretend I've never done anything else.

That it's always been Rory and me—just the two of us against the world and—

You're not your father.

I still, ice pouring through my veins at the cold, female voice in my mind. It blasts through the false reality I was building, steals any of the teasing I was going to allow off my tongue just moments before.

Reality hits hard.

Luckily, though, the two women sitting at the island with me don't recognize the sudden turn in my brain.

They're too busy bonding.

Christ.

This has to be the stupidest thing I've ever done—including punching Pat in full view of the public, fans pulling out their phones and recording the action on the ice.

It's probably circulating social media as we speak.

It's likely going to give Jean-Michel even more reason to dislike me.

Refusing to let him take her to his place, to Chrissy or Rome's either.

Then falling asleep and giving Rory the opportunity to go back to that bastard's house to retrieve her things—thus putting her in Phillip's crosshairs.

Now I'm blasting the Eagles' drama in the locker room back into the public eye when we've been on a winning streak (both in the standings *and* amongst our fan base).

I can see the headlines already.

I can *see* Jean-Michel's disapproving mug.

It's superimposed on the other faces who've looked at me like that throughout my life—former coaches, my parents on occasion, women I've dated, exes, and...Rose.

Who's not just an ex.

But *the* ex who made me realize that I will never have what my parents have.

Because I'm not that man.

Because—

A palm lands on my thigh, squeezes firmly enough that I snap out of my thoughts, realize that I've been leaving my mom and Rory to talk.

Which is fine.

They're both good talkers.

The problem now is that they're both staring at me.

Waiting for me to answer a question I didn't hear.

"Well, for me," Rory says, her voice gentle, her grip on my thigh still firm. "I first saw him on the ice." Her lips quirk as she glances up at me. "I'm afraid I wasn't very nice," she admits, expression contrite. "I thought he was a bit of a playboy and I'm not a hockey fan"—she shrugs, her smile self-deprecating—"or *wasn't* a hockey fan, anyway. But it's hard not to be swept up in the sport when my boss owns the team."

"Oh," my mom asks, "do you work for the Eagles then?"

A shake of Rory's head, sending her blond locks drifting across my arm. "No," she says. "I work for Oak Ridge—the vineyard that Jean-Michel owns."

I know that look on my mom's face.

Apparently, so does Rory because she grins. "Yes, the wine is delicious. And yes, I can get you some."

My mom laughs. "Am I that obvious?"

Rory lifts her shoulder in a delicate shrug. "No," she says. "But that *is* the typical conversational track that occurs when I mention working for a winery. I'm not in production itself, but I do design work—the labels, the signage, brochures, graphics for the website." She smiles. "I get to do a little of everything."

Not planning.

Just letting life tell her what her next task is.

Why do I feel like I've just unlocked some of the puzzle that is Rory?

"She's excellent at her job," I tell my mom. "You should see her designs."

Those fingers tighten on my leg and I feel Rory's eyes on me. I can't keep my gaze from going to hers—not in a million fucking years.

"You think that?" she asks softly.

I brush her hair back from her face, tuck a loose strand behind her ear. "Absolutely."

"Phillip—" She clamps her lips together, eyes sliding closed for a heartbeat.

I bend my head, whisper for her ears only, "That asshole had no clue how fucking amazing you are."

She swallows hard, squeezes my thigh again and then pulls back her hand.

I know she hears me.

But she doesn't *hear* me.

And I know that before all of this between us is done, I need to make sure she does.

"Tell me about teaching, Stella," Rory says a moment later. "I bet that was the definition of *a little of everything.*"

My mom grins and shakes her head before picking up the conversational gambit, telling Rory some of my favorite stories about teaching and her kids and the drama that came from working for a school.

"Oh no, not the finger paint!" Rory says, laughter having her bent almost in half, her shoulder bumping into my chest.

I like that.

Like her close.

My mom nods. "Yup." She sighs, but she's laughing too. "I don't think I've ever seen such a mess."

Rory giggles. "I bet."

"It's just lucky I keep a change of clothes in my classroom because what I was wearing went straight into the trash."

"Oh no!"

A shrug. "It comes with the territory," my mom says, mouth curved. "Luckily, I was pretty good at cleaning up messes, what with six kids and all."

"I don't know how you did it." Rory shakes her head. "I like kids, but a classroom full of them? And I like my clothes. I don't think I could be calm if I lost an entire outfit to finger paint."

I bet she could.

But I don't say that.

I'm happy to sit here, listening to them talk about nothing important and yet everything that really matters—life and laughter and family.

"Speaking of clothes," my mom says, "I noticed yours are in the closet in the guest room, Rory." Her eyes flick to mine. "Is there a reason for that?"

I feel my lungs convulse.

Rory's hand clenches on my leg and I watch panic slide over her like a heavy blanket. "I—um…"

I cover her fingers with my own, link our hands together.

"You know how I am with my closet," I say lightly. "Rory doesn't believe in color coding, so our clothes exist much more peacefully in separate spaces. Isn't that right, princess?"

Rory unsticks. "Yeah," she croaks. "You know how organized he is." She shrugs. "I'm not remotely as organized. Plus"—she smiles—"King was here first and had all those suits. It makes sense he gets the bigger closet."

My mom's gaze flicks from me to Rory.
Then back to me.
"And the wedding dress?"
Rory freezes.
I freeze.
But my mom doesn't.

FOURTEEN

Rory

Stella squeals and jumps toward me, folding me in her arms so quickly that I don't have time to react.

I'm just surrounded in warm, soft *Mom* and it settles somewhere deep inside, soothes wounds so buried in my soul that I forgot they existed at all.

I inhale, commit her scent to memory and then get it together enough to hug her back.

But it's only for a moment because then she's bouncing away, moving over to King and hugging him tight. "My baby's engaged! I can't believe it. When were you going to tell me?" She cups his cheeks in both palms, turns his head from side to side as she kisses both of them. "I'm so happy for you."

King's eyes hit mine over his mom's shoulder.

They're wide and panicked and—

Shit.

Right.

This was a stupid idea.

I'd better come clean. Right now.

I open my mouth, but Kingston beats me to it.

"Mom," he says. "It's new—*really* new"—his eyes flick to mine and away—"so I'd appreciate it if you give us some time to settle."

Stella's head bobs up and down. "Of course. Of course." She mines zipping and locking her lips. "I didn't see a thing."

Only my wedding dress.

God, how could I have been so dumb to have left it in the closet? Hung up and zipped away in the garment bag, yes. Not out of sight, but clearly out of mind.

Ugh.

And why had I left my ring at Phillip's place?

At least that would be helpful in this farce of a situation.

A farce I can't allow to continue.

Dammit.

And I really like Mama Bang.

"Stella," I begin.

"Where's your ring?" she asks like she plucked the word from my mind. "I'd love to see it." She reaches for my hand. "My King has great taste. I bet he did really good."

I freeze.

Because, swear to God, this woman has mind reading abilities.

I think ring, she fixates on ring.

Either that, or a ring is the next obvious conversational topic that comes when discussing an engagement.

Even a fake one.

A throb begins in my temple.

Right.

This has clearly gone too far.

Stella's a nice woman and I need to come clean.

Only when I open my mouth to tell her that my ring is at my ex's house because I couldn't stand the sight of it on my finger, didn't want the reminder of Phillip—even though I could have sold it for a pretty penny—King beats me to the punch.

"It's getting resized, Mom," he says.

"Oh." The disappointment in her tone slices through me and I bite the inside of my cheek, trying to resist channeling my *Big Daddy* vibes—

Can you get the kid a Happy Meal? Somebody get the kid a Happy Meal!

Can you get the MIL an engagement ring? Somebody get the MIL an engagement ring!

"Stella—"

She spins toward me, moving across the kitchen with speed despite her little legs, sweeping me into another hug that has my insides shuddering.

Such a beautiful feeling to be held like this.

King can't possibly know how lucky he is.

"I saw the dress bag," she whispers. "But I didn't peek." Then she winces, her cheeks going pink. "Okay, I had a little peek. A *tiny* peek." A glance over her shoulder, voice dropping so that King can't hear. "That lace on the top is absolutely beautiful."

My heart squeezes.

Hard.

Because—

"That's my favorite part too."

Her face is gentle. "I can't wait to see it."

A lance of pain.

Because she won't.

Still, I force a smile, hug her back when she wraps her arms around me.

"Don't worry," she says into my ear. "This will be our secret—"

She breaks off in a yawn.

"Good grief," she says, pulling back. "You can't take me anywhere now, can you?" She pats my cheek then goes over and kisses King's. "I think tomorrow will have to be pie day, if that's okay with you?"

"Of course, Mom," he says, wrapping an arm around her shoulders, guiding her from the room.

"I'll just help with the dishes—" she begins.

"No, you won't," I tell her. "You'll get some rest and King will do the dishes." I wink. "And maybe I'll deign to help him."

"Careful, princess," he says, narrowing his eyes, though his mouth is curved. "You wouldn't want to start getting me *prickly*."

"I hear your warnings, spreadsheet guru," I tell him, "and I don't heed them."

His lips quirk.

I bite back my own smile.

"Goodnight, sweetheart."

Blinking, I see that Stella's eyes are amused and her smile is wide and she's noted every bit of this conversation.

Dumb, probably.

Especially since this can't continue.

But...

Bantering with King is fun.

So, even though I should end the madness...

I don't.

I just pick up a towel, wave it at him after he's shown his mom to the hall.

"You wash, I'll dry."

Suddenly he's in my face, hands on my hips, body pressed close.

My pulse jumps and my lungs hitch, my stomach going all fluttery. "What are you doing?" I whisper.

A hand tracing up my side. "What I was going to do before the doorbell rang."

"We should talk about this," I murmur as he slides that big, warm hand along my torso, inching it higher and higher.

"Talk about what?"

I wince, and he immediately loosens his hold, that big hand gentling even though that's not what had me grimacing.

"No," I whisper, taking his hand, drawing it back to my side. "You didn't hurt me." The heat of his palm sinks through the material of my shirt, and I go on, "I meant about your mom thinking—" My eyes slice to the side, searching for any sign of her, and even though I don't find any, I drop my voice further. "—we're engaged."

"Hmm," he murmurs, head dropping, his beard catching on the strands of my hair.

That sounded like an awfully casual *hmm*, considering the predicament we're currently in.

One that's my fault.

I sigh, but it's not just because it's my fault. It's also because...his head is still dropping and now his lips are brushing the top of my ear.

"It'll be okay," he murmurs. "She'll go on to visit one of my siblings soon and I'll slip in the news of our 'breakup' when she's suitably distracted." His tongue flicks out and I shiver, my body melting against his. "The heartbreak alone will buy me a reprieve long enough that I'll owe you."

Somehow, I don't think that's possible.

"And in the meantime..." He trails off, body surrounding

mine, those lips moving, drifting down to my earlobe, tongue flicking out to taste me.

"*Oh,*" I murmur, head falling back, giving him access to my throat.

"Christ, you're beautiful," he mutters against my skin.

"King." My hands drop to his shoulders and I don't know if I'm trying to push him away...

Or holding on for dear life before I beg him to use my body any way he wants.

Hot breath raises goose bumps on my nape, my arms. "And you smell like sugar and spice and Everything cookies."

My mouth turns up, nails kneading into his flesh, and I say, "You smell good too."

He lifts his head, eyes dancing. "Who said *I* said you smell good?"

I gasp in mock outrage, narrow my eyes. "How dare you—?"

And that's when he dips his head, lips coming over mine.

More than a brush this time—they're firm and confident, and paired with his palms on my body, his hips pressing me back into the counter, his tongue slipping into my mouth to tangle with mine, it's *oh so good.*

I moan softly, hands going to his head, tangling in the strands of his hair, and—

It's a match into gasoline.

Explosion.

Not thinking.

Just feeling.

Needing. *Wanting.*

His hand comes beneath the hem of my T-shirt and I arch back, breaking the kiss, his name on my lips.

A growl.

His mouth finding mine again—

"I'm just going to grab another one of those cookies before I head off to bed—*oh!*"

We freeze, lungs heaving, mouths a hairsbreadth apart.

I manage to tear my gaze from King's molten blue one, see that Stella is grimacing as she tries to creep out of the room.

Then my eyes go back to King's.

He sighs, looks so put out that I can't help but giggle.

His expression does something wonderful then, something that settles in that same fissure his mom's hug began to heal earlier, drawing the edges closer together, filling it in. Then he cups my cheek, brushes his lips over my forehead, and retrieves the container of cookies.

"I'll be back," he mutters. "And then I'll wash and you dry."

THIS IS AWKWARD.

It's a couple of hours later, and I've delayed bedtime as much as possible.

But my inbox is cleared.

The gala is as organized as I can have it at this moment.

And...

It's getting late.

So, there's no more delaying.

Which brings me to now—standing in King's bedroom feeling awkward as I try to navigate how sleeping next to him for real (or really, for *fake*).

Thankfully, he does something to break the taut silence and us staring silently at each other.

He disappears to his closet.

Smooth? Maybe not.

But effective for breaking the bizarre staring contest? Definitely.

A few moments later, he comes back into the bedroom and walks over to me. It's not until he passes what he retrieved over to me that I realize what he's brought out. And...I melt a little.

Because I remember the sweats and tee he gave me that night, remember being covered in his scent, in the soft fabric that had once adorned his body.

I remember how it made me feel.

How *safe* it made me feel.

So, even though my bag with my clothes is currently shoved into a corner of his closet—my cozy pjs and socks waiting for me—I just take the T-shirt and disappear into the bathroom, thankful that making that walk only hurts if I step the wrong way.

I'm getting better.

Slowly and steadily.

And I'll keep going.

It's the only thing I know how to do.

I close the door behind me, peel off my pants, my shirt, my bra, but leave on my underwear and socks before I pull King's tee over my head.

Spice and male.

Kingston.

Safe.

I inhale deeply, hold that scent in my lungs, committing it to memory.

Then I get it together enough to unzip the toiletry bag I stashed in here earlier, to wash my face—and the makeup that's currently covering up the remnants of the bruises Phillip gave me. I brush and floss and slap on moisturizer and hand cream.

With nothing else to delay me, and knowing that King likely needs to use the bathroom for whatever evening ablutions he partakes in, I leave the awkward-free space of the bathroom and go back out into his bedroom.

Immediately, his eyes hit mine.

Then slowly drift down.

Hot. Liquid.

That stare.

Or maybe that's the space between my thighs.

But he doesn't say anything as he inclines his head to the bathroom, voice on the right side of growl—because I feel it between my legs again—when he asks, "You done in there?"

My heart is thudding against my rib cage, but I manage to exhale, to whisper, "Yes."

He pulls back the covers, and I find that my stare's doing some drifting of its own, dragging over his bare chest, over the sweats that hang low on his hips.

I want to trace along the waistband with my tongue, want to...*whoops* and push them down.

I want...

Well, I *want*.

He touches my cheek and I jump, so focused on the heat blooming in my abdomen that I don't realize he's moving closer, that he's near enough to hold, to stroke, to *lick*.

I shudder.

But he just cups my jaw, tilts my head up.

"I think it's time for you to go to bed, princess," he murmurs.

For *us* to go to bed please.

And to not sleep.

For hours.

"You've had a long week," he says, voice soft, calloused thumb brushing lightly over my skin and making me shiver.

I exhale, though, table those words and just nod. "Yeah," I agree, gently touching the bruise still forming beneath his eye. "You too."

A called-off wedding. A rescue—or two. And now a fake engagement.

We're going to need plenty of sleep to handle all of that.

Gentle blue eyes.

A palm flattening on my cheek.

He leans close.

I hold my breath, wish and want swirling in my belly, and—

He drops his hand and disappears into the bathroom.

FIFTEEN

I know I should be the kind of man who offers to sleep on the floor when I come out of the bathroom ten minutes later, teeth brushed and flossed, face washed, deodorant reapplied so I don't stink up the joint.

I know I should be the kind of man who doesn't offer but just *does* it—takes a pillow and blanket and crashes on the floor, not makes a request hopeful that it'll be turned down, that she'll invite me to share the bed.

I know I *should* be those men.

But I'm not.

I come out with fresh teeth and a decent-smelling body, and I crawl right into bed next to Rory.

She gasps softly, but I don't withdraw.

I don't push it any further either.

I just settle on my pillow, several feet between us, even though I also want to be the kind of man who crawls into bed, draws her against me, and fucks her senseless, morals or the right thing to do be damned.

But she's not ready for that.

It's been a week since the non-wedding—or tomorrow will be, anyway.

She needs time.

So, I just roll on my side, face her, and ask, "What are you thinking?"

She surprises me by not prevaricating, not shutting me down. Instead, she sighs and rolls to face me, hands tucked beneath her head. "That your mom is really nice and I feel like a giant jerk for even suggesting that we lie to her."

My heart squeezes. "It's a little lie."

Her brows lift. "An engagement is a *little* lie?"

Okay, she has a point, so I don't argue further. "I'll fix it when she goes off to visit my brother."

"Which brother?"

"Actually," I admit, "I'm not sure. I know she'll be with Jakob for Christmas, because he's the only one of us with kids, and she'll want to be there for the holiday, but otherwise she goes where the wind blows her."

"Jakob's wife doesn't mind her coming for the holiday?"

I bite back a grimace. "His *ex*-wife is currently fucking her trainer in Hawaii, so she doesn't really get a say in the matter."

Rory winces, her deep green eyes contrite. "Damn," she says. "I'm sorry."

"Nothing to be done for it," I mutter. "I can't say that we liked her all that much, but the way she imploded Jakob's— and the boys'—lives and I can honestly say that I wouldn't mind her getting a severe sunburn in a very sensitive spot."

Lips twitching, Rory huffs out a laugh before her face goes serious. "She cheated then?"

"With that trainer."

"Oof."

"Yup." I shake my head. "Cheated and then decided she didn't want to be a mom any longer, leaving Jakob a single dad to five-year-old twins who"—my mouth curves—"are more than a handful on a normal day, but even more so after all of that happened."

"Poor babies," Rory murmurs.

"Yeah," I agree. "That's not something they'll easily get over." Some traumas slice too deep, create hurts that can't be fixed, no matter how much time has passed.

"Luckily, they have you and your siblings." Her expression gentles. "And your mom. The big happy Bang family."

I tuck a strand of hair behind her ear. "The dramatic, chaotic insanity of the Bang Brothers, you mean?"

"Yeah. *That.*" She grins, but it's cut off by a yawn.

"You're still recovering," I murmur, and before I can stop myself, I trace the yellowed edge of the bruise around her throat, the one she's been covering with makeup, the one I can see now only because she's washed that mask away.

Because it's just her and me.

My heart rolls over in my chest. "You should go to sleep."

One hand slips out from beneath her head, mussing her hair as she stretches her arm out beneath mine, winding our limbs together. She brushes her fingers beneath my eye, lightly stroking the bruise. "You've had a busy week yourself," she whispers. "Saving me." A beat. "Twice." Another. "Plus, two practices. A game. Managing Zeus and dealing with an interloper—*me*—" She smiles. "In your house. Not to mention your mom showing up unexpectedly early." Her thumb traces over my cheek. "That plate of yours is full."

I shrug as well as I'm able to while lying on my side then pull my arm back. "I'd rather it full than empty."

"Right," she murmurs, drawing back herself. "I just..." She shakes her head, stoppers up the question.

"What?" I ask.

"It doesn't matter."

"You're my fake fiancée," I tell her. "I think that means everything in that gorgeous brain of yours matters."

She yawns. "Sorry," she murmurs, dashing a hand over her face. Then touches my hand. "It's just...did I thank you for helping me?"

There goes that feeling in my belly again, the swoosh, the way phantom fingers seem to sweep up and squeeze my heart. "I don't need a thanks, princess."

"I know," she says. Her top shoulder lifts toward her ear and drops. "Or I know that the King I'm getting to know doesn't need one." She exhales softly. "But that King deserves one."

Another squeeze of those phantom fingers. "Princess, you don't—"

"I know." Her palm presses to my chest, above my pounding heart. "But thank you, Kingston Bang. I—" She sighs, closes her eyes for a long moment. "I'm scared of starting over again, but it's a little easier knowing that you have my back."

Christ, she's sweet.

And beautiful.

And my dick is very aware that we're lying in bed next to each other, being nice to one another for a change. The problem is that there are far too few layers between us, and it only takes a bare moment for me to remember the sight of those long, slender legs beneath the hem of my tee as she'd walked out of the bathroom, the way the material had clung to the tips of her breasts.

No bra.

No bra as she's lying next to me—soft and sweet and all too touchable.

Only...her eyes are drooping and her yawns—another one coming as she opens her mouth to seemingly ask me another question. "Sorry," she says. "I just wanted to—"

Another yawn.

And I've had enough.

I peel her hand from my chest, press a kiss to the palm, and gently set it on her belly. "I think your body is telling you that it's past time to sleep."

"I'm fine," she says.

"You're tired."

I roll over and flick off the light, sending the room plunging into darkness.

"King," she says, tone exasperated. "Really?"

I give in to the ache in my chest—those phantom fingers squeezing and squeezing and *squeezing*—and then I reach across the distance between us and tug her back against me.

A soft gasp, her body going stiff for a moment.

"Hurt you?" I manage to rasp, guilt and need tangling together, stealing up my throat.

Silence.

For so long that I almost pull my arm away, almost roll and flick on the light, if only to see her face.

But then she melts against me, all of her soft pressing into me, her soft sigh of contentment hitting hard enough to steal any words, any movement, making it so that I can't do anything except hold her.

Hold her as she says, the words as quiet as the night creeping in, "No, King, you didn't hurt me."

Hold her and listen to her as she slowly drifts off to sleep.

Hold her and claim her as mine and—

Hold her as I allow sleep to coax me under.

SIXTEEN

Rory

I wake up warm and rested, more rested than I've felt in the week since the aborted wedding, in the week of sadness and emotional and physical hurts and...

Nightmares that crept in and tried to steal my slumber.

But no nightmares last night—

Or at least, none that I remember.

I sigh softly, start to roll over.

Start because...I try to move, but I find I can't.

Which is the moment that sleep finally leaves my hazy mind and my eyes fly open.

There's an arm around my middle, but that isn't a surprise. It was there when I fell asleep, same as the big, hockey body had been pressed all to my back. It's just—

The leg between mine, King's thick thigh pushed up against my pussy.

The hard cock throbbing against my ass.

The hand cupping my breast.

I—

Well, I'm turned on, instantly and completely and before my next breath. My pussy grows slick and I feel the material of my underwear, the only thing separating that strong, thick thigh from the rest of my body, grow damper moment by moment.

So damp that I know, if he was awake, he'd be able to feel it.

Same as he'd be able to feel the hard bud of my nipple pressing against his palm.

Hear my breath growing ever more unsteady.

Feel the need coiling in my body, sending me trembling.

I exhale silently, try to regain control, but all I can feel is his sexy body surrounding mine, covering me in his heat, his scent. Desire is a red haze at the edges of my vision, reducing my world to this bed, this man, the way he's got me feeling more with him than I ever felt with Phillip.

Maybe that's why I do what I do next.

Maybe that's why I wouldn't be able to *stop* myself from doing it, even if the world was ending and aliens were descending and nukes were falling from the sky.

I arch my hips—

And sweet baby Jesus, that's good.

His hard cock pressing into me, thick like a steel rod, making my pussy grow even wetter. His breathing is even and steady, but his body moves against mine, grinding closer, his palm closing more firmly around my breast, thumb and forefinger unerringly finding my nipple, pinching it hard enough to make me buck against his thigh.

And then gasp, sparks of pleasure shooting through me.

Rolling my nipple back and forth, back and forth.

That thigh starting to match that rhythm—or maybe *my*

rhythm as I rock against him, already almost embarrassingly close to an orgasm.

Ridiculous.

But I don't stop moving.

Only—

He's sleeping, and I'm grinding against him like he's a sex toy while he's unconscious, while he—

Can't possibly consent.

A bucket of ice-cold water over me, stealing my pleasure, having me go stiff and unsure.

Back and forth. Back and forth. Those fingers don't stop. Neither does the thigh.

Desire and need threatening to steal this clarity, threatening to erase this knowledge of knowing *I can't do this.*

Not while he's sleeping.

Dammit.

I reach up, try to peel his palm away, even though those rolling movements are sending my head spinning, my pleasure spiraling. It would be easy to keep going like this, to come apart.

But it would be wrong.

So, I manage to summon a herculean amount of strength and pull his hand from my breast, to stop rocking.

To start to slide from his hold—

His arm tightens.

I freeze, heart skipping a beat.

And then I find myself on my back, King over me.

His mouth descends and then I have no doubt that he's awake. He takes charge of the kiss, tongue sweeping into my mouth, slick and hot and sure. It tangles with mine as one of his hands slides along my waist, dips beneath the hem of my T-shirt—

His T-shirt.

I gasp at that warm palm trailing on my skin, drifting up, cupping my breast.

No material dulling the sensation, just his body against mine...and it's fucking glorious.

He groans and I arch, trying to get as much of his touch as possible, but he only gives it to me for a disappointing second before his hand disappears.

I protest, and it's cut off.

By the T-shirt being dragged over my head.

"Fuck," he growls, head dipping, mouth meeting my skin. He licks and nips, kisses and drags his tongue over every inch of my exposed torso, slowly making his way up to my bare breast. "You are beautiful."

I gasp.

Then moan.

Then melt as wave after wave of glorious pleasure weaves its way through every single one of my cells, sending my nerves on high alert, every fiber of my muscles tightening, like a spring being twisted around and around and *around*.

I'm so close that I'm going to snap, that my orgasm is going to explode out from me.

But...*he* isn't.

"King," I manage, my lungs sawing and breaths coming in rapid gusts. "I—" A breath. "You." Another. "I shouldn't—" I break off on a moan, head digging back into the pillows. "I shouldn't without you."

He stills, tongue flat on my nipple, lips sucking firmly.

Then he draws back, the suction breaking with a soft *pop*, leaving my nipple so hard that it's almost calling out for his mouth.

"Is it too much?" he asks, eyes half sleepy, but I don't miss the concern, the seriousness creeping into those blue depths.

It *is* too much.

But it's also not nearly enough.

Which is why I know it's not too much in the sense that he means.

"No," I say, reaching for him, the sight of him between my breasts almost too much to handle.

He's beautiful and powerful and sexy as hell.

"Then what?"

"I—" I suck in a breath, release it, steadying my breathing enough so that I can say, "If you keep going, then I'm going to come."

His brows flick up and he holds my gaze for a long moment before he asks, "So?"

"So," I admit. "I don't usually—" I bite my lip. "Not alone. Not without—"

Clarity seems to dawn on his face.

And then he scowls and rears back. "Not ever?"

Had I ever come without my partner coming? No.

Had the reverse been true many, many times? Yes.

Both of which he seems to read on my face because he's suddenly rearing away from me. "Lie back like a good girl," he rasps, hair a mess, eyes no longer the least bit sleepy, hands reaching for the waistband of my soaked underwear, "and let me lick that cunt."

SEVENTEEN

King

I barely resist the urge to tear her panties from her legs, have to clench my teeth together in order to slowly drag the material down her thighs, along her calves, off her feet.

But then it's flying through the air, landing somewhere in my room, and I'm staring at a naked Rory.

Long, lean legs. Lush hips. A narrow waist. The soft curve of her belly, the flare of her ribs, the tempting apple-sized breasts.

A throat I've had my lips on, but not nearly long enough.

A mouth I need the time to worship.

Long lashes resting against the tops of her cheeks.

She trembles, lips parting, eyes slitting open just enough to give me a glimpse of insecurity. For a second, I'd thought she meant that no other man had the pleasure of tasting that slick cunt, that liquid desire I can see—even from here—folds glinting beneath blond curls in the early morning sunshine.

And I'm caveman enough to admit that the thought had sent a bolt of pleasure through me.

This pussy mine and only mine?

Yeah. I'm good with that.

But rage had quickly followed—banking those caveman urges—when I processed what she meant.

She only came—*when* she came at all (because I didn't miss that distinction either)—*with* her partners?

They didn't worship her like the goddess she is? They didn't make her come until she couldn't take any more, until she was limp and sated and her clit was overloaded from sensation?

And then make her come again despite that?

Fucking bastards.

But it's what has my clenched jaw staying clenched, tabling the urge to plunge deep and fuck that slick cunt.

I'm going to make this good.

I'm going to make it fucking incredible for her.

I slowly trace my hand along her side, down her rib cage, her waist, over her hips, and then inside, dipping my finger between thighs I'm desperate to have wrapped around me, her heels digging into my ass as I fuck her senseless.

Patience.

I stroke a feather-like touch through her labia, tracing plump lips, slow and steady, smirking when she arches up, tries to find more purchase in my fingers.

But it's not time for that yet.

"Behave," I chide, pulling back when she presses, waiting until she settles, then rewarding her with a brush of my thumb over her clit when she melts into the mattress. "Let me make you feel good."

She's restless, her gaze locked on mine. "I need…"

"I know what you need," I tell her. "Now"—I reach in, pinch her nipple hard enough to make her gasp—*"behave."*

"You're a dick," she snaps, but her eyes are sparking with desire.

"I'm going to give you *my* dick."

Just not right now.

She rolls her eyes, but she's grinning.

Until I brush her clit again, and then she's moaning, lips —both sets—damp and plump and tempting. My mouth waters, but I'm going to get her to come this way first. Then with my mouth. Then my fingers *and* my mouth. Then—

Right.

I should probably stop thinking about all the ways I'm going to make her come.

And actually *make her come.*

I press my thumb a little harder, circle her clit, gauging her gasps, the rocks of her hips, what has the color on her cheeks growing and her lips darkening with increased blood flow. I watch her nipples bead and harden further, feel the slickness in her pussy grow, her breathing speed up.

"King," she whispers.

And I hear it.

The hitch in my name on her lips, the one that has my cock aching, like those phantom fingers in my chest have left my heart alone and are wrapping around my dick, stroking firm and fast, coiling my orgasm at the base of my spine.

I grind my teeth together, stave it off, keep hold of my control.

And I keep at her clit, rubbing firm and sure and—

"King!" she cries out, probably far too loud considering that my mom is right down the hall.

But I can't bring myself to care.

Not when I get to watch her orgasm slide through her—

tightening her ass, flexing her hips, curling her fingers and toes as her thighs tighten around me for a heartbeat. Two. Three.

And then she goes limp.

Fucking perfect.

Tart and sweet. Sass and kindness. My prickly princess who only blooms for me.

It's dangerous thinking—I'm fully aware of that. Fully aware that this has only one way to end, and that's with my heart becoming roadkill because I can't give this woman all that she needs, all that she deserves.

And she deserves *everything*.

"Holy." She's breathing like she just ran a marathon. "Fucking." A long inhale that has her tits jiggling and my cock growing even harder. "Shit."

"Again," I mutter.

Those emerald half-mast eyes fly open, lips parting in surprise. "What?"

"I haven't tasted that slick cunt, princess."

Another breath, shorter, more staccato. "King," she whispers.

I don't listen to the note of warning in her tone, just palm each lush thigh, push them wide, and I get my mouth on her.

Sweet.

So fucking sweet.

Barely any hints of tart, and just wet enough for me to drink her up, for my tongue to slide freely through her folds. I dip inside her entrance, tasting that slick channel, feeling her shiver, those internal muscles contracting around me, and then I'm sliding my mouth away, dragging my tongue up to her clit.

Circle. Tease. Press. Push her closer to the edge.

Back down and inside.

Clit. Tongue fuck. Repeat until I feel her fingers in my hair, until she's both keeping me close and pushing me away, until I feel her thighs trembling, hear my name chanted in increasing frequency.

"King. King. King," she cries hoarsely. "Oh God. *King.*"

My tongue is fucking that slick pussy so I get to feel her convulse around me.

Fucking glorious.

She slumps down to the mattress, chest heaving, tits bouncing, and—God—I want to fuck her.

But I'm also not done with her.

I wipe my chin, kiss my way up to her mouth, tasting her lips in a lazy, slow caress, waiting until the sweat begins to dry on her body, until her breathing stabilizes, until clarity comes back into her eyes.

Then I kiss along her throat, nibble at the princess-like ear, slide my lips along the sleek column of her throat—gently. Carefully. As though my mouth can make the bruises there go away.

I drift lower so I can taste each delicate collarbone.

Nip at the soft globe of her breast.

"King," she warns quietly.

I suck her nipple deep in answer.

"King!"

And then I'm making my way back down between her thighs, using my mouth and fingers in tandem this time, using all that I've learned from my previous use of each of them. I put it all together to drive her relentlessly up to that peak, not slowing, not stopping, just forward, forward, *forward.*

One finger. Two. Three.

Sucking at her clit, her labia.

A flash of teeth.

My name on her tongue again.

And then her cunt is clamping down on my fingers, her hips are grinding against my face, my beard, fucking me as much as I'm fucking her.

And then—

She shudders.

Her grip on my hair tightens painfully.

And...she comes apart.

I grin against her pussy as I slowly coax her down the other side, bringing her to a gentle landing, waiting until she slumps back on the bed, hair a mess, sweat on her forehead, between her breasts, limbs lax and akimbo.

She exhales, eyes peeling open—

Just as my alarm goes off.

Fuck.

Question in those emerald irises.

"Practice," I tell her.

She sighs, opens her mouth, probably to apologize.

I halt her with a kiss.

"Another time, princess, yeah?" I murmur.

She gives a jerky nod, clearly not in control of her facilities.

I smirk.

Because, yeah, I'm a self-satisfied asshole.

But mission accomplished.

I'm going to leave her limp and satiated...

And—

I slip my hand back between her legs.

—with one last orgasm.

EIGHTEEN

I never thought I was the type of woman who'd be fucked senseless.

But...

I grin.

Mission accomplished, I guess.

King was...

A force of nature. A god. A...king?

Yes to all of those.

And he hadn't even taken off his pants.

I hadn't even been able to taste him, to touch him beyond the silken dark locks I gripped as he worked me with fingers and tongue and then fingers *and* tongue—

And again.

I shift on the mattress, muscles sore, clit on fire, and yet feeling the slightest bit empty.

Because I didn't get the hard press of his cock stretching me, didn't feel the powerful thrusts of his thighs pushing mine wide, didn't experience the slap of his balls against me as he fucked me good and fierce and deep.

Because I know he'll be all of that.

Know he'll be *more*.

But after that last orgasm—my fourth (and what kind of sex gods were at work here to make that a real-life thing?)—I hadn't been able to so much as move.

Not a hand. Not an eyelid.

Nothing.

I'd just laid there as he gently brushed his lips over mine, giving me a taste of myself when his tongue tangled with mine, the evidence of his unmet desire pressing against my hip before he'd slipped out of bed, tucked the blankets over me, and disappeared into the bathroom.

Something I only deduced because of the door closing and the sound of water turning on dimly reaching my ears.

And I hadn't even heard him leave.

The pleasure-induced haze he'd left me in transforming into a pleasure-induced slumber.

I'd woken with the sun much higher in the sky than normal, managed to stumble to the bathroom, not feeling the bruises, the healing cuts on my feet, and showered.

Using King's soap.

Surrounded in the clean, spicy scent of him. The water sliding over my skin just like his fingers and tongue had hours before.

Now, I'm using my concealer—I've become intimately acquainted with it—to cover the yellow bruises on my cheek and jaw and throat. There's not much to do about the abrasion on my cheek, but luckily that's mostly healed, and I gave up on wrapping my ribs a while ago, tired of the restriction that came with the tight bandage, especially when they were feeling better.

So loose clothes, my comfiest bras, and more makeup than I normally wear.

And no heels.

Mostly because King had stolen them and stashed them somewhere...

And honestly?

I didn't want to wear them right now anyway.

I dab one more spot, ensuring the bruises are completely covered no matter the lighting, and then add some blush, liner, and mascara before calling it good. I don't know if Stella's going to be downstairs, but I want to be presentable if she is.

"That's as good as it's going to get," I murmur, capping the mascara and moving from the room.

I tug the blankets up in a halfhearted attempt at making the bed, knowing instinctively that King won't care if it's perfect, if the comforter isn't evenly folded over, the pillows straight, not a wrinkle in sight.

He doesn't sweat stuff like this.

Hell, he'd probably just make a note to add it to one of his lists in his Life Planner.

☑ *Give Rory orgasms.*

☑ *Leave her in a pleasure-hazed slumber.*

☑ *Make bed when she manages to crawl her ass downstairs.*

Check. Check. Check.

I grin, smooth out a particularly bad wrinkle in the comforter, then go downstairs to find Zeus.

The crate in the bedroom is empty, but I know that King has a few gates up on the first floor, making a safe space for Zeus without giving the mischievous fluff ball full reign of the house. I'm not sure, though, if he had time to walk the pup.

What with my multiple orgasms and all.

My grin widens and I hurry down the stairs.

He's a good pup, but hours alone in the house is still a recipe for disaster...or at least, for the shoes on the shoe rack.

But when I turn the corner, I see that my walking services aren't required.

Zeus—still wearing his harness, though his leash is folded on the counter—is sitting like a little angel next to Stella, who's bent over a cutting board full of green apples.

"Hi, sweetheart," Stella says glancing up from the apple she's peeling.

Using a knife, the skin coiled up in one long spiral. Her eyes meet mine, but the knife doesn't stop.

And she doesn't cut off her finger either.

Just keeps peeling that apple.

"Hi," I say, feeling more than a little awkward.

"Woof!" Zeus says, springing up and sprinting toward me, his little fluffy booty shaking.

"Hey, baby," I croon, crouching down and scratching him exactly as I've discovered he likes—just behind his adorably large ears and massaging upward...along with plenty of butt scratches.

He melts under my touch, reminding me of how effectively King had made *me* melt not all that long ago.

When I straighten after giving him a good long rubdown, I see that Stella's watching me, her eyes gentle and her mouth quirked.

"Is this for the famous apple pie that everyone has been raving about?" I ask, moving toward the stack of apples, both peeled and unpeeled.

She nods. "It sure is."

I should probably leave her be, should get to work, let her make this for her son.

But my feet won't let me make the move.

And then my mouth opens, tongue and throat forming the words.

"Will you teach me how to make it?"

"CHEESE?" I ask incredulously thirty minutes later as I watch Stella layer a thin layer of white cheddar over the pie crust—store-bought because, quote, *"No one who's actually busy in real life has time to make homemade pie crust."*

"Just pies?" I'd teased.

She'd given me a good-natured wink. *"Pie filling."*

"From scratch," I'd pointed out.

That had earned me a light swat...and another apple to peel.

Then she'd asked me about work and we'd talked about nothing and everything.

Until it came to...

Cheese.

She smiles up at me, hands still layering. "Yes," she says as though imparting state secrets—and I suppose she is considering how much I heard about the deliciousness that is Stella's apple pie over the short time I've known her son. "It melts beneath the apples and makes everything creamy." A sigh, clearly appreciative of all the healing properties of cheese.

(I approve).

"And it adds a contrast to all of the sweetness in the filling. You can make it without it," she says, nodding at me to pick up the bowl of apples we've peeled and sliced and coated with sugar and cinnamon, "but it's not nearly as good."

"I'm excited to try it," I tell her honestly after I've dumped the apples into the cheese-filled crust. I set the bowl in the sink and start to wash up.

"We'll give you the first slice," she says as she slides the pie into the oven. "With ice cream."

"That sounds delicious."

She blows on her knuckles, buffs them on her shoulder. "Oh, it will be. Maybe we'll eat the whole thing and not leave a crumb for King and his buddies." Her grin is so mischievous, so much like King's when he's pushing my buttons that I can't help but grin back, my belly filling with butterflies. "It would be the least that little stinker deserves after all the gray hairs he gave me."

I open my mouth, intending to ask her for her best story—purely for fake fiancée research purposes (and not for blackmail), but her phone starts ringing.

"Excuse me," she says, hitting the button to silence the call. "What were you going to say?"

"Oh, that's okay." I snag the sponge, start scrubbing the sides of the bowl. "I'll clean up here. You can go ahead and—"

She swipes the sponge from my hands. "Nice try, honey. You cooked and did the dishes last night. The least I can do is clean up after myself today."

"It wasn't a big deal," I hedge. "Plus, you'd traveled all day. I'm sure you were tired."

Stella dries her hands on a towel then reaches over and touches my cheek. "You're a sweet girl."

I suck in a breath.

"I was tired, but I could have managed. It was nice of you to be understanding of me barging in though, and to go a step further and cook and clean." Her touch turns into her cupping my cheek. "I see it, and I appreciate it."

"Stella," I whisper.

Because I don't know what to say to that.

"Add in hanging with your fiancé's mom all morning, learning her son's favorite recipe, *and* fighting over doing the dishes?" She smiles, squeezes my arm. "Thank God one of my boys finally picked right."

Guilt slices through me, and I have no clue how to respond.

King didn't choose me.

He's not my fiancé...even though I kind of wish he was.

Because that would mean that Phillip had never been and—

Her phone rings again, and she glances down at the screen with a sigh. "I guess I'd better get that." She narrows her eyes at me. "No dishes, missy, and I mean it." She points a finger at me then scoops up her phone and walks out of the room, her voice echoing back to me.

I smile.

But I do the dishes anyway.

Because they're dirty and need to be washed, and it's not like I'm going to disappear into King's office without a word, expecting Stella to serve me my pie.

Something I'm glad of when she comes back into the room, her brows furrowed with concern.

"Is everything all right?" I ask.

"It was my friend, Cathy," she says and I push down the shiver that name induces. Just because my stepmom Cathy was the worst doesn't mean there aren't perfectly nice *other* Cathys in the world.

Stella sighs, and I set the sponge in the holder, turn to fully face her.

"We're supposed to meet later," she says, "but Cathy wants to get together *now*, apparently."

I draw my brows together, confused as to why she sounds a bit put out, especially when it comes to meeting her friend.

But she goes on, clarifying. "Unfortunately, she has to want that when I have a pie in the oven."

"Oh," I say, the pieces sliding into place. "I can watch the pie," I tell her.

"What about your call?"

I have several work meetings today, but nothing critical—hence me hanging in the kitchen and peeling apples with my fake future mother-in-law.

I shrug. "I'll grab my laptop and take it from here." I nod to the island. "Plus," I add with a smile when the furrows between her brows don't ease, "that means I get first crack at that slice."

She softens, palm coming up to touch my cheek again. "Sweet," she murmurs before dropping it away, gaze gliding over the sink.

I wince.

Because, yeah, I did those dishes.

She sighs softly, but her lips are turned up as she walks over to the oven and peeks inside. She fiddles with the timer then turns back to me. "When that goes off, let it sit for thirty minutes if you can wait that long. Then enjoy."

I nod. "Got it."

"Thank you, honey." A beat as she pockets her phone. "You'll tell King I'll see him tonight?"

"Of course."

Another smile and pat of my cheek, and then she's disappearing upstairs, coming back down a few moments later in a nice blouse, her jacket folded over her arm.

We exchange goodbyes.

And then she's gone, leaving me in an empty kitchen, the delicious smell of apple pie in the air.

I look around, almost expecting her to pop back in.

When she doesn't, I go down the hall and retrieve my laptop.

Then I wait for the timer to go off so I can pull out the pie.

But I only manage to give it fifteen minutes before I carve out a slice.

Then nearly die from the nirvana of that first bite.

She's right.

The cheese makes all the difference.

NINETEEN

King

It's later than I want it to be when I'm pushing into the house, body sore and aching.

Ego smarting.

Because Coach—who hadn't been on the ice for my fist fight with Pat—had seen the video.

And he hadn't been happy.

At all.

My ass still stings from the verbal beatdown.

And Pat, fucking cancer in the locker room with his idiotic minion, Duncan, at his side, had sat in the other chairs in the conference room smirking at me as Duncan supported his bullshit story. Saying that I'd acted unprovoked and taken it too far (just because Pat, the fuck, had both eyes blackened and a broken nose to my single shiner).

Smirking while my ass was handed to me.

Over and over again.

Fun times.

I hadn't thought the post-practice meeting was going to be *great*.

But I hadn't thought that it was going to involve the two assholes spinning a story and barely holding back laughter when Coach bought it, hook, line, and sinker, and proceeded to ream into me.

Fun fun.

If I'd known we needed to bring in witnesses, I would have accepted Cam or Rome's offers to come with me.

Except, Cam's family is in town and they live on the opposite coast. I'm not going to keep him when he wants to soak up as much time as possible.

And Rome wanted to get back to Chrissy—I'm not going to fuck with their free time, not when we have far too little of that during the season already.

I know plenty about how a lack of time together can make relationships implode.

My temple pulses with a burst of pain.

Because fuck do I ever know about how this job can tear people apart.

You're not your dad. You can't make this work.

Another time. Another relationship. Another woman.

I sigh and hang my keys on the row of hooks just inside the door, unzip my Eagle-branded jacket and hang it above them.

I didn't ask my friends to come with me because...it was my fuck up.

My shit to deal with.

"Stupid," I mutter, knowing that I wouldn't let that slide with Rome—that he and I have been through enough now to start building lines of communication...and that means calling bullshit on each other when necessary.

But I'm not ready for him to call bullshit on me now,

especially with Rory in my house, with how much I want her...with all the memories that's churning up.

I grind my teeth together.

Table that shit.

My mom is here.

Rory is here.

I can focus on that and the potential shitstorm my newfound engagement with Rory might bring, can focus on the impending matchmaking that will happen if my mom finds out it's a farce.

Better that than the bullshit in my head.

Better that then—

Soft music reaches my ears and all thoughts of relationships imploding and my mom's horrible matchmaking attempts (and how the women she sets me up with have a penchant for stealing my stuff and showing up unannounced at my door) fades.

Because...

Music is playing in my kitchen, drawing me down the hall like a siren's call.

It's not my mom's music, isn't the random mix of 80s metal and 90s rap. Isn't a track that came far before me and my siblings' time, nor is it one of the poppy songs she mixes in that we love to give her a hard time about.

It's a newer ballad, a soft and sweet song about love that I've heard Chrissy play at her house more than once, singing along softly as she cooks or handles one of her rescue cats.

And Rory's usually singing alongside her.

She's singing today too, I see as I turn the corner and look into the kitchen. Her cell is on the island, the music slightly tinny from its speaker. And Rory...

My heart skips a beat.

She's dancing.

Hips moving in a tempting rhythm that has my cock growing hard, my heart skipping a beat, my hands clenching into fists, needing to touch.

But instead...I watch.

I wait.

She's fucking beautiful as her body twists and turns in a sensuous rhythm. I can almost taste her on my tongue, almost feel those soft curves beneath my palms. There's cinnamon and sugar in the air, and the soft floral scent of her shampoo. Her laptop's open on the island. My mom's pie on the far counter. A pot simmers on the stove.

Domestic.

The entire scene is domestic, and my heart thrums, the beauty of coming home and seeing this, seeing *Rory* like this, embedding itself into my soul.

Beautiful.

Absolutely fucking perfect.

"...and that's why I love you..." she croons quietly, hands moving along her sides, ribs and feet clearly not bothering her any longer. She raises her arms, twines them over her head. "Forever and always..."

I don't realize I've moved.

Not until I capture her hand in mine, lacing my fingers through hers as I draw her back against me.

She gasps, head jerking up, eyes coming to mine, and then I feel it—

She melts against me, her back to my front, her fingers softening, head dropping back against my shoulder.

And *that* lands right beside the vision of her dancing alone.

Slowly, I lower my arm, drawing hers down with it, wrapping both of mine around her middle, bringing her even closer against me. My body starts swaying, matching the movements she'd been making just moments before, mirroring the song's rhythm.

It's instinctual and impossible to resist.

We rock together through the chorus and then I turn her during the verse, pressing her front to mine, encircling her in my arms, tucking her head beneath my chin.

Cinnamon and sugar and flowers.

Soft and sweet and cautious.

Her hand stays above my chest for several long moments before it settles above my heart. "Your heart is racing," she murmurs, barely audible over the music, over the song winding down.

"Because I'm holding a beautiful woman in my arms," I tell her, smoothing my hand up her back, drawing her closer. So close that I can feel the sweet kiss of her breath on my throat, that my beard catches on the silken blond strands of her hair, that I'm drunk on her presence.

My words have her fingertips pressing into my flesh, her breath catching. "You've dated plenty of beautiful women," she whispers.

"I haven't dated *you.*"

"Not dated," she teases. "Just put a ring on my finger. Or not," she adds lightly, lifting her left hand with her naked finger and laughing quietly, and the sound of that coats my soul in the sparkling beauty of *her.*

Rory, bright and beautiful despite everything.

Rory, a woman I'm scared to want.

But who I do—something that increases with every heartbeat.

And still, I don't let her go.

I hold her, rotating slowly, the music filling the room even though I barely hear it. I'm focused on her.

Every breath.

The way the lights overhead glint off her hair.

The scent of flowers drifting off her skin.

The cinnamon and sugar of the pie in the air.

The soft bite of her nails into my chest. The way her pelvis rocks against mine, reminding me of this morning.

The feel of her body against mine.

The slick heat of her on my tongue.

The clasp of her around my fingers.

The sound of my name on her lips as she came.

My cock stirs and I draw her even closer, burying my face in her hair, knowing I'm not being the least bit sly when I inhale deeply, bringing the intoxicating scent of her into my lungs.

Holding it as close as she is to me.

Thankfully, she doesn't comment, just melts against me, just lets me hold her.

But eventually, the ballad fades out, transitions into an upbeat pop number and we slow our movements, pull apart. "Speaking of rings," I say as I reach into my pocket, pull out the box I'd picked up on the way home.

Her mouth drops open. "What—?"

"My mom won't believe it without a ring," I tell her, though my heart is beating strangely fast. Probably because that feels like a prevarication, a convenient excuse to have bought her something nice for no reason except...that I wanted to. "And I figured you wouldn't want to wear your old one."

That makes her shudder and I know I made the right call.

Know that it wasn't the bullshit that's been swirling in my head that made me pull over, made me stop and look in the window of the jewelry shop.

Made me buy the ring.

It was *her*.

I place the box in her hand and she holds it for a long moment before opening the lid.

Then stills, plump pink lips parting in surprise.

"Okay?" I ask softly.

She doesn't move—except for her eyes. Those flick up and meet mine. "Yeah," she whispers. "It's more than okay."

"Good," I say, knowing I should come up with something better, something more meaningful.

But it's all I can do to keep my hands steady as I slip the ring from the black velvet interior of the box, as I settle it on her finger.

It catches slightly on her knuckle before I manage to slip it over, not stopping until it sits at the base of her ring finger.

"Perfect fit," she whispers.

Every thought in my mind shatters, scattering this way and that, panic whipping through me, all calm sent spinning by a miniature tornado.

But then I catch sight of that ring glittering in the overhead lights...

And everything settles.

Perfect fit.

TWENTY

The ring feels heavy.

It shouldn't, considering it's just a ring of metal and stone, albeit the diamond ringed by pale blue gems is large—ridiculously large under any circumstance, but also ridiculously large for a *fake* engagement ring.

This is pretend.

And I've got two carets sitting on my finger.

My charm bracelet looks silly next to the glamorous piece of jewelry, and I fight the urge to take it off.

That drags me to my senses more rapidly than a bucket of icy water over my head.

I hid who I was once.

I'm not doing it again.

The bracelet is staying, no matter what.

Warm fingers wrap around my hand, and King draws it up to his mouth, presses his lips to the back of it. "Perfect fit," he murmurs, and those words echoed back to me, glide like silk over my skin, the gentlest of kisses.

I throw my arms around his shoulders, press my body flush to his, and I kiss him.

Not gently.

Not gliding my lips over *his* flesh.

Instead, I kiss him with every bit of longing that's been inside me since the moment I first saw the gossipy TikTok about him, about King Bang, the bachelor hockey player. The blogger had expounded on all of his talents (which were more about the way he looked and who he'd dated and less about his skills on the ice).

Not that I know much about the sport even now.

I'm learning, and Chrissy and Jean-Michel are good teachers.

But...a bunch of giants swinging sticks at a little rubber disc doesn't appeal to me all that much, and it probably won't ever.

I like it when they score.

And when they fight.

And—

A soft growl against my mouth.

"Pay attention," King orders fiercely, arm wrapping around my waist and dragging me flush against him. He nips at my bottom lip, making me gasp, and then promptly takes advantage of my distraction to slip his tongue in, teasing mine, kissing me until my head is spinning and my knees are jelly.

Something he must sense because that arm around my middle tightens and he lifts me, setting me on the counter.

I gasp, but it's surprise mixed with heat, frenzy with plea-sure, need with beauty.

I'm not thinking straight—clearly, because who in their

right mind could be thinking straight with a man like Kingston Bang surrounding her, touching and stroking, kissing and tasting?

And that's why I don't realize.

Why I don't sense the metal clasp of my bracelet catching on the fabric of his shirt until it's too late.

We're both too far gone in the kiss, both too wrapped up in each other, in the moment, in the kiss that's sparked like fire through my veins.

I encounter resistance, my first sign, but I don't process it quickly enough, stilling as he's moving, those big muscles flexing, all of the strength in his athletic body already in motion.

He grips my hips and tugs me toward the lip of the counter, ass resting on the edge.

But my body is moving the other way, seeking purchase in the stability of the granite surface.

And...my bracelet, the cheap, tarnished silver that a little girl loved—*loves*—so deeply...

Gives way.

Metal flexes, snaps.

Charms slide from the thin chain, scattering this way and that in a cacophony of broken memories that wake Zeus from his deep, past-his-bedtime slumber and sends him from his bed in a mess of nails clawing the floor to find purchase, barks to fend off the imaginary scary intruder, and then—almost as rapidly—excitement in realizing he'd slept through his master's arrival.

"Wait," King orders through the chaos, steadying me, nudging me back so that I don't topple from the counter. "Zeus, wait."

There's laughter in his tone.

But only for a second, his hands tightening on my waist for a heartbeat before he lets go in a rush.

"Zeus, no!"

I'm spinning, reeling, blinking at the sudden change.

Kissing to chaos. Cradled close, protected to...alone on a cold, hard counter.

Then he's bending.

And I process.

"Oh God," I whisper, scooching to the end of the counter, looking between my naked wrist and the charms scattered on the floor.

Charms that are being chewed up like a scattering of tasty kibble by Zeus.

"Oh my God," I say, still whispering as I push off, settle my feet on the ground. "My—"

Tears are stinging the backs of my eyes, even before I realize that King is bending, gripping his mouth, swiping a finger inside.

And that cheap, tarnished chain is retrieved from his mouth.

But one glance tells me enough.

It's ruined.

And something inside me, one of those long-buried fragile and hidden pieces...

Shatters.

"No," I whisper, dropping to my knees, hands darting in all directions, trying to gather up the pieces.

But they're wet and chewed and broken.

Like the chain.

Like...me.

Chewed up. Dropped into a puddle on the side of the road. Broken into a million pieces.

Loss and grief and change.

Nothing permanent.

Nothing that's precious to me is safe.

Not ever.

"Excuse me," I whisper, pushing up to my feet. "I—"

King glances up from his spot next to Zeus, lightly chastising the pup.

"Not his fault," I say. "I—"

I should have known better than to care, to expose those soft, *real* parts of my soul to the world.

I. Should. Have. *Known.* Better.

Keep it locked up in a tiny wooden box, safe and sound and tucked away.

"I need to go," I whisper.

"Princess," he begins.

But I don't sit in that endearment, don't allow myself to feel it, and I don't stay.

I just turn for the hall, shove my feet into my Crocs—Crocs King bought me so I'd have something comfortable to wear after he'd hidden my heels. Crocs that are gentle on the mostly healed wounds on the bottoms of my feet.

Crocs that made me think I could be something different, just for a little while.

But...it's fake.

It's not for me.

It's—

Go. Now.

My purse is on the table, my keys easily accessible in the front pocket.

I have them out and in my hands a moment later, am turning the knob to open the door when I sense King behind me.

"Rory," he begins, but I put my hand up.

"I need to go."

Zeus is in his arms, eyes wide and sad and guilty, sending my heart thrumming, guilt churning anew in my belly.

But I don't feel that as much as the drive to leave.

To escape.

"Okay," King says, lifting his free hand, holding it out to me as though I'm a panicked animal.

And I suppose I am—or at least, I'm acting like one.

"Okay," he repeats. "I get that you need to go. I just—"

I tug the door open, step outside, feeling the cool lick of the night's air on my heated skin.

"Are you coming back?" he asks, jarring me from the sensation, from that sweet kiss of night.

I close my eyes against the sight of him standing there, concern and fatigue etched into the lines of his face.

I think about his shit week. I think about the stress of all those failed dates and him not wanting to disappoint his mom.

I think about waking in the warm, comforting circle of his arms and the rage on his face when he saw the bruises that Phillip gave me.

And...

I nod.

"Yes," I whisper.

Then I turn and run away.

And, like usual, I don't have any plan of where I'm going.

TWENTY-ONE

King

I sigh and bring Zeus against my chest, watching through the kitchen window as Rory's car zips down the driveway, its taillights disappearing into the midnight darkness.

"You messed up, bud," I mutter.

He whines and looks up at me with those big puppy eyes.

"Or maybe *I* did by encouraging you to be a floofy vacuum," I tell him, scratching him behind the ears and setting him on his feet. I follow him down, getting on my hands and knees and searching for errant pieces of Rory's bracelet.

Unfortunately, there aren't any to be found.

Which means that I might be conducting a different search for charms in the morning, and I'm not looking forward to it.

Which means that my dog has just destroyed Rory's last possession from her dad.

"Fuck," I mutter.

"Woof," Zeus barks softly, coming over and leaning on my leg and foot, a warm weight that's become familiar.

He did that the first time I went over to Chrissy's house and saw the menagerie of rescue animals she was keeping—in this case, a litter of corgi pups.

Adorable and *troublesome* pups.

But Zeus was more chill than his siblings—in charge in a confident, relaxed way that told me he'd be a good fit for my life.

The rest is history.

He loves me, but he's also cool sleeping in the other room on his cozy pillow.

Not that he's not aware of where I am at all times. He's just...cool.

Calm for a corgi—minus the consumption of Rory's priceless artifacts.

"You're cool, aren't you, bud?" I ask, nudging him off my foot, if only to scratch him properly.

The garage door goes, the noise rumbling through the house and sending Zeus's ears perking. Mine would do the same if I could, and I push up to my feet, move to the window over the sink, hoping to see Rory's car in the driveway, to watch her pulling back in.

Changing her mind.

Wiping the look of her panic and fear from *my* mind.

"Woof?" Zeus barks again.

But it's not Rory.

It's my mom zipping into the driveway, parking and getting out, walking toward the front door. I inhale, shake off the moroseness clinging to my limbs and force myself to plaster on a natural smile by the time she's walking into the kitchen.

"Hi, baby," she says, moving over to me and rising on tiptoe to press a kiss to my cheek. "How was your day?"

Shit. Shittier. And I dropped a shit-ton of cash on a diamond ring that was significantly bigger than something I should have bought, especially for a fake relationship. Then... perfect. For a moment, my day had been perfect.

Holding Rory in my arms.

Soft and warm and smelling of apple pie and flowers.

Our bodies melding together, swaying to the music.

Beautiful. Perfect.

And then...shit again.

But I don't tell my mom any of that. Fuck no, I don't.

I just kiss the top of her head and squeeze her lightly. "Great," I say, nodding to the pie on the counter. "Especially because I have pie."

She steps back and glances over at the pastry delight, mouth curving. "Of course," she says.

"Of course what?"

Her eyes meet mine. "Of course Rory pulled it out at the perfect time."

I frown.

She grins. "That golden-brown crust." One shoulder lifts and drops in a shrug. "I couldn't have done it better myself."

My brows drag together further.

Thankfully, she takes pity on me and explains.

"Cathy"—a friend she'd made on one of her earlier visits to town—"wanted to meet early. Your pie was in the oven, but Rory offered to watch it." A nod to said pie. "And of course, she pulled it out at the perfect time. *I* couldn't have done it any better—and I don't just mean the baking or the prep work she helped me with before that. I mean"—she takes my hand, squeezes—"all of it. Rory is a lovely person and...you did good, King. I'm proud of you."

Guilt slices through me so quickly that it takes everything in me to not flinch back.

Proud of me.

For faking a relationship.

For pining after a woman I shouldn't want.

Shouldn't because Rory's just out of a relationship, and because...Rory deserves a man who isn't gone half the year, isn't potentially dragging her from city to city when her life, her work, her friends, her animals are here.

Because she deserves that fairy tale.

Because I know I'm not the man to give her that.

Not. Your. Father.

I grind my back teeth together, exhale silently through my nose. "Thanks, Mom," I say softly, scooping up Zeus and starting to back into the hall. "Not to rush off"—*lie*—"but I've got to pack for the flight in the morning." I hitch my head toward the stairs. "I'll tell you goodbye tomorrow before I go."

She's quiet for a moment, those eyes on me, studying me, Mom Radar apparently pinged, even though my voice is natural.

Even though I have lots of experience lying like this.

Lying through my heart pounding in my chest and my fingertips tingling and my throat so tight it seems like a miracle that I'm able to get any words out at all.

But even *if* that Mom Radar is triggered, she doesn't call me on the lie.

She just moves close and touches my cheek, her eyes sad. "My sweet boy with the big, vulnerable heart." She drops her hand, sadness drifting away when Zeus squirms in my arms, wriggling his long, hot dog shaped body in order to kiss her on the chin. She laughs, stealing my pooch and cuddling him close. "Zeus and I will make you some treats to share on the plane before I head home to see your dad."

"You're leaving already?"

She kisses Zeus on the top of his head, gaze drifting up to mine. "You're good, baby," she says. "And you and Rory need your space."

"I—"

"I'll be back for Thanksgiving." A smile. "And I'll be here long enough that you'll have time to get sick of me."

"Never."

"My sweet boy," she murmurs again. Then shakes her head. "Go pack, baby. I'll get to baking."

I kiss her cheek, pat my pooch on his fluffy butt. "Thanks, Mom."

"Anytime, baby."

And then I go into the hall, take the stairs.

I do pack a suitcase.

Which centers me enough so that I can go back down and help my mom with the brownies, stealing more than my fair share, even as I consume half the pie.

My stomach full of carbs and refined sugar—so much so that I feel sick—I soak in this time with her, catching up on all the gossip about my siblings, chatting with my dad, who calls her telling her that he and the team he coaches are en route to home from the road trip he was on, listening to her lunch date with her friend Cathy (and surmising that their friendship seems to be cooling, likely because the blind date she'd set up with Cathy's daughter, Stacy, had been a disaster).

Something else to feel guilty for.

But before that takes hold of me, she's distracting me with a story about the twins and some Silly String and Jakob coming home to a mess that...

Suffice to say, reached epic proportions.

We laughed, we reminisced, we ate, and while I love these moments and I love my mom, I can't lie.

My focus is on the front door.

On the empty driveway.

On the fact that my bed stays empty when I go to sleep that night.

And remains that way when my alarm goes off early the next morning.

TWENTY-TWO

Rory

The knock on my door has me glancing up, seeing that Jean-Michel is standing in the doorway.

"Getting an early start," he says, gaze searching mine.

I tap at the keyboard, saving my work, then push the tray in. "I have a lot to catch up on."

His gaze flicks down to my hand then back up to my eyes, something flaring there that sends a shiver down my spine.

It's deadly.

That look is...deadly.

"Apparently"—those eyes flick down and back up again—"so do I."

I still, stomach twisting and confusion spinning through my mind. Then my own eyes drift down to my hand and—

The ring.

Shit.

"King's been busy."

Three deadly words.

"It's not what you think," I blurt immediately, folding like a cheap suitcase.

He steps into the room, closes the door behind him. "What do I think?"

"It's only to get his mom off his back with the match-making for a little while," I say. "We came to an agreement. He helped me with Phillip, so to get his mom to lay off the blind dates, I'm providing...an *anti*-dating service?" The last is said like a question, even though it isn't one.

To my surprise, Jean-Michel doesn't explode, doesn't scold me for being stupid and faking an engagement that is pulling the wool over a perfectly nice woman's eyes, for lying to her when she doesn't deserve that.

His head cocks to the side, stare fixed on mine. "That's why you're staying there?"

I blink.

"Why you're staying at King's house?" He lifts his brows. "The fake engagement."

Right.

I don't admit the fake engagement is a recent development, that the reason I've continued to stay with King after those first few days is a weird combination of not wanting to inconvenience Jean-Michel or Chrissy or Rome and... wanting to soak up more of King, more of the way he makes me feel.

Especially because he's nothing like what I thought.

I nod so abruptly that I probably resemble one of those bobbleheads that the team gives away on random fan nights. "Yeah," I say quickly. "That's why."

"Hmm," he mutters, crossing his arms and leaning back against the doorway. "And I'm guessing that's why one Mama Bang is currently in the lobby with a huge tray of brownies for you and the rest of the staff?"

My throat convulses. "I'm sorry what?" I manage to squeak out.

"Where's my future daughter-in-law?" I hear echoed down the hall.

Shit.

"Please don't—" I begin, but Jean-Michel shocks me by moving to my side, squeezing my shoulder lightly.

He bends down, stares deeply into my eyes, expression gentle. "All I've ever wanted is for you and Chrissy to be safe and happy."

My heart squeezes.

Because Chrissy had been through so much.

"You don't have to worry about me," I whisper. "I'm fine."

He exhales, tugs a lock of my hair. "I know," he says. "You and my girl are always *fine*. Been through hellfire and back and you're fine." He shakes his head, pats my shoulder then mimes zipping and locking his lips. "For what it's worth, I'm a vault."

Relief floods me.

That's worth a lot, a whole freaking lot.

"Thank you," I tell him. "It's just for a little while and—"

Something dances across his face that has my brows dragging together.

"What?" I ask.

He shakes his head, turns for the door, but I swear that he's gone from deadly to smiling and that...well, that doesn't make any sense. "I'll go get your future mother-in-law."

I open my mouth to correct him, but I don't get the chance because he's opening the door, moving out into the hall.

He doesn't get far, pausing just over the threshold, extending a hand. "Stella, I'm Jean-Michel. Your future daughter-in-law's"—a look in my direction and I watch Stella move into the open doorway—"boss."

"And my son's," she says with a laugh. She lifts the tray in her hands. "Brownie?"

He smiles indulgently—something I only get to see from the hardened businessman because he points it in my direction—then takes one of the brownies from the tray. "Thank you."

"You're welcome."

And then Stella's bustling into my office, offering me my own brownie—which is far too delicious for my waistline—and plunking herself in my desk chair. "So, why didn't you come home last night?"

I END up driving Stella to the airport, eating far too many brownies, and finding myself all that much more charmed by her.

Thankfully, she bought my excuse of needing to help with the rescue. Something that isn't exactly a lie—there's always work to do there—but something that was less than the truth the night before.

I needed to run.

My bracelet.

From my dad.

This is why I shouldn't have worn it.

Because I always ruin the good things.

And I did again.

The song in the air, the beautiful feel of King holding me, him slipping that ring on my finger and how all of it—*all of it* —felt right.

Only for the moment to be shattered.

Because, for one second, for a heartbeat in time, I wanted it to be real.

Would have begged the universe for the chance.

It reminded me quickly enough.

Because that's not for me.

It wasn't Phillip handing me a ring and all but ordering us to get married. It wasn't me compromising what I wanted because Phillip's family and keeping up appearance were more important than what I wanted.

It was...a fantasy, a perfect moment in time and space.

And then it was done.

"Stupid," I whisper, sending Zeus's ears pricking from where he's sitting next to me on King's couch, my computer in my lap, my glass of wine on the side table next to me. "Fucking stupid."

Because I'm sitting on King's couch, in his house.

Because I'm here instead of Chrissy's after I drove his mom to the airport.

There's no reason to be here.

Except for Zeus.

Except...I could have brought him to Chrissy's. He would have loved to spend time with his sister, Athena, whom she and Rome adopted.

But I hadn't.

Instead, I dropped Stella, promised to see her in a few weeks, and drove back to King's place.

To pack up my stuff and leave. I'd carry on the charade when Stella visited, but for now, I needed space.

Until I saw the note and a bottle of wine from Oak Ridge on the counter.

My favorite wine from my place of employment.

And then there was the gift certificate to a local spa pinned beneath it.

And the apology note was signed by Zeus—or with his paw print, anyway.

So...I didn't leave.

I couldn't.

For better or worse, I gave into what I wanted, stopped thinking, and just...

Stayed.

But I know that it's going to come back to bite me.

TWENTY-THREE

King

My body feels like I got run over by a train.

And hell, maybe it had.

It's always like that when we play the Sierra.

A tough, brutal battle.

The only benefit is that the flight is all of an hour and we don't get home horribly late.

The bad news?

Some idiot decided that we should have a home and home matchup—meaning that we played in the Sierra's arena last night, and now they're coming to play in our arena tomorrow.

Flight. Morning skate. Game. Flight. Light practice. Morning skate. Game.

That's a lot of hockey over three days.

But that's the life of a professional athlete—living and breathing the sport so that it takes over my life, determines when I eat and what I eat and when I sleep and what I do with my free time.

Who I date—or don't.

Who I enter into a fake relationship with—no matter how dumb.

I should just let Rory off the hook. She set my mom at ease, got her flying home and leaving me to my peace (and limiting her attempts at matchmaking).

I should let her go.

But when I walk through the door into the house and find her sleeping on the couch, Zeus at her side, sprawled out on his back, tiny legs flapping in the air, snoring like he swallowed a chainsaw, something tightens in my chest.

Just a little bit longer.

Then I'll turn her loose.

Plus, even though Phillip was arrested, he's out on bail and currently licking his wounds (according to Jean-Michel's security team). So, she might not be safe yet.

Which is the truth.

But also a convenient excuse that I cling to as I scoop up Zeus, taking him out for a quick potty break before tucking him into his crate in the bedroom.

And it's one that I continue to cling to as I slip my arms beneath Rory's lush body, cradle her against my chest, and bring her upstairs. I don't miss the open bottle of wine I left her, or the glass with dredges of the white next to it. I don't miss her laptop on the coffee table, her shoes tucked beneath. I don't miss that she's made herself at home, nor the relief that floods through me at the thought.

Instead, I just pretend that I'm holding her carefully because she's fragile and recovering, because she needs to be protected at all costs.

Not because she's precious to me.

Even though—

"No," I mutter, and the word paired with my movements in lifting her from the sofa have her brows drawing together in an adorable frown, her head rolling slightly from side to side on my arm.

Shit.

But before I can somehow find a way to soothe her back to sleep, her lids peel back, sleepy green eyes coming to mine.

I tense, thinking about what Phillip did, thinking that it might be disorienting or scary to wake up with a big brute of a man holding her, manhandling her, manipulating her body without her permission.

"King," she murmurs before I can apologize, can set her onto her feet.

Crack!

I almost wince as a sharp sensation lances across my chest. Not because it's painful, necessarily, but because what I'm feeling is so raw and vulnerable and...more than a little scary.

Then her eyes slide closed again and she burrows her face into the crook of my arm and—

She goes back to sleep.

To. Sleep.

Crack!

This time I do wince at the sharp, shuddering sensation that ricochets through my chest.

But, thankfully, she's not awake to see it.

* * *

I DREAM of flowers and soft, springy summer grass cushioning my body.

Sun dancing across my closed eyes and the cool wind just barely ruffling my hair.

I dream so deeply that when I wake, I have a moment of disorientation.

I'm in that dream, that peace, the vision dominating my mind.

But then...I'm awake but living that dream.

Sunlight glints in through the open shutters of the windows, streaking across the carpet, the end of the bed...

And over the woman in my arms.

I inhale, and it's flowers in my nose.

I flex my arms, and it's soft curves against me.

I look down and—

Crack!

Rory's beautiful green eyes are open and she's looking up at me. "Hi," she whispers.

"Hi," I whisper back, everything in the world going hushed.

My mom's not here. We don't have to pretend.

But stopping myself from cupping her jaw, from tilting her face up while I bring mine down is impossible.

Our lips meet, and that fantasy, that dream becomes real life.

In the form of her soft moans, her body melting against mine. She lets me roll her onto her back, legs parting, our pelvises aligning. I can feel the heat of her cunt through the thin layers of material separating us.

But I want more.

I want *everything*.

I slide a hand between us, slipping it beneath the fabric of her T-shirt, finding silken skin and soft, warm flesh, gentle curves. "Okay?" I murmur when her breath hitches, eyes going wide.

Her lungs inflate on a long, slow breath, and I start to pull my hand back.

"No," she whispers, fingers wrapping around my wrist, pressing slightly, flattening my palm against her.

"Princess?"

Her throat works, but then she presses her palm against her again. "It's better than okay."

And then she's sitting up slightly, reaching for the hem of her shirt, yanking it up and over her head. It flies across the room, but I'm not tracking it. Instead, my gaze is glued to her, to those gorgeous curves and sun-kissed skin and—

She reaches for my shirt, tugging it off before I can pounce on her, tossing it away.

Then her hands are on my bare skin, softly tracing over my body. So softly that it's almost teasing. So softly that the delicate caresses set fire to my veins, to my flesh, to my nerves.

And that's before her hand slips into the waistband of my underwear, those soft, delicate fingers wrapping around my cock and squeezing hard enough to make my vision haze.

"*Fuck!*"

The little minx just grins.

And starts stroking.

My brain shuts down, but I have enough control to reach down, to try to slide her hand off. Because her first.

Always *her* first.

"No," she says, her free hand coming to my chest, pushing me back, clambering on top of me. That hand continuing to move without hesitation. "Last time was me. This time is you—"

The squeak she makes as I reverse our positions is adorable, and makes me smile even when all I want to do is fuck her until she can't remember her name.

"No," I say. "This time is you."

She shivers.

"And then you again."

Another shiver, her lips parting on a shaking exhale. But I see the protest flickering in those emerald eyes.

"And then you *again*."

More protest in beautiful green irises.

Which is why I add, "And *then* me."

The objection fades.

"Yes?"

Teeth working her bottom lip.

Then a nod, her cheeks coloring, her body arching beneath mine.

I come down over her. "I need the words, princess."

"Yes," she whispers.

And that's enough to splinter the last of my control.

I bend down and kiss her.

Her lips part immediately and I sweep my tongue inside, tangling it with hers, swallowing her moan. Fucking beautiful. Fucking perfect.

Perfect as I kiss her long enough until my lungs protest.

Perfect as I drag my lips over her skin, as I kiss her breasts, as I push her pajamas down and slip my fingers between her legs.

Perfect as I encounter slick heat, as I push into the tight clasp of her cunt, as she rocks against my hand, her head pressing back into the pillows, neck arched, eyes clamped closed.

Perfect as my name tumbles off her lips, as her pussy clamps around me. And again.

And *again*.

Perfect as I reach for the nightstand and snag a condom, as I roll it down the length of my cock.

I pause with just the tip of my cock inside her. "Princess," I say, waiting to move until her eyelids slowly peel open, until her stare locks with mine.

Then she nods again.

And I push home.

For a second, the world stands still.

Heat. Slick.

Perfect.

But then it starts moving again, or I'm moving, or—

We're moving together, bodies and mouths and breaths in sync. I give and she takes. Slow and steady and deep.

Until slow and steady and deep isn't enough.

Until the next moment, my next breath, my next heartbeat hinges on...

Her.

"King!"

Her body convulses around me, pulsing in a hypnotic rhythm that drags me over the edge.

I thrust—once, twice, three times and—

I'm gone.

TWENTY-FOUR

Rory

"Oh my God!" I groan, slamming my hands back against the shower as King buries his face between my legs and fucks my pussy with his tongue.

Sex is...

Incredible.

I'd heard about it being mind-blowing.

But...I hadn't ever experienced it.

Not until the last twenty-four hours anyway.

From the moment that I woke up before King, watching him sleep like a total creeper, but also totally mesmerized by the way his face was softened, how his thick lashes had rested on the tops of his cheeks, his hair mussed, a lock hanging over his forehead that I wanted desperately to tuck back into place, my life had shrunk.

But not in a bad way.

Because this man had blown my mind.

Repeatedly.

Giving me so many orgasms, I actually lost count.

And yes, I'm sore.

And no, I'm not going to stop him and his delicious tongue and fingers and lips and teeth from working their magic.

Partly because I still have the taste of *his* orgasm on my tongue, the salty musk of him in my nose and on my taste buds.

Because he finally let me get my mouth on his cock.

And it had been glorious.

But now he's back to being generous, working my body with the intense focus I've seen him display on the ice.

And with me.

And...I wonder with how many other women.

The thought lances through me, a cold bucket of water over my head, threatening to douse my desire.

King growls, withdrawing his tongue and turning his head to nip at the inside of my thigh currently resting on one of those broad shoulders. "Pay attention." Sharp blue eyes lock onto mine and I shiver at the demanding, heated look within them.

It doesn't matter what he did with other women.

It only matters what he's doing with me.

"Better," he says, flicking his tongue over the stinging flesh before turning his head again.

He sucks on my clit, and does it hard enough that I jump, that I'm not thinking about anything that isn't his mouth on my pussy, his tongue and fingers slowly driving me insane.

Driving me into oblivion.

"King!"

My head thunks back against the glass, but I don't feel it, not with the orgasm barreling through me, not with his mouth on me, his fingers in me. Stubble brushing along my thighs, a big palm cupping my ass, keeping me pressed against his mouth as pleasure flows through me, wave after wave after *wave.*

Eventually, it stops, slows to a halt, and my knees wobble, threaten to give way.

But King notices.

Of course he does, his arm banding around my hips as he slowly draws away from me, leaning back on his heels and cradling me against him.

The water flows over my body, soaking the hair I hadn't intended on washing this morning, but I can't bring myself to care, not with him holding me like this, not with the fairy tale of the last day. Not with—

He shifts slightly and I gasp, eyes flying open. "You're hard."

The smile he gives me...God, it shouldn't make my pussy throb, shouldn't stoke the embers of desire that have just been banked by my orgasm.

But it does.

Because, God, he's fucking pretty.

He doesn't bend me over the bench set along one side of the shower, doesn't thrust deep and fuck me hard and fast again.

He settles me on that bench, the cool tiles a soft bite on the backs of my thighs, and then he proceeds to wash—and condition!—my hair. After, he loads up the loofa with shower gel and soaps me up before carefully rinsing me off.

Butterflies whip around my belly, their delicate wings creating a maelstrom that threatens to steal my breath.

Because he's treating me gently again.

Because he's caring for me. Carefully. Softly. Sweetly.

And...I've never had that.

"King," I whisper as he directs the handheld shower head

toward my feet, ensuring that the last of the suds are rinsed, that the bottoms of my feet are clean and free of soap.

So I don't slip.

Those butterflies turn into tiny little birds, flying around my insides, thumping against my lungs.

"King," I say again.

"It's okay, princess," he murmurs, touching my cheek for a brief moment before he uses the loofa to brusquely wash his body, rinsing off the suds in quick, efficient movements.

He says it's okay.

But it's not.

How can this be okay?

How can he show me this, get me used to this, and I just… move on with my life when it's done?

Fingers on my jaw, tilting my head up. "Too much, princess?"

Yes.

And no.

Not nearly enough.

In fact, I have the feeling that it will *never* be enough.

"Too much," he says softly before I can reply, picking the answer out of my mind. Or maybe from my expression. I've never been good at hiding my emotions, at obscuring what's in my heart.

And right now, my feelings are too big, too much…

Too fucking perfect.

"I'm fine," I whisper.

His expression gentles, but he doesn't argue with me, just turns off the shower and wraps me in a towel. And even before I manage to push up to my feet, he's lifting me in his arms, carrying me over to the vanity and setting me on the counter.

He steps back, snags his robe from the back of the door,

and a heartbeat later, I'm engulfed in soft flannel that smells of him.

"There," he murmurs, slipping the towel free and tying the robe shut.

"Wait," I say when he starts to turn, hand extended like he's going to hang up the towel.

I take it from him, and then—heart pounding because this is a small thing but it feels like a very big thing—I drag the fabric of the towel over his chest, scooping up water droplets, drying his skin.

He goes still, so still that he resembles a statue.

I want to say something, anything, but my heart is in my throat.

And I know this small thing—all of the tiny pieces of our time together—are going to destroy me.

"Thanks, princess," he murmurs a heartbeat after I finish.

I nod, settle the towel in my lap. "Of course," I whisper.

And then I stop, gripping the material tight.

Because I don't know what the hell to say next.

Because I'm an awkward mess and I don't know what to *do* next.

Because the world is topsy-turvy and small things are huge and—

Fingers on my jaw again, drawing my gaze from my hand clenching at the white cotton back up to King.

"Come to the game tonight?"

My fingers convulse. "Wh-what?"

His hand shifts, palm cupping my jaw. "I want to look up and see you in the stands, princess," he says.

My pulse thunders in my veins. "Really?"

"Yeah, baby." A beat. "Really."

"But the guys," I sputter. "Th-they'll see me there, see the ring and they'll kn-know that—"

I'm not making any sense.

I've gone to plenty of games. I don't have to wear the ring.

But...this is different.

This is me going for *him*.

It means something.

And that's terrifying.

"I don't care about the guys." A beat. "Or if you wear the ring." His fingers flex and he seems to be warring with himself. "I care about *you*."

I inhale so sharply that I choke on my own spit.

"Shit, princess," he mutters, patting my back. "Just breathe."

He's patient while I regain my breath, and when I take a moment to find the courage to meet his eyes.

And when I finally do, I see that he's persistent.

Determined.

Because when I've finally caught my breath, when I'm no longer choking, when I'm finally holding his gaze again, he asks,

"So...will you come tonight?"

TWENTY-FIVE

King

Sitting in the penalty box and trying to get a glimpse of Rory up in the owner's box high overhead hadn't been my plan.

But waking up and spending a full day and a half fucking her every way imaginable also hadn't been on the docket either.

"Who are you looking for?" Pat says from next to me. "I saw some hot pussy in section one-oh-two, but I'm not sharing."

Right.

Because that's the extra layer of joy to this game tonight.

Sitting in the box next to Pat.

He'd taken a cheap shot on a guy on the other team—a player who's as much of an asshole as Pat is so I couldn't give him too much shit for that. But a couple of the guys on the other team hadn't appreciated that gesture much and I—as a halfway decent teammate who knows that Pat's an asshole but still plays an important role on the ice—had stepped in to make sure he didn't get pummeled when he went full turtle on the ice.

For all his talk of pussy…

Pat was sure a dick. Or maybe a ball sack.

Vulnerable to the smallest bit of contact.

"Or maybe," he drawls and I grind my teeth together, "you're looking for a certain woman who you're fucking."

My head whips away from the stands, glare fixing on him in an instant.

Too fast. Revealing too much.

As made evident by the asshole's smirk. "Yeah," he says. "I knew you'd get in there."

"Fuck off, Pat," I mutter, gaze turning to the Jumbotron, counting the seconds until I can get the fuck out of here. Five minute penalty for fighting. Five minutes too long to sit next to this asshole.

Then, to add to my misery, it's not strictly just five minutes. I have to wait for my time to count down, but then I also have to wait for a whistle before I'm allowed to leave the Naughty Box.

"For someone who's getting his dick wet, you're sure in a bad mood," Pat says gleefully.

As gleefully as I'd put my fist right through his face.

Christ.

I need to get out of here.

"Do you ever get tired of being an asshole?" I grind out.

"Nope," he says as the whistle blows and he stands up.

I flick my eyes to the clock, see that the hockey gods have been nice enough to grant me freedom from this box of hell, and jerk to my feet, reaching for the handle and yanking open the door—and doing it so quickly that the metal edge slams into Pat's shoulder.

Ha.

Fucker.

He grunts, but I don't apologize, just hop onto the ice, skate to the bench, and sink down beside Rome. My captain glances over at me. "How was *that?*"

Cam—on my other side—snorts. "Five minutes of hell."

That.

Exactly that, but—

"Doesn't matter," I mutter. I nod out to the ice. "We're down a goal and not much time is left in the game. We've got to get our shit together."

Rome nods in agreement, but he's already looking at Cam. The youngest brother of the Jackson siblings sighs, screwing up his mouth, and I know he's thinking. His—the Jackson brood—isn't a family of hockey players like mine is, but they're still obscurely famous for being connected to their adopted sister and Hollywood superstar, Sophie Jackson. Cam may be the youngest and on the quiet side, but the kid's got a great mind.

He can draw up plays that are effective and creative, and he can do it fast.

Case in point?

Taking the next fifteen seconds before we hop onto the ice to toss three ideas our way.

One of which means that I'm cutting to the right when the puck ricochets off the boards and between the skates of a defenseman on the other team.

It means that I'm already skating balls out past him before he can react.

It means that I beat everyone to the corner, scooping up the puck and cutting hard to the net.

The other team is closing fast, and their goalie knows exactly where I am, gaze locked on me, squeezing that post, cutting off any decent angle for a shot.

Which is fine.

Because I have no plans on shooting.

Just faking one.

Which I do, watching the goalie react, flinch, bracing for the puck.

But I'm already dropping it back...

To Rome streaking in.

He doesn't pick it up, just lets it slip by as he skates hard at the net, distracting the goalie as...

Cam receives the puck, flicks it back to me...

I shoot...

It sails into the top corner of the goal, sending the netting flying up, the red light flashing, the buzzer going.

The crowd roars as Cam and Rome barrel into me, hugging me and smacking my back as we collide with the boards.

Cheers and fans banging against the boards.

"Fuck yeahs!" from my teammates.

That high that only comes from when something goes really, really right.

"One more, yeah?" I say as we skate toward the bench.

Cam nods, mouth curved up into a grin. "About that," he says as we sit down. "I've got an idea."

One I have no doubt will work...

And it does.

The very next shift we have, we execute Cam's tic-tac-toe of a play, sending the crowd roaring again, the buzzer going, the goal song blaring through the arena's speakers.

Nothing beats this high, especially when I manage to sneak a glance up at the owner's box and see Rory and Chrissy jumping around like adorable lunatics. They're smiling, but I can't see much more of their faces other than the white of their teeth.

It's enough though.

That flash of white on Rory's face, the evidence of her pride and happiness.

Stupid, huh?

That I don't feel whole until I see a woman amongst twenty-two thousand people smiling down at me.

But it's true.

The whistle goes and I tear my gaze away in time to see my teammates lining up for the face-off. Less than two minutes left in the game now. We just need to keep our shit together for a little while longer, hold on to the lead, and we'll get those two points.

The puck drops, but my eyes drift to the man next to me.

The one who's staring at me.

Rome.

Who leans close and mutters, "You gave me a talking to not all that long ago."

I grind my teeth together, threatening to cut through my mouth guard, but I don't take the bait he's just laid out. Instead, I focus on the game.

I'm one of six siblings. I know *all* the tricks to get me to spill my guts.

In fact, I'd used them on Rome just weeks before.

"And in that talk"—he pauses, and I feel him looking at me, but I don't tear my stare away from the action on the ice —"you said you're not interested in settling down."

"I'm not."

A beat. "Then what the fuck are you doing?"

I don't even know how to begin to answer that.

Because I don't know *the* answer to it.

Rome waits a long moment, but I keep my eyes on the ice as we scoot down the bench, moving toward the door leading onto the offensive side of the rink. Then he sighs quietly. "Just don't hurt her, yeah?"

I open my mouth—

Freeze.

Because I don't know if I can keep that promise.

TWENTY-SIX

Rory

I'm standing outside the locker room, feeling a little nervous.

Because...

King is inside and he asked me to come and...I'm wearing the ring.

Stupid, right?

I just broke up with my fiancé and I'm nowhere near ready for a new relationship, and further that, King hasn't given any indication that he wants one—

Aside from demanding I stay at his place.

But that's just him being a good guy. He's got a protective streak. He's demonstrated that time and again.

And anyway, he's made it clear to everyone far and wide that he's not interested in a relationship. It's why I despised him so much after seeing those posts.

A case of social media being true.

Only...it's not.

I bite back a sigh. None of this matters. We're only

staying together now to save him from those matchmaking efforts of his mom and because Phillip is out there on bail somewhere and King's place is safe...

And King is a good guy.

Just not *my* guy.

Even if he fucked me senseless for twenty-four hours.

When someone shows you who they are, tells you what they want...

Well, I've learned that's something I need to pay attention to.

Ha.

Sure, I have.

Right around the time that Phillip closed his hands around my throat and started to squeeze.

Stupid.

I swallow hard, trying to shake off the feeling of that hand, the fear that's shredded my insides, but it doesn't want to let go easily, doesn't want to pull the barbed spikes from my heart, my mind, my soul—

"Hey, gorgeous."

I jump, hands clenching into fists, jaw clamping together so tightly that I bite the inside of my cheek hard, drawing blood, the sharp tang of copper clinging to my taste buds. But even as I'm processing that razor-edged flavor, I'm looking up...

And seeing Patrick Buchanan standing in front of me.

Wearing a smirk, his eyes cold, and his body far too close.

I know that Rome, King, and Cam can't stand this guy. I know that Chrissy thinks he's an arrogant jerk who spends his spare time trying to fuck with Rome and King and Cam and the rest of the locker room.

I know that—despite that—she also doesn't find him particularly dangerous.

But my spidey sense is tingling.

After Phillip...well, let's just say that it's been honed to a fine point.

I note the sharp edges of his expression, his body nearly brushing mine, the way he came so close before announcing himself.

I don't like it.

And...I don't like him.

I don't know him...and I don't like him, and that's enough. My instincts are screaming to step back, but I don't have room to because he's come close, because he's positioned himself between where I'm leaning back against the wall and the open space of the hall, his big body boxing me in.

Trapping me.

Like Phillip had.

Yup. Definitely a creep.

And maybe a dangerous one.

But...I've been through worse. Phillip. My sisters. My stepmom.

The verbal abuse.

The...physical.

So, I know that I might bend, but I also know I won't break.

I straighten my shoulders, lift my chin. I may be a nice person, may have a soft heart for those I care about—furry or otherwise—but I was raised in a den of vipers.

I can deal with a hockey player, even one who makes my spidey sense tingle.

Which—despite the situation—makes my lips twitch.

Because as a certain gorgeous hockey player with a protective streak a mile wide pointed out not that long ago, I am very good at being a prickly princess.

Something I channel right in this moment, lifting my chin

and managing to stare down my nose at one Pat Buchanan, even though he's a good foot taller and, likely, at least a hundred pounds heavier than me. "Can I help you?" I ask all...well, *prickly princess-like.*

He grins wolfishly, body swaying closer. "I can think of a whole lot of ways that you can help me, gorgeous."

Barf.

Just...*barf.*

"No thanks," I say dismissively, deliberately sliding my eyes from his and turning my head away.

I want to escape, but considering that Pat the Asshole (as King has coined him) is still between me and escape, I'm not exactly free to do so. Instead, I scan the open space behind him, looking for my way out...or maybe for someone—like King or Rome or Cam or, hell, Jean-Michel since it's his freaking team and he's always managed to look out for me in the past—to come rescue me.

Alas—and now I really sound like a prickly princess—what I can see of the hall remains empty.

Where's that hot hockey player on his white horse (or motorcycle) to save me?

Ugh.

I guess this prickly princess—no, this *cactus queen* is going to have to save herself.

The humanity.

But at least the sarcasm has centered me, pushed down the fear, bolstered the spikey.

I put up a hand. "You're too close," I say firmly. "Back up."

Unfortunately, my words don't have an effect on Pat.

In fact, he just leans closer, dropping a palm onto the wall next to my head, so near that I can scent his cologne—or rather, his cologne changes from clinging to the air to filling my nose, inundating my senses.

Blegh.

"Don't be like that, gorgeous," he says, his other hand lifting and tugging lightly at a strand of my hair. "I'm a nice guy."

A *nice* guy.

Double blegh.

It's always the ones who say they're *nice* guys who are creeps.

"Don't touch me," I order, slapping his hand away.

And it has absolutely no effect on him. In fact, it seems to urge him on. He settles that hand on my waist, draws even closer. "We could be so good together," he drawls, bending his head and nearly succeeding in pressing our mouths together.

Luckily, I turn in time to avoid him then shove at his chest, blurt out the only thing I can think of, "I don't think my fiancé will like that very much."

Pat stills, brows shooting up. "I heard the wedding was off."

I don't even know this man, other than that he plays for the team and he's a total asshole, but he somehow knows that Phillip and I broke up?

I don't like that.

Not even a little bit.

"No," I lie. "It's not."

A shrug, those big shoulders lifting and falling indolently, like me telling him I'm engaged doesn't matter. And I guess, to him, it doesn't. "Come on, gorgeous," he cajoles, "your fiancé isn't here. What he doesn't know won't hurt him—"

"But *this* will hurt *you*."

I barely have the chance to feel the relief coursing through me at the sound of King's voice.

Because then he's between me and Pat.

And his fist is flying.

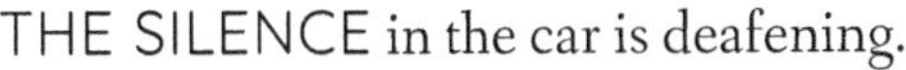

THE SILENCE in the car is deafening.

And uncomfortable.

And...deafening.

"Is your..." I begin as we wait at a signal, the red light interminably long. Especially when his head whips in my direction, those eyes locking with mine, pinning me in place. Those blue irises are flints of ice, cold enough to make me shiver, but somehow I manage to push out, "Is your hand okay?"

Said hand flexes on the steering wheel, the quiet groan it makes drawing my gaze to those knuckles standing out in sharp relief, the tight grip on the leather, the tension ratcheting up in his body. But all he replies with is a terse, "Yeah."

Then the light turns green and he looks forward again.

And...

Right.

That's clear indication that he's done talking, I suppose.

Cool. Cool.

I'll just stare out the window and pretend this terse silence doesn't exist.

Pretend that he didn't clock a man for cornering me, for scaring me, that he didn't lay the asshole known at Pat Buchanan flat on his ass with just one punch.

Pretend that he didn't protect me...again.

But all that pretending is fucking useless.

Because he *did* protect me, and my heart—already soft and vulnerable and open to him...

It feels like I'm in danger.

But it's a danger I yearn for, that I'm desperate for, that I know I'm going to run headfirst into.

"Are you mad?" I whisper.

His head whips to the side, eyes flicking to mine, seeming to see too much in that flash of contact before he turns back to the road. "At you?"

I inhale. Exhale.

Be brave and kind.

"Yes. You're probably going to get in trouble again and it's my fault." I nibble at my bottom lip. "I'll talk to Jean-Michel. Explain what happened. He'll—"

"*No.*"

I freeze.

His big chest rises and falls on a breath. "No," he says again. "I'm not mad at you." He touches my cheek. "Thank you, but I don't need you to talk to Jean-Michel."

Maybe he doesn't need me to.

But I'm going to do it anyway.

He sighs. "You're going to do it anyway, aren't you?"

"I have an in with Jean-Michel," I say. "You know that."

And I'm not going to let King take the fall for doing something kind (and yes, I consider planting his fist into Pat's face a kindness.

"Stubborn."

I settle my hand on his thigh. "Prickly, remember?"

Which, thankfully, makes him smile.

At least for a second.

Because then it fades again and I realize that there's something else at play here.

Something I missed.

"So," I whisper, squeezing the firmly muscled leg. "Who are you mad at?" A beat. "Besides Pat?"

His gaze flicks to mine then back to the road, and for a second, I think he's not going to answer me. "Yeah, I hate that fucker," he mutters. "But—" Another breath. "I hate more that he scared you and I wasn't there to protect you. I'm never fucking there at the right time—" His teeth click together and he shakes his head, cutting off the flow of words.

"I—"

Frankly, that's not something I ever expected him to say—how can he think that when he's come to my rescue time and again?

It doesn't make sense and I want to press him to explain, but one look at the set of his jaw and I know this isn't the time. Instead, I stick with the facts. "You were there. You stopped him."

A shake of his head. "He had you cornered, princess. If I hadn't walked out of the locker room when I did..."

I shiver, and I know he sees it because he loosens his grip on the steering wheel for a second, covers my hand with his own.

But it's a fleeting touch, there and gone in an instant before he's back focusing on the road, back clenching the steering wheel with both hands, back not looking at me.

He was there, and he'd stepped in.

He had my back. Just like before with Phillip. But, based on the tautness of his jaw, his grip on the steering wheel, the fury emanating from his frame, he's not going to be receptive to that sentiment, to me trying to convince him exactly how thankful I am for him.

How deep he's woven himself into my soul.

So deep that only Chrissy exists there. And Jean-Michel. And my pups.

And Rome.

And...now King.

Before Jean-Michel and Chrissy, no one else in my life had stepped in like that—not after my dad had died.

No one protected me, looked after me for no reason except that I'm a living being and worthy of love and protection and kindness, just like every other person and animal on this planet.

But King did.

And I know exactly how precious the gift that he's given me is.

The least I can do is look after him in turn.

To make him understand.

To give him this part of me...and hope that, at some point, he'll see I'm a safe place to seek solace in return.

Be brave and kind.

"Phillip wasn't mean in the beginning."

The steering wheel protests again, but I keep going.

"He never handled me roughly or hit me, not until the day of the wedding and he saw me in the dress and..." I close my eyes. "He wasn't happy. I'd gone against his and his mom's wishes in choosing my dress, by choosing the style I wanted."

One of the "many ways I disobeyed them."

A tiny victory on a war of attrition I didn't even know I was fighting.

Losing myself.

Losing what was important to me—my pups, my rescue, even pulling back from Chrissy and Jean-Michel.

And lying to myself that it was happening at all.

"I don't know if it was the stress of the day that pushed him over the edge," I say, hating that I have to admit the next, "but I do know it was inevitable that we got there. He was always going to hit me. Because there were red flags from the beginning that I ignored—stupid stuff like not splitting responsibilities even though he promised, him flying off the handle when I tried to hold him to those promises, becoming unreasonably angry and giving me the silent treatment for days when I broke down and did the chores anyway. Because he was *going to get to them*. Because I undermined him." I sigh. "And I ignored it all because *I loved him*."

"Princess—"

"I know," I whisper, squeezing his thigh again. "I was dumb. I didn't recognize that it didn't matter how I changed, how I tried to make myself smaller, how much I tried to cater to him, it wasn't enough. Wasn't *ever* going to be enough. And I—" I swallow hard. "Truthfully, I didn't think I deserved anything better. Didn't think I deserved someone who was happy that I found joy in things like a TV show or book or—worse—my rescue. I thought it was normal for my partner to make fun of me for"—I do finger quotes—"*being emotional* because I cried when a dog I loved was adopted out. I thought not being willing to share the house with any rescue dogs was a boundary I needed to respect, no matter that it destroyed a part of me to not be able to help them, no matter how dire their circumstances were, or how much guilt I had when I needed to rely on my fellow volunteers more than I felt like I should."

Red flags.

So many of them.

And I was blind to it all.

Okay, not blind. I *ignored* them.

Because I thought that was as good as it got, as good as I deserved, and King has shown me in just a few short weeks that I deserve more.

So. Much. More.

Dumb that I couldn't see it before, huh?

It's just...

I'd forgotten.

"You made me see that I deserve better," I whisper. "You didn't have an angle, didn't need something from me. You just...stepped in, and I need you to know I appreciate it."

"Ror—"

"Because I had the bad, and because I know what that's like, and—"

Courage now.

"You've shown me what it's like to have good," I whisper. "Because I haven't felt this settled and safe... since my dad was alive."

"Rory," he whispers, voice hoarse. "*Princess.*"

Too much.

It's *too* much.

And that's why I make the decision to pause there, to transition our conversation to something lighter.

"Don't you mean *Prickly* Princess?" I tease.

He jerks. "What?"

"I've decided to own my Cactus Queen title."

"Rory," he says, slowing to a halt at a stop sign and looking at me. "Baby, I—"

Damn. He's not going to let me change the subject.

Probably because I'm handling it with all of the finesse of a sledgehammer.

I reach up, touch his cheek. "I just want you to know that I value you," I say softly. "That I appreciate what you've done, and that you're a good man."

That has his eyes sliding closed, a mix of pain and pleasure sliding over his face.

"And if you ever want to talk about anything—"

Like the reason pain and pleasure crosses his face when I say he's a good man.

His eyes flash open and he leans back, pulling away from my touch as he proceeds through the stop sign.

"*Prickle* Princess," he says after a moment.

"What?"

"Not Prickly, but Prickle."

An odd mix of disappointment weaves through me, but I don't push.

I should have, I realize later.

Should have demanded answers.

All of them.

But I'm raw and vulnerable and I've depleted my well of courage.

So I grasp on to the light and don't miss the relief that darts through his expression when I ask, "Not Princess Pricklesticks? Or Spiny Sweetie?"

He snorts. "Okay, so that wasn't my finest moment of creativity." A shrug. "But having five siblings means that quantity over quality is more important sometimes."

"And what *are* those times?"

"When lobbing insults," he says, flashing me a grin that coats my skin in sunshine even though it's pitch black outside, "and consuming food."

"After tasting your mom's apple pie," I say, "I would agree that's a situation that requires quantity."

"Definitely," he agrees, finally loosening his hand from the steering wheel and settling it on my thigh. "I can think of another situation that *requires quantity*." His palm is big and strong and has my pulse speeding up. "Though, quality is important too."

Orgasms.

It's orgasms.

I see that thought, that *intent* write itself into the lines of his face, the grip of my thigh, the blazing heat of his gaze when it meets mine, just for a second.

My breath catches.

Because if he just slides it a tiny bit northward...

Yup. Orgasms.

I shiver, but not in fear.

Something I know that *he* knows because his blue eyes heat, the icy fury from before turning into a hot spring, a bubbling temptation encouraging me to dip a toe into the waters.

The light turns green and he looks away as he pulls forward.

Taut silence.

But not anything like the tense ride it had begun as.

Instead...it's anticipatory.

And when he pulls into the garage, hits the button to close the door behind us, then turns toward me, ordering, "Get naked..."

I not only oblige.

But I've already begun even before the words reach my ears.

TWENTY-SEVEN

King

This woman's mouth is sin.

And heaven.

She pulls back, tongue dancing along the tip of my cock before drawing it deeply into her mouth, so deeply that I feel the back of her throat closing around me as she swallows me down, can see tears clinging to her lashes.

I want to drive deeper, to grip her hair and fuck that lush mouth.

But she's naked and blowing me after I got to eat her out on the hood of my car—giving light to a fantasy I didn't know I had.

A fantasy we're going to reenact again.

Right after—

I give into the urge to dive my fingers into her hair, but it's to pull her off me, not drive deep. I flip her around, press her front on the hood of my car, kick her legs wide, and have just enough control to roll on the condom from my wallet before I plunge inside that tight, wet cunt.

She gasps.

I groan. "Fucking perfect," I grunt, thrusting into her. "You are. So. Fucking. *Perfect.*"

"King!" she moans, hips pressing back against me, ass jiggling, head thrown back, mouth parted as my name dances off the tip of her tongue.

Beautiful.

Mine.

"Oh my God!" she cries out. "King. I—"

She's close.

Damned close.

Which is good, because I'm going to come.

I grip her waist, change the angle just enough to ensure that she topples over the edge before me, and then allow her clamping pussy to drag me under.

"King," she groans, meeting me thrust for thrust as we both come down, as our movements slow and grow lazy, nuzzling my throat when I find the strength to pull out, to hold her close, to carry her up into bed.

Once we're both under the covers, the condom's taken care of, and the house is locked up (and our clothes retrieved from the garage floor), she settles her hand on my chest, just over my heart.

"You played great tonight," she whispers.

"Thanks," I whisper back, lazily tracing my hand over her skin, making random patterns. "And thanks for coming."

"Of course." Her lips press to my flesh, and for a long moment she doesn't say anything else. But then, as my eyes are drifting shut, she murmurs, "What did you mean earlier?"

You're not your father.

Fear coils at the base of my spine, but I push the voice down, ask, "What do you mean?"

It's a casual question, but she reads right through it, through me. "Earlier in the car, honey," she says. "You said you're never there at the right time, but..."

I grind my teeth together, want to slam the door closed on this discussion.

Except...she gave me so much in the car, shared so fucking much, was so fucking open and brave and vulnerable—

How can I possibly keep my idiotic trauma to myself?

It's nothing like what she went through.

Nothing.

I open my mouth.

"Because—for me—you seem to always be there at the right time."

That jolts through me.

"Princess," but I don't finish the denial that's clinging to the back of my throat because she pushes up, those deep green eyes locking onto mine.

"Don't," she says. "I promised myself that I wouldn't push you, but fuck that." Her hands come to my cheeks. "Don't deny it or put me off. You meant what you said in the car."

"I—" But I just clamp my lips together, bite back the words.

Because what the hell can I possibly say about it?

Oh, you poor little brokenhearted boy, are you too scared to love again?

Fuck yes, I am.

And what will I look like in the eyes of this incredibly brave woman if I admit that?

A fucking coward.

Especially when she goes on, proving exactly how strong she is. "I accepted Phillip's treatment of me because I thought it was the best I could have. No," she whispers. "It was what I thought I *deserved*."

"Princess," I say, sitting up and drawing her against me. "You can't honestly think that you deserve—"

"They left me," she murmurs and my arms tighten, drawing her gaze back to mine. "My mom." A breath. "My dad." Her throat works. "And my stepmom, stepsisters didn't want anything to do with me when my dad was gone. They were cruel to me. They..." A breath. "They loved to see how much they could take from me, and...I got used to giving it, used to thinking that was all I could have, all I deserved. I thought the derision, the cruelty, the ostracizing, the pulling more than my fair share of weight at home, even the stealing from me was normal. It wasn't until I really got to know Jean-Michel and Chrissy that I realized how dysfunctional my dynamic at home was and I cut contact with them. But did I use that knowledge when it came to Phillip? Nope." She tosses her hands up. "I fell into the same damned patterns."

Shit.

I draw her closer, bury my face in my hair, hating the sadness on her face, in her eyes, in those terrible words. "I'm so sorry, sweetheart," I say. "But you can't expect yourself to be perfect in every moment. To make the right choice every single time."

"Maybe not," she says. "But doesn't the same go for you?"

I freeze.

"Why do you hold yourself to a different standard?"

Because what's tangling through my mind is nothing compared to what she endured.

And I need to get the hell over it.

She leans back. "I'm starting to come to terms with that

little girl inside me, learning to wrap my arms around her and give her a hug, tell her that what she thinks isn't true. Because of Jean-Michel and Chrissy. Because of Rome and Cam. Even because of your mom and how she accepted me with open arms without really knowing me." A breath, her hand on my cheek again. "But mostly, I'm starting to realize all of this because of you."

That hits like an actual blow to the abdomen, stealing my breath. "Princess, I didn't do anything."

"Except you did." She shakes her head. "You've really—"

Another blow, just a different variety.

"—helped me understand how this—how a relationship—can be. How a man can treat a woman. What I deserve." She laughs, but it's not amused, not really.

It's sad again, and I fucking hate it when she's sad.

"I was engaged," I blurt.

Because this moment, what we're building—it doesn't feel fake.

It's fucking...

Something.

She stills, those green eyes befuddled and beautiful and I just want to kiss her again, to fuck her until we're both senseless so I don't have to feel what I'm feeling. But, Christ, after everything, I owe her honestly.

"I was engaged," I say again.

She stills.

"No one knew," I admit. "Not my siblings. Or friends. Not even my mom. I..." I shake my head. "Rose didn't want me to tell anyone because she didn't think it was going to last."

That stillness becomes somehow even more still.

And fuck, I want to retreat, to get the hell out of this room and away from her eyes that are seeing far too much.

"She said I wasn't enough to make up for being gone all the time, that I'm not my dad, able to keep a family together even though he wasn't always physically there." I sigh. "She wouldn't wear the ring. Wouldn't come to my games. Wouldn't—"

My throat closes up.

Because I can't do this.

I fucking *can't*.

It's too fucking pathetic.

"King, honey," Rory begins and that sits like barbed wire on my bare skin, digging in, hurting me despite the fact that I should have been over this bullshit years ago.

I shrug, even though it feels like very non-shruggable series of events. "It doesn't matter," I whisper. "It was all a mindfuck. She was cheating on me the whole time and when she found a teammate with more money, more fame, she was gone." I shrug again. "Like I said, it doesn't matter. I'm over it."

Which is a lie.

Something I can see she knows even though she's too nice to call me on it.

"Right," she murmurs, running her fingers over my cheek, her nails through the strands of my beard. "Right," she says again, starting to shift out of my hold. Giving me space. Not pushing. "I mean that seems like a lot." Her throat works. "But you know yourself—"

Do I?

Because this shit between us is supposed to be fake.

And it feels like anything but that.

"I just..." Her throat works again. "I'm here."

I touch her cheek. "Thank you."

Emerald eyes drifting back to mine, disappointment swimming in their depths.

And…that feels like shit.

But I can't give her the rest.

Not right now.

"What happened to my Prickle Princess?" I tease, capturing her hand, keeping her in my arms, desperate to see her eyes fill with anything but that disappointment.

"Excuse me?" she whispers, brows pulling together in an adorable furrow.

"The Cactus Queen wouldn't let my bullshit excuses slide," I say lightly, tucking a strand of hair behind her ear, brushing my thumb over that tiny v between her brows, wanting to smooth out the confusion, the hurt, the sadness.

Hell, who am I kidding?

I just want to touch her and keep her close and safe and…*mine*.

Before that thought sends panic snaking up my throat, stealing my ability to breathe, one half of her mouth quirks up, and she says, "The Cactus Queen will let that bullshit slide when it's late and we've both had a long couple of weeks." Her hand comes back to my jaw, fingers pressing lightly into my skin, and she sighs softly. "And because you don't owe me an explanation, King. God knows you've done more than enough for me already."

Something that feels even more wrong.

That she thinks I wouldn't give her more.

That she thinks I wouldn't give her this.

That she thinks I wouldn't give her the world.

"It's really not a big deal," I say, hating the sympathy that creeps into her eyes, hating the way it makes me feel. "Plenty of other people have dealt with a shitty breakup and come through unscathed."

"But not you." She nibbles at her lip. "Or not you in *this* situation."

You're not your dad.

God, I've heard that so many times over the years.

Too many fucking times.

And not just from Rose.

She just...somehow made that feeling stick.

"Not me," I agree. "I...well, I fucked it up. She deserved better and I couldn't do enough for her and—"

Christ.

My voice cracks. My eyes sting.

Over a decade old breakup.

I really *am* pathetic.

"*She* deserved better?" There are embers of fury in Rory's green eyes now.

"I—"

Fuck. Why did I open this shitshow up for discussion?

But before I can pull back, Rory asks quietly, "How didn't you do enough for her?"

I freeze, force myself to meet her eyes. Thankfully, there's no sign of pity in the emerald depths and that means I'm able to take a breath, to let the words come.

"I'm away half the year," I remind her. "And most of the other months are dominated by me training or at practice or watching tape or getting ready to play. Even when I'm here, I'm busy and unavailable."

Her brows pull together, the embers sparking into a tiny inferno in deep green irises. "Because you have a *job?*"

I peel her hand from my jaw, press a kiss to her palm. "Hockey dominates my life and leaves room for little else."

"Except rescuing a pup"—she nods to Zeus sprawled out on my feet—"and keeping a schedule"—to my binder, currently sitting on my nightstand because I'd spent the morning before the game doing some planning and prep work for the next couple of weeks—"and rescuing runaway brides from the side of the road."

I inhale sharply.

Exhale.

You're not your father.

"It's not that simple."

A long pause. "Was it different before?"

I tilt my head to the side, link my fingers with hers because it feels better to touch her, to hold her. "What do you mean?"

"Did you always plan your schedule and make time for your family?"

"I—" I frown.

She reaches over me, scoops up the binder, battered from —*yes*—years of use. "Because this bad boy looks well-loved."

"I—"

"How long have you had it, baby?" she presses.

I fight the urge to look away.

"How long?" she asks again.

"Since I moved away from home."

"So you have a demanding job that takes you away from your family, and I see evidence of you making them a priority —something that would presumably carry over to a woman in your life." Her fingers squeeze mine. "What I *don't* see evidence of is you neglecting the people you love."

My throat is tight.

"Especially because you made *this*"—she touches her chest—"little runaway bride feel very much like a priority even though we've spent the last months bickering and circling each other because I'd taken it upon myself to be the most Prickly Princess of all time." Mouth curved, she leans down, brushes her lips over mine. "But I know it's not that easy, that just because someone says something, it doesn't heal those wounds deep inside. I just…" A breath. "I don't see that—you being neglectful and a bad partner—being a reality. I think…" Another exhale. "I think maybe she was like my stepmom and stepsisters. Just…not a good person."

Rose *wasn't* a good person.

I'm not so fucked up that I can't see that, but—

You're not your father.

I exhale again, hate that it's shaky. "I'm not my dad."

Her hand convulses and I hate myself a little bit, but the rest of the words just tumble out.

"I've never been my dad, not on the ice, not off it. I'm not going to hit records or be a stabilizing presence in the locker room or coach a team to the championship year after year. I don't have it in me to make a woman feel as special as I should when I'm away for more than half the year, to balance a big family and make everyone feel loved and seen." I grind my teeth together. "But I know my limitations and I do the best with what I've been given."

It's why I'm not getting married.

Not ever.

Why I'll humor my mom.

But not with anything permanent.

Fucking liar.

Because if Rory wanted permanent, if Rory loved me, if Rory was mine, I'd—

"So that's why you've been avoiding the matchmaking from your mom." Her hand flexes in mine. "Because you're like me."

My eyes flick up, holding hers.

"You think that you don't deserve happiness."

Those words—

They blast through me.

My skin feels tight, embarrassment creeps out of my

stomach, crawls over my flesh, leaving me itchy and uncomfortable.

"That's not it," I grind out. "We're not—" I break off because that's the panic talking.

"Alike?" she asks.

Rory's nothing like me.

"You're good, and I'm...*not*."

Christ. I inhale, mouth opening. Wanting to take it all back. To not ruin this.

But then Rory's expression closes down.

And she pulls her hand from mine.

TWENTY-EIGHT

Rory

Has this man lost his fucking mind?

I push off his chest, turn for the edge of the bed, fury on his behalf burning in my stomach.

He saved me.

Literally.

And he thinks...

Unable to keep my eyes away from him, my gaze is drawn back over my shoulder.

And I freeze.

Because the look in his eyes...well it's not one I thought I would ever see on the cocky hockey player's face.

I turn and crawl back into his arms, disturbing Zeus, who gives me a small disapproving "woof!"

Mentally promising him all of the belly rubs later, I clamber onto King's lap, cup his face in my hands, and hold his head steady. "You are a wonderful man," I whisper, hating the disbelief that blooms in his eyes at the words. "You are," I say again, brushing my lips over his.

Not deeply.

Not with the intense spark that ends with us both being naked.

But long enough to watch the pain of the past disappear.

He covers my hands with my own, peels them from his face and presses a kiss to each palm. My heart squeezes hard. "Thank you," he murmurs.

"King," I begin, knowing that the past is riding him, that there's some part of him that doesn't believe me.

A few words in one conversation aren't going to make that better.

So, I bite back the urge to keep digging, to convince him of the conviction in my heart, to convince him of what I've seen through his actions.

Kingston Bang is a good person.

I can have that printed on a billboard and I still don't think it will sink in.

So...I'll just have to convince him of that fact.

He deserves *more*.

"Thank you," I say. "I don't know if I ever explicitly thanked you for what you did with Phillip—"

"You did."

My eyes lock with his, those pools of warm blue water that I want to dive into, to spend eternity floating in. "I hope you know that I really—"

"I do."

"And that I don't know what would have happened if you hadn't—"

"You would have been okay." He tucks me against his chest, kisses the top of my head. "You would have been okay because you're a fighter, a survivor." Fingers under my chin. "And you have Jean-Michel on your side."

That has me grinning, thinking about all of the ways that Jean-Michel has looked after me over the years. Rescuing me from a shitty job. Treating me like a daughter. Praising my work. Encouraging me to keep pushing. Supporting my rescue. Even keeping my secret from Mama Bang. "More like a grumpy, domineering fairy godmother who's determined to get his way."

King stills.

Then he does the most wonderful thing...

He laughs.

"What?" I ask as Zeus wakes up enough to crawl up King's chest, fluffy wriggly body bouncing as he joins in on the excitement.

"Nothing," King says, still chortling. "I'm just picturing Jean-Michel, killer businessman who dominates the board-room and can eviscerate you with a look, sporting fairy wings and a magic wand."

I giggle.

"See?" he teases, tucking my hair behind my ear. "It's funny."

And, God, I really love it when he does that.

A gentle tuck, roughened fingertips running over the shell of my ear, caressing the sensitive lobe.

Running down the front of my throat.

I shiver, and—as always—he notices.

And he does something about it, tucking me against his chest, drawing the blankets over us, coaxing Zeus to lay down in front of me, so I'm the filling in a fluffer-man sandwich.

It's sweet.

It's...pretty much all I've ever wanted—to feel safe and secure and protected.

My throat is tight and my eyes sting but I push that down and I commit this moment to memory.

Because who knows when I'll have it again?

Who knows how long it will last?

But I do know exactly how precious it is.

And that's why I tuck this feeling away, why I vow to keep it safe.

"Why is Jean-Michel your fairy godmother?" he asks as he wraps his arm around my belly, drawing me even more flush against him.

I give it to him.

King had taken away any hope of me hiding anything from him when he saw the bruises on my throat, when he tended the cuts on my feet.

When he shared what was eating him up inside about his ex, his dad.

I don't know it all, and he doesn't know everything about me either.

But...we have these slender threads of understanding connecting us now—cactus to Prickly Princess to Cactus Queen, runaway bride to safe spot to land, cocky bachelor hockey player to wounded nice guy with a heart of gold.

And brusque billionaire to...

Fairy godmother.

So, I send out another thread to the man holding me, knowing that it's going to strengthen our connection, knowing I'm playing with fire.

But I give into it anyway.

And I tell him the story of knowing Chrissy in high school, but not being all that close even though I liked her a lot (because Jean-Michel is the aforementioned scary). I tell him of our reconnecting later and my chance meeting with her dad during a presentation I was putting on with my former employer.

"If you think that Jean-Michel is brusque, you should have met Donovan. He was—and still is—the biggest asshole I've ever had the displeasure of knowing."

"Where does he work?"

I freeze at the deadly tone, and then roll toward him, hand resting on his chest, able to feel his heart beating steadily below. And, yup, I was right. He's scowling, eyes threatening murder.

Inexplicably, that has my mouth tipping up, warmth blooming in my belly.

I've seen that look on his face before, and probably, a man committing acts of violence on my behalf shouldn't give me the warm fuzzies, but it does. The furious expression on his face settles me. In fact, half-expecting him to demand Donovan's last name, social security number, and contact information *amuses* me.

"Don't worry," I say, touching his cheek, losing my battle to contain the rest of my smile.

He scowls.

I go on, "Jean-Michel took care of him."

King's scowl fades and the fury in his body softens.

Though, not by that much.

I want to laugh.

But I don't.

Because...this man who would come to my defense in a heartbeat thinks that he's not good, not worthy.

It makes absolutely no sense.

And it's why my new mission is to make him see how much value he brings to the world, to the lives of those around him.

To...me.

So, I tell him the story of Jean-Michel stepping in when Donovan decided to berate me in front of a boardroom of higher-ups. I tell him about Jean-Michel taking a look at my work and poaching me from Donovan's company on the spot.

I tell him about how Donovan's company went bankrupt —somehow, because obviously my fairy godmother couldn't have possibly (*cough*) have caused it to go under by becoming a direct competitor instead of a collaborator.

And then I tell him more.

About Chrissy and my friendship, and him funding my first rescues. I tell him about the dinners at his place with Chrissy and I cackling and taking over the TV, and how he'd never liked Phillip but had still helped my ex get his current job. I tell him about Jean-Michel going to bat for me when I pushed for a change in marketing and how he never made it feel like I couldn't talk to him, no matter the hour.

I tell him how all of that made me miss my dad.

And how much I loved that I could have someone like him in my life.

And how I also hated it...because it hurts to remember what I lost.

I don't stop there, though.

I keep going.

I tell King everything that I've ever hidden away like a deep, dark secret.

I give him more than I've ever given anyone.

Because I'm in too deep.

And I have no hope of pulling back.

TWENTY-NINE

King

I listen.

And I rage.

That she went through so much.

That she had so little.

And when she finally finishes telling me about how Jean-Michel recognized her talent (not a surprise from the shrewd businessman) and all that the grumpy fairy godfather has done for her over the years, my respect for the man has grown.

He sees Rory, all that soft and sweet and bright inside her.

And he's looked out for her, protected that gentle core.

I need to find a way to thank him.

But what does one do for a grumpy billionaire fairy godfather who has everything he can possibly want?

"And then—" Her words are interrupted by a giant yawn,

so I table the thought and smooth back her hair, tucking an errant strand behind her ear. She smiles...

And promptly yawns again.

"I think it's time for sleep, princess," I say softly, rubbing my hand slowly up and down her back, loving that my touch has her slumping against me, that it garners yet another yawn as sleep tries to steal her under.

"*Prickle* Princess," she corrects.

"I thought you hated that name."

"It comes from you"—her lips brush over my throat—"and I don't think I could ever hate any part of you."

I freeze, her words striking with the impact of a nuke.

But luckily sleep takes her before she realizes what she's done to me, her breathing going slow and steady.

And I'm left lying there in the dark, thinking that I'm playing with fire and that...

She's perfect.

And that's...

Well, that's the fucking problem.

MY PHONE BUZZES, and I manage to peel open my eyes to see that sun is pouring through the windows.

Early.

But not *that* early.

If I hadn't exposed my heart last night, hadn't been fucking vulnerable and open and then spent the subsequent hours thinking about Rory being vulnerable and open right back.

And that asshole of an ex-boss of hers.

And that I need to make a list of everyone who's wronged her so I can make sure they pay (even if Jean-Michel has already done the same as her revenge-seeking fairy godfather).

If not for all of that, I would have likely been awake far before this hour.

Something my brother, Jakob—his name popping up as I glance at my cell's screen—would assume, considering he knows this life and knows me and how I prepare and recover from games and that I'm a creature of habit that likes to get up and start the day, not allow it to waste away.

He just doesn't know that my recovery of late has been spending my nights fucking the beautiful woman softly snoring next to me.

I hit the button on the side, stopping the vibrating, rejecting the call, and start to set the phone back on when it starts going again.

Buzz. Buzz.

I sigh, jab at the screen.

Then grind my teeth at the text message that's appeared.

Jakob: What's this about an engagement?

Christ. Maybe he *does* know how I've been spending my post-game recovery.

Though—frankly—it's a shock it took this long for my mom to let the cat out of the bag...and then for Jakob to reach out and give me shit.

Buzz. Buzz.

Jakob: You trying to give Mom more confidence in playing fucking matchmaker?

He should know by now that nobody *allows* our mom to do anything.

She does what she wants, *when* she wants—hence her

breezing in and out of town, visiting her kids like the tiny tornado she is.

Do I have a choice?

No.

Or more importantly, would I ever tell the woman who sacrificed so much to raise us no?

Also...no.

Still, my fingers race across the phone screen.

Me: It's not like that.

I can almost hear Jakob snort despite the hundreds of miles between us.

So, I keep my fingers moving.

Me: She didn't have any part in this.

Something that's true, but also something that's completely the wrong thing to say because it'll only bring more questions.

Ever since Jakob's divorce, he's been as anti-relationship as me.

Of course, he doesn't know the circumstances of *my* particular brand of bullshit—seemingly buying into the *hockey is my life* lines I've fed everyone around me—but, sadly, we had a similar implosion of the committed relationships we thought would last forever.

Mine being my ex making me realize that I'll never live up to the grand expectations in my mind, never be able to live up to the legacy of my family...and then going on to fuck someone else. While Jakob's ex-wife chose a far more cliché path of expression, fucking her personal trainer and then moving to Hawaii to *find herself.*

Fun times.

But this is why I shouldn't have sent that text.

If my brother knows that Mom wasn't behind my relationship...knows that there's something more, something deeper—

Cue panic.

Mine.

Because if he knows that this isn't my mother's influence, then—

My cell starts ringing again.

That.

He's going to want to know every fucking detail like the nosy sibling he is.

I groan softly and push out of bed, careful to not wake Rory as I slip out into the hall, waiting until I've quietly closed the door behind me before I swipe my finger across the screen.

"Tell me you're fucking kidding," Jakob snaps.

"Quiet," I mutter, holding the cell away from my ear—because, Goddamn, my brothers are loud. "Rory's sleeping."

A blip of quiet, filled with befuddlement before he roars, *"Excuse me?"*

"Jesus Christ," I mutter, moving more quickly down the hall—

Come to me, coffeepot.

I need sustenance for this conversation.

And copious amounts of caffeine.

I shove in a pod, stick a mug beneath the spout, and slam down the top, listening with relief at the sound of the coffee brewing, the hint of the earthy scent hitting my nose only moments later.

"Tell me, King," Jakob snaps.

I swap the mug for an empty one, even though it'll mean

more dishes to wash once I'm fully caffeinated, and quickly down the contents, sighing in relief when the hot brew hits my taste buds. "Is there a reason *you're* pissed about this?" I mutter.

"Yes," he says, the word still snapped out, but the rest of what he says is drowned out by the sound of his boys. They're loud enough in the background that I hold my cell away from my ear again.

Jesus.

They come by it naturally.

"Yo!" Jakob shouts over the din, "I'm on the phone. Take it outside and solve it with Thumb War, yeah?"

My lips twitch.

If I had a penny for every time I heard my mom say that over the years, I would have...

Well, a lot of pennies.

Mostly because I'm the oldest and smartest and only participated in Thumb War battles I knew I could win.

Those being *not* against Annie.

Because, swear to God, our little sister is sneaky as fuck and has major Thumb War skills.

I chuckle, but the noise on the other end of the call dies down and I reach for the mug that's now mostly full, sucking back more coffee and bracing for the firestorm of my younger brother.

"So, you don't have anything to say about it?" Jakob grinds out a moment later.

"Well"—I take another sip, lean back against the counter—"I probably *would* have something to say about it if I could hear you over your hellions."

A snort. "You know that we Bangs aren't quiet."

"This is true."

"I thought you'd sworn off women," he says. "I *thought*

that you were going to make sure Mom stopped with this happily-ever-after bullshit that she's been pushing on us."

I sigh, set down my mug and rub my temple, try to soothe the throb that's begun there.

He's not wrong.

I did promise those things—right after my laptop was stolen by my mom's last setup-gone-wrong.

It's just I promised those things...

Before Rory.

"It's not like you think," I begin, intending to tell him that she's different, that I've never met a woman like her.

"Dude," he says. "You know that every woman is a greedy parasite that wants to suck you dry before she flits off to the next better thing."

I *used* to think that.

Before Rome and Chrissy.

Before...Rory.

"Rory—"

"Rory," he mutters. "Christ, is her mom's name Lorelai and you're going to have lots of teen drama at the local small town coffee shop?"

I frown. "What the fuck are you talking about?"

He blows out a breath, the sound echoing through the speakers. "Never mind. Just ask Annie about the crappy TV shows she made me watch after you moved out sometime and then you'll get the full rundown."

That clears up my frown.

Because I've been subjected plenty to Annie's brand of entertainment...and dealt with the mind melt afterward.

"Annie aside," I say. "Rory's full name is Aurora—"

A humorless laugh. "And it gets worse. She shares her name with a fucking princess. Jesus Christ, you've seriously lost it now, man. Don't make the same mistake of marrying a spoiled brat like I did—"

I want to argue.

To tell him that what I have with Rory isn't that.

She's not a princess. She's far from spoiled. She works her ass off, has overcome so much.

That I only call her princess, only treat her like one because she fucking deserves it—deserves the world.

But my brother is a stubborn fuck.

And he's nursing a broken heart.

And he's not going to see reason, no matter what I tell him about Rory, no matter how hard I try to convince him that she's different.

That she makes me feel different.

Which is why I cut him off.

"Just shut up for a second and listen to me."

Jakob's diatribe halts.

And I say words that feel completely wrong—

"It's all fake, man."

THIRTY

It's all fake, man.

I mean, he's not wrong.

And it was my idea in the first place.

And it *is* supposed to be fake.

But...

Ouch.

Because last night, I'd thought...

Well, I know *I'm* in deep, but I thought that maybe something changed for him too. He'd shared, had listened to me when I shared, and—

I thought we were becoming something more.

It's all fake, man.

Fake.

Not real.

I lean back against the wall, hand to my chest, as though that will keep the pieces of my heart together. It's better I know. Better I have this information. I can continue forward with a clear mind. Keep up the charade, but protect myself while I get back onto my feet.

Even if...some part of me wants it to be different.

Wants it to mean more.

Wants to stay.

Had started thinking of the future he and I could have together, this man who knows almost all of my secrets and hadn't turned away.

It's all fake, man.

Right.

This is why I don't make plans. This is why I just keep my head down and continue moving forward. It all goes away and if I stop moving, if I allow the present to wrap around me like waves kissing the bow of a ship and then dragging it under, sinking it into the dark ocean depths.

Taking me down with it.

No.

I need to stop standing on board, arms waving for someone to save me, all while waiting to drown.

I need to take charge of my life.

I *need* to swim my ass to shore.

King's voice rumbles on, but I force myself to turn away, to head back up the stairs, to accept what I already knew.

This isn't real.

This is a fairy tale—the white knight rescuing the damsel from the side of the road. It's been nice to live in this world, this moment for a little while, but the real fairy tales have grim endings.

I need to step out from between the pages of the book, need to get back to reality.

It's time to find an apartment, finish up my design work for the gala, focus on my pups.

Time to forget this whiplash of men—terrible to wonderful.

Time to...move on.

———

THE KNOCK at my office door has me looking up, seeing Jean-Michel leaning back against the doorframe.

He's decidedly casual—for him anyway—in a button-down with the sleeves rolled up, a pair of jeans and boots.

Out walking the vineyard, inspecting the vines, the wine production.

Finger on the pulse.

Always.

This man somehow has the uncanny ability to keep track of all of the varied pieces of his business ventures.

I guess that's what makes him so successful.

And it's also probably why he's appeared like my fairy godmother—some magical part of him sensing that I'm unsettled, that I'm a mess, that there's something going on with me that he needs to fix.

"It's late," he says.

I glance out the window, see the sun sliding behind the hills in the distance.

"So says the hockey team owner who was traveling with the guys and then spent all day working his other job." I nod to his boots. "What are you going to do? Trade those for dress shoes and head off to a board meeting?"

The flicker in his eyes has me knowing that I'm right.

Not that he acknowledges it.

He just tilts his head down the hall. "Want to walk the space for the gala?"

My heart squeezes.

This man is ruthless.

But he's also kind.

And I know he's checking in on me because he's worried about me and wants to take my pulse.

Well, know what?

He's had his own brand of shit dropped into his lap of late, what with his ex-wife showing up and trying to implode his life, his relationship with Chrissy, and his businesses.

So, in the vein of finally stepping into my own life and making decisions that will have me—pardon the sports reference—jumping in the game rather than waiting around for someone to extend a hand and draw me onto the ice, I decide that maybe my fairy godmother needs some magic of his own.

And that's why I'm already on my feet and moving toward him before I tell him, "Yeah, let's walk it."

"AND THE BARS will be set up here and on the far side of the room," I tell him, scanning the digital map on my tablet and then looking up and studying the space again.

Something about the setup feels wrong, but I can't put my finger on it.

Then again, I'm the design brain for graphics and menus, gift bags and photo backdrops.

Space planning isn't in my wheelhouse—

Thankfully, it *is* in my fairy godmother's.

"No," he says, reaching over me and tapping the screen. "That's not going to work. You need to double that at least." A beat and he studies the map. "No, with this amount of tickets sold, you'll need at least six."

"Six?" I exclaim.

"This is a charity event and auction," he says, pulling out the notebook and pen he always keeps in his back pocket and sketching out a layout of the room, complete with those six drink stations. "You want people to spend money." Another beat before his eyes flick up to mine, his mouth curving up in one corner. "Which means you need people to drink all of the free wine that your boss is donating."

"Fr-free?" I sputter. "Jean-Michel, that's not what we agreed to."

In fact, what we *agreed to* was that he would give my rescue a wholesale discount on the wine.

And that I'd pay the rental fee for the event space.

Especially because he's "giving" me the team for the night—making the event sponsored by the charity arm of the Eagles organization doesn't strictly make it mandatory for the players to attend, but it does encourage them.

Strongly.

He lifts one muscular shoulder, drops it again as he continues laying out the room in an efficient manner that speaks of exactly how many events like this he's attended. "Maybe not, but that's what we're doing."

"Jean-Michel—"

"And you're not paying the rental fee for the space."

"*Jean-Michel!*"

His head tilts up, eyes hitting mine. "Did I tell you that Phillip has decided to take the relocation offer with his company?"

I still, almost able to feel that hand on my throat again.

Almost able to see the anger in Phillip's eyes.

To feel the fear that had coiled in my belly, spread from fingertip to toes, burst out of every cell, that had me running the moment Phillip left the room, climbing out a window and sprinting down a deserted road.

"Hey," Jean-Michel murmurs, gently settling his hand on my shoulder. "It's taken care of."

I swallow. "It shouldn't have to be."

Those fingers squeeze.

Gently.

Not like Phillip's had squeezed.

"No, Ror," he says. "It shouldn't have."

I take a breath, release it in a long, slow exhale.

And then I push that aside.

Forward.

Saving myself.

But not spitting on the help the people I love give me, not refusing to grab the life preserver.

I can find a balance—

It's all fake, man.

In some things.

"Thank you," I whisper, eyes stinging.

His brows come up. "For what?"

And that dislodges King's voice.

Because this man is impossible. A total silver fox with a body that's more fit than most men my age (excluding a certain group of yummy hockey players who've recently been folded into my circle—or, rather, me into theirs). And more than being in shape, Jean-Michel exudes a certain...

Sex appeal.

There.

I said it—or *thought* it, anyway.

I shouldn't have—said *or* thought.

But I did.

Because Jean-Michel has daddy vibes.

Gross, considering he's a father figure and those vibes don't do it for me, but...

I can't deny it.

He's a total hottie who deserves someone to love him.

It's not something I've ever allowed myself to think before. I mean, how can I? Chrissy's my friend and I was with Phillip and...

Still, I don't miss that there's something different about him today.

Like he was frozen solid behind a wall of ice, impenetrable and not exactly unfeeling, but also...

Not open at all.

But, for some reason, that ice has melted.

And he's exposed to the world.

"Are you okay?" I ask softly.

His hand drops to his side, snapping his notebook closed, clipping the pen onto the cover. "What are you talking about?" He tucks them away. "I'm fine."

Liar.

"The team's finally getting itself together—no thanks to more than a few people behind the scenes who need to get *their* shit together or get the fuck out," he says. "But I don't have time to get into that. Let's figure out the rest of this so I can get to my meeting."

Gruff words, but I don't miss the tightening of his shoulders, the muscle flicking in his cheek.

Be brave and kind.

Kind isn't the problem. I'd fight a war for this man, to protect that big heart hidden inside the often grumpy and stern exterior. What he'd done for his daughter, for me, for so many others in his periphery was astronomical. And now that Angela, his ex-wife, had popped up back in his life, throwing so many parts of it into chaos, he might need a fairy godmother of his own.

And...

Maybe I needed to be the one to return the favor.

So...now it's on to brave.

"I'm *talking* about your ex-wife showing up."

He stills, teeth clicking together audibly.

I touch *his* shoulder. "Are you doing okay with her being around again?" After leaving him and Chrissy when Chrissy was a baby and being MIA until recently...

And now trying to contest a divorce that had been granted years before.

Because if it *wasn't* final, then the assets she could get her hands on—

Well, Phillip might have fucked with me, might have wronged me terribly.

But Chrissy's mom?

Angela might fuck with Jean-Michel, with Chrissy, and with everyone under the umbrella of Jean-Michel's many businesses.

The pressure to keep it all together must be—

Astronomical.

Plus, Angela is as much of a bitch as my stepmom, Cathy.

"I'm fine," he says again.

"Right," I tell him, crossing my arms and fixing him with what I've begun to think of as my Cactus Queen glare, "and that sounds *so* convincing."

To Jean-Michel's credit—although that muscle in his jaw ticks again—he doesn't snap at me. Instead, he exhales, shakes his head, and turns for the door. "There's an apartment in my building that's opened up." A glance over his shoulder. "Since Mama Bang headed home and you don't need to play make-believe anymore."

Nothing else could have stopped me in my tracks quite as effectively.

Something I know *he* knows since he pauses, rotates to fully face me, and turns the tables.

Effectively.

Confidently.

Because...

That's Jean-Michel.

"Unless, it's *not* pretend."

THIRTY-ONE

King

"Good God," Cam says, shoving the oversized apple turnover into his mouth with all the grace and manners of a farmyard animal—something I only know because I'm doing the same with my apple-cinnamon donut.

And seriously, I love the fall.

Apples of all varieties.

Empty calories and refined sugar and loads of carbs accompanying them.

Fucking chef's kiss.

"If the woman wasn't married"—Molly, the owner who opened a chain of restaurants, cafes, and bakeries around the Bay Area—"I'd get on my knees and beg her to marry me," I say through another huge bite.

"I think you might have better luck if she wasn't married and you got on your knees and begged to do something *else* to her," Rory says innocently from next to me.

Cam freezes.

I glance at her with narrowed eyes.

Rome's mouth hitches up at the edges.

Chrissy...well, the woman who knows the *other* woman who's joined us in our pursuit of all these empty calories and delicious carbs the best, starts cackling.

Rory, meanwhile, takes a dainty bite of her pastry and smiles like she's an innocent angel.

"Liar," I murmur, leaning in to whisper the word in her ear. "She'd be begging *me*."

"Who says?" she asks, but I don't miss the little shiver, the way gooseflesh prickles on her skin.

"*I* say." I flick out my tongue, taste the sweetness of her and smirk when she squirms in her seat. "And *I* say that you want me on my knees later," I murmur, nuzzling at that *oh so sensitive spot* just behind her ear.

Am I aware that everyone at the table is watching?

That they've seen Rory still wearing the ring I bought her? That they know this shit is supposed to be a ruse to get my mom off my back?

Yes to all.

Do I currently give one fuck that what I'm doing is contrary to all of that?

Nope.

Not one fucking bit.

I press my lips to her skin and she squirms again. I clock another shiver wracking through her frame, know it's because of me, because of my touch. Know that I can get her to do it again later—*multiple times* later—then straighten, return to my donut.

I know that I'm smirking like an asshole, proud like a caveman of the reaction I coaxed from her.

And I don't give a fuck.

Same as I don't give a fuck about the knowing look that Chrissy and Rome exchange.

Probably because the truth of what I feel for Rory is there in my belly, my heart, my soul.

She's different.

I can be different with her.

I can be…myself.

I didn't get the chance to tell her that last night, considering she worked late.

Nor this morning, when Rome and Cam and Chrissy descended on my house and the allure of the delicious delights of Molly's had drawn us out of bed after only two orgasms for her.

And I'm going to make sure she knows she can do the same.

"Hmm," she murmurs as she delicately sets her apple tart down, mischief in her eyes before she looks away and wipes her fingers on a napkin. She turns enough to settle her hand on my thigh, her slender fingers burning like a brand through my jeans. "Or maybe you want me on *my* knees," she murmurs, hand sneaking higher.

My dick goes hard.

Just like that.

Rock fucking *hard*.

And I know if I don't get her to behave herself, I'm going to take that hand of hers, peel it from my thigh, and haul that sexy ass off to the bathroom.

And make her shiver.

And moan.

I capture that misbehaving hand and lace our fingers together, lifting it so I can press a kiss to the back of it.

Then I settle it back onto my thigh and lean close again. "Behave," I order softly.

More mischief in green eyes, along with a dash of stubbornness.

Of...*prickliness.*

The Cactus Queen about to make her appearance.

I grin, tap the tip of her nose, murmur, "Or do you only take orders in the bedroom, princess?"

Her nails bite into the fabric of my jeans.

And...yup. I want to be naked, want to feel that bite on my bare skin, want—

"Kingston?"

Rory goes ramrod stiff next to me, but I'm so busy doing the same at the sound of the slightly abrasive, nasally voice I'd endured for several hours on a date my mom had set up for me a few months back that I hardly notice it.

Because—

"Oh my God, Kingston, it *is* you!"

A taloned hand reaches forward, gripping my shoulder with so much force that I have to release Rory or risk both of our chairs toppling backward. I squeeze her fingers, settle her hand back in her own lap, then push my chair back and stand, turning to greet—

"Stacy," I say, hoping I manage to keep the dread from my voice, my expression as I lean in and press a kiss to her cheek.

And nearly choke on her perfume.

Jesus.

I lean back, even though she seems to want to linger close, those long, fake nails digging into my shoulders.

Thankfully, I'm stronger—albeit not by much, considering the force it takes to break this woman's grip.

"How are you?" I say when I'm clear of the cloud of her perfume.

Her bottom lip comes out, and I know she's going for a cute pout.

The trouble is...it isn't cute.

It's annoying as shit.

I'd seen it pulled no less than a dozen times in the couple of hours we spent over a meal together—the final time being when I'd put her in a Lyft and sent her on her way.

Alone.

Hoping to never see her again.

And...yet here we are.

"I'm terrible"—pout—"especially since I haven't seen you"—another pout—"since our dinner together."

Where she ordered the most expensive thing on the menu, took all of two bites of it, was rude to the waiter, and spent more time taking a selfie than talking to me.

Yeah, I'm not a fan.

Nor that my mom is friends with Stacy's mom, Cathy.

"Life got busy," I say, snagging the top of my chair, putting a little distance between us. I hitch a thumb over my shoulder. "Well, it was good to see you, but I should—"

For the first time, those predatory eyes move from me, seeming to notice that I'm not alone at the table.

I almost laugh at the excitement blooming on her face when her eyes hit on the men—puck bunny extraordinaire, this one—and the almost immediate subsequent sneer that takes its place when she sees Chrissy.

But it's the fury replacing that when her gaze drifts to Rory that has me taking a step to the right, putting myself between my princess and the woman who looks ready to gouge her eyes out with those long, red talons.

"What the fuck are you doing here?" Stacy says in frosty, clipped-out words.

Not to me.

To...Rory.

"Hi, Stacy," she replies quietly. "You're looking well."

And I fucking hate that I've heard that tone before.

That it was the same one she'd used with that asshole of hers.

Stacy doesn't respond—or not verbally anyway. Instead, her gaze drifts down Rory from head to toe in a long, slow drag, her mouth curving into a derisive sneer that has me clenching my back teeth together.

Then she sniffs, clearly dismissing Rory as she turns back to me.

And yeah, no, that doesn't work for me.

Neither does the way her hands are contracted into claws, like she'll cut a bitch if Rory dares so much as move.

"As you can see," I begin quietly, and although the words aren't loud, I make sure to inject plenty of ice into my tone.

You fuck with Rory—who seems to know your skinny ass for some reason—and you fuck with me.

And I'm a hell of a lot meaner.

Something I make evident in my eyes when Stacy glances back in my direction.

The veneer between fake sweet and bitch is being scrubbed away.

And yeah, no, I'm not going to expose Rory to that.

"As you can see," I say again, drawing my chair back and starting to sit down, "we're eating. It was good to see you, though." I plunk my ass down, turn my back on her.

Dismissing her.

Unfortunately, she doesn't go away.

"What are *you* doing here?" she snaps.

Not directed at me.

At Rory.

Who's gone even stiffer, whose hands are clenched into tight fists on her lap.

Whose skin is pale and lips are pressed flat and...her eyes won't come to mine.

Fuck. *That.*

"You need to go," I tell Stacy.

Another sniff, this one sent in my direction.

Fuck this bitch.

Especially when she reaches for Rory's arm and snaps—

"Not until I talk to my sister."

THIRTY-TWO

Rory

It's like I'm back in that house again.

Trying to be small and quiet.

To go unnoticed.

So their cruelty…

Well, so it wouldn't touch me.

But just like every other time I wanted to hide and they were determined to find me, to unleash whatever unpleasant emotion that was bothering them onto me, it doesn't matter how small I am.

They still see me anyway.

She sees me.

"Not until I talk to my sister," Stacy snaps, hand jerking out, fingers and long nails curved like claws.

I've felt them bite into my skin plenty of times before.

But today, they don't make it that far.

King's hand shoots out in a flash of movement, faster than my eyes can track, but suddenly his hand is next to me—

faster than her. His strong, thick fingers grip Stacy's wrist, staying it less than an inch from my shoulder. "I don't think you need to talk to your sister right now."

His tone is cold, far colder than I've ever heard it.

I look from his fiercely protective expression and over to Stacy's mulish one.

She'll create a scene.

In an instant.

And...dammit.

I love Molly's. I don't want to be embarrassed to come here, don't want to be remembered as the woman whose sister threw a hissy fit and ruined everyone's lunch and delicious apple treats.

I want...

To have peace and enjoy some yummy food with my friends, with the man I care about.

Because I don't have forever with him.

Because...

It's fake.

Which means...I need to corral her outside, let her get her anger out, and then find a way to get rid of her.

Yay.

So. *Much.* Fun.

Biting back a sigh, I reach up and cover King's hand with my own. "It's okay," I tell him. "I'll talk to my stepsister."

His eyes flash to mine.

And the way our stares connect—and hold—give Stacy her opportunity.

She breaks his grip on her wrist, jerks forward and clenches my hand tightly enough that I gasp in pain and try to pull back. "What. The fuck. Is *that?*" she snaps.

The ring.

She's looking at the engagement ring.

King's engagement ring.

The fake one.

But...she doesn't know that.

Shit.

"Don't. *Fucking.* Touch. Her," King growls, grabbing Stacy's finger and pulling it back far enough that she cries out and immediately releases my hand.

Her eyes are fucking terrifying.

They promise retribution and—

King's already on his feet, stepping between us, Cam and Rome flanking him. A wall of hockey players coming to my defense. The big brothers I never had. The man I never had either.

And, perhaps for the first time since my dad died, I feel safe, protected, and...wanted.

In a way that even my fairy godmother Jean-Michel can't compete with.

My throat goes tight, eyes stinging.

Stupid.

Because it's not real.

I mean, yeah, King is a good person. They all are. I know they'd stick up for me no matter the situation...

But they'd stand up for anyone in this situation.

Good. People.

It's not about me.

Even if what I feel in my heart is more.

It's family.

It's...love.

It's *everything*.

"Breathe," Chrissy whispers, crouching next to my chair, her arm slipping around my shoulders. "You're good."

She knows about Stacy and Desiree, knows how they treated me.

Not all of it.

But enough to know.

Because like recognizes like and she's been through enough of her own horrors to know—

Well, to know *enough*.

"I'm okay," I tell her, eyes flitting to hers for a moment.

That moment is long enough to see that she doesn't buy that for a second.

But I'm already looking back to my sister, barely visible through that wall of hockey players and—

"What's going on, my darling?"

I still, dread boiling in my belly, that voice like nails on a chalkboard.

"What is it?" Chrissy murmurs.

"My stepmom," I rasp out. "I can't do this. I—I need to go."

Chrissy opens her mouth, but doesn't get the chance to reply because—

King is there, hand on my jaw, tilting my face up and studying it for the barest heartbeat before he glances over at Chrissy. "Pack our stuff up. I'll get it from you later."

Eyes wide, she nods.

He takes my hand. "Let's go."

"But—"

"Aurora Grace!"

I shudder, but childhood instincts kick in and I freeze.

"No," King mutters. "We're going."

His arm goes around my middle and then I'm on my feet and being propelled toward the door.

"Aurora. *Grace*."

"King," I whisper, a weird mix of guilt and relief warring through me when he doesn't stop moving me forward and out onto the sidewalk.

"Just keep those feet moving, princess," he orders gruffly, directing us down the sidewalk and behind the building to where his car is parked in the bakery's lot.

"I—"

"Aurora Grace!"

"Christ," he mutters, picking up the pace and getting us both to the car before they catch up.

Unfortunately, it's *at* the car where they do catch up.

Stacy and Cathy and—oh great, the whole club's here—Dessie stand there glowering at me like they did when I was a little kid who was suddenly all alone in the world and they were teenagers and a grown woman who could have shown kindness.

Like Chrissy had.

Like Rome and Cam.

Like King.

But they hadn't.

And that truth settles somewhere deep inside me, healing that old wound that never closed, that oozed old hurts and insecurities.

Why *couldn't* they have been kind?

Why *couldn't* they have looked after me?

But...maybe it wasn't about me after all.

Because Jean-Michel and Chrissy, Rome and Cam, and... King.

None of them had a problem—

"What are you doing with her?" Stacy grits out, her expression frankly scary.

"Do I need a reason to spend time with my fiancée?" King snaps.

Which doesn't help the scary.

Not at freaking all.

Stacy looks like she's going to bust out a long sword and

skewer King. Or me, when her gaze drifts back to my hand and then up to my eyes. Hers threaten retribution. "I thought the wedding was off."

A wedding they hadn't been invited to.

A wedding they'd showed up at because Phillip and his mother had decided they needed to be invited.

To keep up appearances.

God, why had I wasted so much time with that—

"She's not marrying that asshole," King mutters.

Yup. Asshole.

Stacy stills, scary flaring, growing into something...

That has me stepping a little closer to King.

Without looking at me, without taking his eyes off the viper-like chaos in front of me, he clocks my body nearing, and tucks me more tightly against his side.

God, I love this man.

The thought ricochets through my brain in a thousand directions—all of them violent and tearing and frightening and...

Beautiful.

A beautiful sort of violence.

Because it shatters through the veneer of what I had with Phillip, what I thought I deserved.

Because it pierces through the cloud of my childhood sweeping in like a tornado, threatening to destroy everything I've tried to build since moving out.

Because...

King is different and he makes me feel different and—

It far eclipses anything—*anything*—I felt for Phillip.

And...it's fake.

"I thought you weren't interested in settling down."

Heart pounding, mind still reeling from that beautiful violence tearing through me, I look back at my stepsister.

"I'm not," King says. "Because what I have with Rory is so much more than that."

Jaws fall open—and not just Cathy, Stacy, and Dessie's.

Mine is on the pavement at his declaration.

Which means it's easy for him to open the passenger door and coax me into the car.

Easy for him to get in himself, to start up the engine, and pull out of the spot.

What I have with Rory is so much more.

But...it's fake.

It's all fake.

Isn't it?

THIRTY-THREE

King

The silence in the car is disturbed by my phone ringing.

I start to reach to decline it on the screen, but Rory stills my hand. "It's your mom," she says softly, those green eyes unfathomable. "You should always take a call from your mom."

Except when I'd dropped a bomb on a woman I've grown to care about.

After she'd been confronted by one of the psychos my mom had set me up with...and that woman, who'd made a single blind date a nightmare that wouldn't quit, had a mother who *my* mother was—for some reason—friends with.

What the actual fuck?

Hell, maybe I *did* need to talk to her.

To tear into her.

I jab my finger at the screen, snap, "Hello?"

"King?"

"Yeah, Mom," I mutter. "You called me, remember? Yes, it's King."

There's a long pause. "Is this a bad time?"

"I've just seen Stacy again." A beat. "And Cathy."

Now the quiet grows.

"Did you know that Stacy is Rory's stepsister?" I grip the steering wheel, navigate us onto the freeway that'll lead back to my place. "And that Cathy's her stepmom?"

Rory inhales sharply, eyes clenching closed.

I reach over, take her hand.

"What did you say?" my mom asks.

I take a breath, struggling for calm because this isn't her fault. Not really. She's misguided and pushy but...who the fuck could have predicted the world is this small? "Your friend, Cathy's daughter, Stacy." I pause for a second, make sure she's picked up all of that. "She hasn't just lost her mind, she's also a total bitch. She practically assaulted Rory in the middle of Molly's when she saw the engagement ring."

"She's Rory's *stepsister?*"

Something about my mom's tone...well, it has me freezing, my anger and frustration fading away.

Concern rippling up instead.

"What?" I press.

Silence again. Then, "Is Rory there with you?"

A breath from the woman next to me. "Yes, Stella. I'm here."

Silence. Then a quiet sigh. "I'm sorry that happened, sweetheart," she says. "Cathy"—a breath—"well, she didn't have very nice things to say about her stepdaughter and"—regret filling the car—"clearly she's mistaken because you're wonderful Rory, and I think...I think it's likely that Cathy's not the friend I hoped she was."

"You think?" I mutter then promptly feel like a dick.

Because my mom sucks in a sharp breath that rattles through the speakers.

Because my mom lost her best friend not long ago and...she hasn't fully recovered.

Hence, all of us putting up with her matchmaking.

"I'm sorry," I tell her.

"No, I am," she says.

"Mom—"

Rory squeezes my hand. "Stella, it's okay," she murmurs. "My childhood was messy and...well, it's too much to get into at the moment. Suffice to say, I don't have a relationship with Stacy, Cathy, or Dessie, and I haven't for a few years now."

It's not okay.

None of this is okay.

I can't protect her from this shit. I can't make it so the bad stuff didn't happen.

I can't—

You're not your father.

I can't make it okay.

And Christ. That burns through me.

But I shove the voice down, focus on what's important. "It's not okay."

"King," Rory murmurs, squeezing my hand. "I'm fine."

"I—" My mom exhales, the sound rattling through the speaker. "King is right. It's not okay."

"I don't mean you, Mom," I begin. "I mean, I'm over the matchmaking for sure, but"—I look at Rory—"it's not okay for them to treat you like shit."

She nods, but I see the battle in her eyes.

It's hard to hear that.

To accept it.

Because those inner demons are assholes.

"King's right." Another breath. "Look, I...it sounds like

you both need a moment, and I think it's better that we discuss this in person." Her voice gentles. "I was calling to confirm my visit and flight times since Dad's team is playing on Thanksgiving Day. I wanted to take some food requests and see if you needed help planning the wedding and..." She pauses. "But I understand if you'd both like some space right now."

A visit from my mother.

I can't think of anything I want less right about now.

But then she keeps talking.

"I-I know I owe you an explanation, honey. About a lot of things. And—"

Her voice cracks.

Dammit.

Rory's fingers tighten in mine. "Stella," she says gently. "This isn't your fault. It's a crappy misunderstanding and—"

"I should go," my mom says. "I'll check in with you both in a couple of days and—"

I slide to a stop at a signal and glance at Rory, and with that single look, I know we're both in consensus. "Come for Thanksgiving, Mom," I say softly. "We can talk about it over apple pie."

"I—"

"Please," Rory murmurs, concern in her eyes as they cling to mine. "Your trip was cut short last time. I'd love to spend more time with you. *Really.*" Teeth pressing into her bottom lip before her chin comes up and she nods once, as though she's made a decision. "And if you stay through the weekend, you can go to the gala with us."

"I shouldn't," my mom murmurs. "I've already over-stepped and you're a young couple, you need privacy."

"Mom," I say gently, nodding back at Rory. "Fly out. And

stay for the gala." A beat because I know she's going to put us off. "Please?"

Her next breath is shaky. "I don't have a dress."

"So we'll go shopping," Rory says gently. "I need to pick up some accessories for mine anyway."

"I—"

"I'll book you a ticket, Mom," I tell her. "You just get on the plane."

A long silence as I half expect her to disconnect the call.

But then she just sighs again, says, "Okay."

And *then* she disconnects.

I push the button to open the garage door, pull inside, park, and look over at Rory.

Her expression is gentle. "I'm okay."

Okay.

I fucking hate that she's *okay*.

I want her to be great, to be perfect.

Which is why I turn the engine back on, reverse right the fuck out of the garage, and—

See about making sure she knows she's exactly that.

TO HER CREDIT, it takes Rory a solid five minutes to ask, "Um, want to clue me in to what the hell you're doing?"

"Prickle princess coming out?"

"Cactus Queen who will spike your ass is out and ready to play." She pretends to jab at me with her finger.

I grin. "Well, her Royal Spikiness can just wait to find out."

She snorts, but there's something careful about the way she settles her hand back into her lap that I don't love.

Hell, who am I kidding?

I fucking hate it.

The distance. That she's cautious to touch me. That she's worried about what my reaction might be.

Considering her stepsister's shit fit that's not a surprise.

Considering her asshole of a fiancée, also not a surprise.

Considering all she'd lost...newsflash, it's *still* not a surprise.

But I hate that her actions are carefully calculated—that she clearly spends a lot of mental energy trying to make sure that she's not stepping outside of some irrational boundary one of the assholes in her life drew up.

I hate that she can't just relax and be herself with me, especially when I've been more open with her than any other person.

I've seen glimpses of it—the real her.

But I want it one hundred percent of the time.

Because...I want her.

And I'm fucking terrified I won't be the man she needs—

Fuck that.

The thought tears through me so fiercely that I almost miss the turnoff.

You're not your dad.

No, I'm not.

You're not enough.

Maybe not, but I'm not going to leave this woman out there, exposed and vulnerable to the world. Not when...

She's mine.

May the hockey gods help me.

But. She. Is. Mine.

The thought burns like acid through my veins. It's terrifying and intoxicating. It makes me want to pull this car over, get out, and scream up at the sky.

I want to break shit, break it until all the memories are in pieces so small I can't remember them.

Because...she's mine.

Not for a little while.

Forever.

I pause, wait for lightning to strike me down for just thinking that.

And when it doesn't, I breathe...and then I reach over the console and pick up her hand, lace our fingers together, lifting her hand and pressing a kiss to the back of it, just beneath the huge-ass diamond ring I'd bought her.

Fake.

But not.

It's not fucking *fake*.

THIRTY-FOUR

The soft kiss on the back of my hand is seared into my skin.

And that pulsing sensation that skates over my flesh for the next five minutes distracts me for the remainder of the drive.

I barely feel the centripetal forces pulling on my body as we wind our way to the top of a hill, barely notice the rusted metal gate that's pushed to the side, thus allowing us to keep driving up.

I don't notice much of anything—aside from that feel of King's mouth on me—until we slide to a stop and he turns off the engine.

Then...

I notice *everything*.

Shamrock-colored hills spreading out in all directions, large dark green oaks dotting them in irregular intervals, and a bright blue sky filled with floofy, cotton candy-like clouds floating slowly across the horizon.

"Come here," he murmurs, taking my hand and drawing me to the side, up along a shaded path.

"Where are we going?" I ask as we walk under the canopy of leaves, our shadows mixing with the dappled sunshine.

He slips his hand from mine, wraps his arm around my shoulders, tucking me close, enveloping me in the warmth of his body, the spice of his scent. My soul immediately settles.

"Wait just a little longer, princess," he says softly. "Please?"

I nod, whisper, "Okay." And maybe it's not so much that my soul is settling, but rather that it expands a little, as though the tendrils between us are growing, leaving my body, drifting over, clinging to the edges of him.

Wanting to feel him.

Wanting to sew him into my being.

Wow...that's not creepy at all.

Which is easier to think about than the fact that—

I want this to be forever.

I clamp my eyes closed.

Which is not a smart thing to do on a path filled with rocks and random tree roots.

Because, yup, I promptly trip.

But I barely move, barely have the sensation of falling before I'm held even more tightly.

Kept safe.

Protected.

"Easy now, princess," he murmurs, stroking a finger down my cheek, seeming to wait for me to open my eyes.

And when I do, I'm dropped into deep blue pools.

Beautiful man.

"I don't want this to be fake," I blurt.

Horror floods through me.

Because…

I. Just. Said. That.

He stills, and I wait for him to drop his hand, for him to set me away from him.

But…

He doesn't.

Instead, he says the most wonderful thing.

"I don't think it's been fake from the moment I picked you up from the side of the road."

My heart skips a beat, words stoppering up in my throat. "But—" Then I clamp my teeth together, bite back the words that will make me sound like even more of an idiot.

He doesn't let them stay buried, though.

Of course not.

"What?" he asks.

I nibble at the corner of my mouth. "I—"

Ignore it. Pretend I hadn't heard it. Be happy with him admitting this isn't fake.

That's incredible.

Wonderful—

All of a sudden I'm pressed back against the trunk of a tree, pinned carefully between King's big body and the bark, his hands cushioning my head and back from the roughness. He bends, puts his face in front of mine. "What, princess?"

I inhale, debate for a second.

Then figure…what the hell.

"I heard you on the phone, King," I say. "It's okay." I shrug. "You don't have to protect my feelings, I swear. I'm a big girl. It's time that I move on and get my feet under me and—"

His lips hit mine, stealing my breath in a kiss that leaves my heart racing. "What the fuck are you talking about, baby?" he asks again.

"I overheard you."

His brows drag together. "When?"

"In the kitchen the other day," I murmur. "I heard you on the phone with someone and you were talking about me." I grind my teeth together. "Talking about *us*."

That frown stays in place.

"And you said we were fake."

His expression smooths out and then he's pushing back, taking my hand again, drawing me back up the path. "My brother," he says. "I told you his wife cheated on him and left him with the kids." A glance over at me and I nod, completely befuddled at his change in demeanor, that he's relaxed now. But then he goes on, "Jakob's not exactly seeing straight when it comes to women right now." A breath moving through that big body of his. "And I lied to him so I didn't have to listen to him rant." Another look. "And because I didn't want to deal with what I was feeling." His fingers squeeze mine. "What I *am* feeling."

"King—"

"It's scary," he says, drawing me out into the sunshine and toward a bench.

I'm struck by the beauty of the valley in the distance, the beauty of his eyes as they meet mine.

"It's scary and after what happened with my ex, after every fear of mine was validated—I'm not good enough, I'll never be good enough—" He sits, drawing me down next to him. "But that fear is smaller than the fear of losing what you bring to my life."

I shake my head. "I haven't done anything, honey. I'm just—"

"You made me feel," he says, cupping my cheeks in his big, warm hands. "You made me realize that there's more that I want. That there's more I can *have*. But I think"—he shifts, pressing his forehead to mine—"I knew that from the moment I met you. It's why I pushed your buttons so much. I was desperate to find something wrong with you."

My heart lurches in my chest, throwing itself against my rib cage.

Throwing itself at this man.

Offering itself up on a silver platter.

"King," I whisper.

His mouth hitches up. "I know," he says softly, straightening slowly and reaching into his pocket. "I was delusional to even think that this was something else, that it was fake, that it might mean nothing. I'm clearly a dumbass." He pulls his hands out. "Because I bought this weeks ago after Zeus ate—"

"My bracelet," I whisper.

"I know it's not the same," he says. "I just..." He takes my hand, peels open my fingers, then places the new charm bracelet gently in my palm. "I thought it might be something to remind you of the good your dad gave you."

The beautiful view is hidden behind my tears.

Yup. I'm a sap and sobbing through this moment is likely ruining it.

But I can't help it as I turn my bleary eyes to the thin silver chain of the bracelet.

"The clasp is reinforced so it should withstand any persistent pups," he says softly, gently lifting it from my palm and showing me the clip. "And the charms aren't wooden but they're—"

"Perfect," I whisper, touching a finger to each of the charms in turn.

Big Ben. The Eiffel Tower. A koala. The Colosseum. A boat.

The Golden Gate Bridge.

All of the charms from my father.

And new ones.

A dog bone.

A crown.

A hockey stick.

And a...cactus.

The laughter that bubbles up and out of my throat is watery, and the tears that slide down my cheeks are hot and copious and drip off my chin.

"Shit," King mutters, drawing me close. "I'm sorry, princess. I didn't mean to make you sad."

"Sad?" I ask, eyes still leaking but vision clear enough to see his face, to see this beautiful man. "No one has ever done anything this nice for me."

His chest inflates on a breath, worry dragging over his features.

And I find myself desperate to take it from him, to make him smile, to make him *see*. "I'm touched, King. Beyond words." My mouth curves. "And that's coming from a woman with Jean-Michel Dubois as my fairy godmother."

"God*father*," he says.

"What?"

"I've been calling him your fairy godfather because he's scary as shit, but he's worked magic in your life."

Magic, yes.

And I'm so freaking grateful for it, for him.

But not as much magic as the man in front of me has sprinkled over my life.

"Fairy Godfather." I tap my bottom lip. "I like that. Maybe I'll get him a T-shirt printed with it."

King grins, says dryly, "I'm sure he'd love that."

I smile back at him, heart full because...he sees me, he wants me. This...

Isn't fake.

"He'd wear it to all his board meetings," I quip.

Laughter in the air and then King sobers, touches my cheek again. "I'm sorry I made you cry."

"I'm not," I say, covering his hand with my own.

"My beautiful non-prickly princess." A kiss to my forehead. "Can I put it on you?"

I nod, holding my breath as he wraps the bracelet around my wrist and fastens it. Because this feels bigger than the ring somehow, bigger than anything that's come before.

Be brave and kind.

And when he presses his lips to my wrist, just above the bracelet, the words...just come out—

No planning. Just blurting.

Just some small part of me hoping that the universe won't take this away.

Because this moment, this man...

I *need* to say it.

"I love you," I whisper, watching the shock flash across his face, tangle with renewed worry. "I know it's scary. I know it's too soon and that it complicates everything and—"

He sweeps me up against him, drops his head so that his mouth is a millimeter away from mine. "You are fucking *perfect.*"

And then he's kissing me.

And then he's giving me something that I know I'll never, *ever* forget.

"I love you so *fucking* much."

THIRTY-FIVE

King

My heart is pounding like a locomotive as I lower my head, take her mouth in a kiss that encapsulates everything that I'm feeling.

Love.

I fucking love this woman.

And I want to keep her.

And I thought it, said it out loud, and...

Nothing bad happened.

She sighs, lips parting, and I sweep my tongue inside her mouth, tasting her, taking from her, giving back.

I tug her onto my lap.

"King!" she gasps, hands going to my shoulders, legs straddling my waist.

I drop my forehead to hers, loving the dazed look in her eyes, the way her nails knead at my shoulders when I drag my hand up her side, how her pelvis shifts, rocking against my dick.

Which is hard.

Because...it's Rory.

She leans in and this time she kisses me, all eagerness and heat and need, those hips rocking against me and—

Christ, I'm going to come in my pants like a teenager.

"Princess," I murmur, cupping her hip, drawing her to a halt.

"I want you," she whispers. "I love you and I want you and—" Her eyes blaze with need. "More than I've ever wanted anyone."

Heat scalds through me and my dick twitches.

I want her too.

So fucking much.

But it's the middle of the morning and we're on a public trail and any idiot could walk up and—

She moves then, doing it faster than my desire addled brain can process, flicking open the button on my jeans, yanking down my zipper—

"Princess—"

She wraps her hand around my dick and—

Look.

Frankly, I don't try very hard to stop her.

Because her fingers are wrapped around my cock and they're stroking and then...

Her mouth joins the party.

And *then* I'm really not thinking about stopping her, about drawing that warm, slick mouth off my dick, peeling the fingers free.

No fucking way.

Teeth and tongue, lips and suction.

A hand dipping into my underwear to cup my balls, and—

I stiffen.

Sweet baby Jesus, I'm going to come in her mouth.

On the side of a hill.

On a public trail.

In the middle of the day.

"Princess—"

She hums, her hand tightening, and—

Shit.

I know I have one second—one fucking second—to gather the remnants of my control, to pull them into something tangible, to—

"Fuck," I growl, gripping her shoulders, pulling her off.

Pop!

"Dangerous," I mutter, not missing the pride on her face, the mischief in her eyes. "And...convenient."

Confusion sliding through her expression.

Until I reach for the hem of her dress, drag it up.

"King—"

"Shh," I order quietly, dragging her underwear down those lush thighs, wanting to taste the sopping cunt that's partially obscured by blond curls, but knowing that it will have to wait until later.

I nudge the fabric, send it down along her thighs, allow it to drop to her ankles.

Then I'm coaxing her to step out of them, tucking them into my pocket.

Drawing her back onto my lap.

Pushing inside.

We both gasp.

And then she's rocking again, the tight clamp of her pussy all around me. Hot. Slick. Convulsing tightly.

"King!" she cries, head falling back, eyes closed, hair a glimmering golden cape spread out behind her.

Beautiful.

Mine.

And then I'm lost in the pleasure of her, of this moment, of her love and the feelings in my heart and...

The fact that my future—our future—can be different.

Which is exactly the moment that I hear voices echoing up the trail.

"I STILL CAN'T BELIEVE that you almost got me arrested," she grumbles later that day.

We're curled up on the couch, a crappy action movie on in the background that neither of us are paying attention to. Because...things have changed and we're both being careful of that.

Aware of it.

Protecting it.

"No one saw anything," I remind her.

Because I'd swept her off my lap, tucked myself away, and straightened her dress before any of that could happen.

Her underwear was still in my pocket, though.

I grin.

"You're proud of yourself?" she asks, all prickle princess.

"I like your exhibition tendencies," I tell her, leaning close and nuzzling her throat. "Because as you know," I remind her, "you're the one who started it all."

She scowls, cheeks flushing, but I don't miss the pride in her eyes. "Rude," she grumbles. "It was totally your fault."

"So says the woman who stuck her hands down my pants..."

"It was one hand," she exclaims. "*One* hand—*ack!*"

I flip us, pinning her between my body and the couch cushions. "But five fingers," I murmur, trailing my tongue along her throat, pressing a kiss to the hinge of her jaw. "All wrapped around my cock."

"Four," she groans, nails scoring over my back.

I freeze, snag one of her hands, drawing it between us. "One. Two. Three." I kiss the tip of her thumb then her pointer and middle fingers. "Four." Her ring finger. "Five." I nibble at her palm. "Am I missing something?"

"Yup."

She doesn't go on, so I weave my hand into her hair, tilt her head back and kiss her throat. "You have five fingers, princess."

She shudders. "A thumb isn't technically a finger."

I freeze.

Then laughter boils up and over, filling the space between us.

This woman is fucking funny.

And sweet, her cheeks reddening, her teeth nibbling at her bottom lip.

But there's uncertainty drifting into her eyes, clinging to the edges of gorgeous emerald.

She doesn't plan for the future, but she told me she loves me.

She's lost so many things that were important to her, but she still found the courage to give me those words.

"Fuck, I love you."

Her eyes widen, the uncertainty disappears, and I know that I never stood a chance at keeping my distance from this woman, know that all the distance I erected, the times I pushed her buttons, every moment I clung to the fact that I'm not my dad...

It was all bullshit.

Because I was scared of getting hurt.

Scared of loving someone and having it go bad.

And because of that...

I almost missed out on this.

If I hadn't seen her on the side of the road that day, hadn't pulled my bike to a stop, hadn't seen the bruises...

I might never have had her like this, might have never seen this side of her.

Might have never had the chance to love her as she should be loved.

Because I'm going to love her *so fucking good* that she'll never have any doubt where she stands in my heart.

"Even if I'm right about thumbs?" she asks.

Teases.

Because she's here with me. Because, somehow, she can give that to me, even after everything she went through.

"I'll show you thumbs," I tease back, dragging my hand in, dipping my fingers (and said thumb) under the waistband of her pajamas, pressing my lips to hers and kissing her with every part of what I'm feeling—which is a whole fucking lot.

"This isn't fake," I growl when I pull back, holding her eyes, needing her to see the truth in mine, "and it never has been."

"No," she whispers. "It's not." A beat, her palm pressing to my cheek. "And it hasn't been from the beginning."

All the fear in me—not that there's much of it left, Rose's voice in my head fading to a faint whisper—settles and I cup her hip, turning us so that she's cradled against my chest, so that we can watch the movie we've been ignoring.

She doesn't protest, just scooches closer and relaxes against me, her contented sigh hitting my ears. Zeus, who was displaced during my shifting, jumps back onto the couch and settles in front of her.

And...this moment is small.

It's a valley overlooking a gorgeous view. It's giving a

meaningful present. It's scoring a goal and seeing her dancing like a fiend in the stands.

It's a dance in the kitchen.

It's teasing and an inside joke.

It's...us.

And *that's* why I know it's perfect.

THIRTY-SIX

Rory

I'm a woman in love.

It feels weird to say that still.

Even a week after having first said the words out loud.

Hell, it's weird to even think it.

To actually *feel* it because I know now that what I *had* been feeling in my relationship before wasn't love, not truly.

It was...

Not right.

And honestly? A part of me is still terrified. Scared this is all going to be snatched away. That I'll be left devastated and heartbroken and alone.

That I'll have to go on living without King.

But as much as I'm scared, I'm also...

At peace.

Because even *if* it all goes wrong, I'll still have had this time, these moments, the memories.

And right now, that's enough.

Especially because every day with King has been better than the last.

Cuddling on the couch. Watching him play at the arena. Hydrangeas in a vase on the island, the man having somehow discovered my favorite flower. Walking Zeus together on the trails that back up to his house. Coming home from a long day at work and finding the fridge full of my favorites, a slow cooker loaded with dinner on the counter, a note with the channel his game will be playing on tacked to the fridge. Pastries from Molly's. Spa appointments booked for Chrissy and me so we can have a girl's night.

And King.

Gentle touches to tuck back my hair behind my ear, kisses stolen as we dance in the kitchen, and...

Orgasms.

Lots and lots of orgasms.

Smiling, I turn off my playlist, drop my empty coffee cup in the sink, and snag my purse from the hook that King designated as mine—oh, my sweet, organized man. I tuck it over my shoulder as I walk down the hall and pull open the door, hitting the button to send the huge metal paneling rattling up when I remember I left my laptop on the island.

Maybe I need King to make me a Life Planner too.

Chuckling, I let the door swing shut, bustle down the hall, snag my computer, and hurry back into the garage.

I need to get to work.

"Rory—"

I freeze, the voice sliding like ice down my spine, panic gripping me for a heartbeat before my fight-or-flight kicks in and I drop my stuff, whip back toward the house.

My computer makes a sickening sound as it crashes against the concrete floor, my purse scattering its contents alongside it.

That doesn't matter.

I leave it all as I slam back inside, kicking myself for not being aware of my surroundings as I push the door shut behind me.

Or try to.

Because—

Then *Phillip* is shoving it inward.

And I'm not strong enough to stop the momentum, not strong enough to keep him out.

Heart in my throat, I release the wooden panel, let it crash open against the wall.

I leave that too, knowing it probably damaged the Sheetrock, having the inane thought that it *had* to happen right after King spent time repairing the hole he made when he punched the wall in the bedroom all those weeks before.

I sprint down the hall, intent on the front door and escape and—

I don't get there.

A hand grips my shoulder and yanks me back, fingers digging into my flesh so hard that I cry out in pain.

"Stop!" I shout. "Let me go!"

"You've ruined it," Phillip snarls.

"Let. *Go.*" I grab at his hand, wrench back a finger like King did to Stacy at the bakery, getting her to release me.

And it works.

Phillip grunts, grip loosening enough that I slip free, that I run for the front door again.

Unfortunately, I don't get far because this time, he grabs a handful of my hair and yanks me to a halt.

Fire burns along my scalp and I cry out, hands coming up to grab at his wrists, trying to staunch the pain, to find a way to get him to let me go. But his hold just tightens and—

"*Woof! Woof! Woof! WOOF!*"

Nails scrabble on the floor as Zeus's tiny fluffy body turns the corner. His teeth are bared and eyes fierce as he launches himself at us.

No.

At Phillip.

Who shrieks. "Ow! *Fuck!*"

The grip on my hair loosens enough that I'm able to pull free. I look down, see that Zeus has attached himself to Phillip's ankle and—

My ex kicks out with his other foot.

The *crunch* is sickening.

Zeus yelps as he skids across the floor, slamming into the cabinets.

Maybe I should have run.

Taken my chance.

But Zeus.

The little fluffy pupper that I rescued from a hoarder's house. The pup who's sweet and gentle as his sister is an adorable terror.

I can't leave him.

I scramble over to the pup, covering his body with my own, grunting when Phillip's foot connects with my ribs.

For fuck's sake, I only just finally stopped feeling the occasional twinges from my previously bruised torso, finally stopped feeling the bone-deep ache and the odd burst of pain when I stretched the wrong way.

Now I was going to have to go through all of that healing again.

Which is another insane thing to think about when I'm currently being assaulted by my ex.

I get that.

But it still slides through my mind before the next time he makes contact with my side.

I grunt and Zeus whimpers, the noise enough to snap me out of my bullshit.

Not standing on the bow of the ship waiting for rescue.

Swimming my ass to shore myself.

With a corgi in tow.

Grinding my teeth against the fire in my side, my scalp, I tuck Zeus close, cradle him away from Phillip, and brace—

Another kick that knocks me against the cabinets.

I shove the pain down as he winds up again, the motion giving me enough time to get my feet under me, to start pushing upward and—

"You. Do. *Not*. Hit. Other. People!"

I blink—halfway up—almost unable to believe what I'm seeing.

Who I'm seeing.

Mama Bang.

Standing there in the kitchen, holding a hockey stick.

Or rather...swinging it.

At Phillip.

Each of those clipped-out words accompanied by her slamming the stick against Phillip's back.

And shoulders.

And head.

Phillip's eyes are wild and then he whips around, reaching for the stick. But Mama Bang, but Stella—damn, she's fast—darts back and holding the stick like a lance. "Don't you dare, you piece of shit."

Zeus is shaking.

My body is aching.

Stella is standing like a tiny warrior ready to battle.

Phillip is the dragon ready to be slain.

I react without thinking, setting Zeus on the floor and then carefully grabbing the vase from the counter.

I lift it and...

Slam it down onto his head.

"WE'VE GOT to stop meeting like this," I joke as Dr. Halston shines a flashlight in my eyes.

Grinning, she clicks it off then reaches into her bag. "You remember the deal with the salve?" She passes a new tin of it over to me.

I nod, eyes flicking over to where Jean-Michel is talking with the head of his security, Pascal. "Yes. Thank you."

Alarm system upgrade? Imminent.

And I'm not going to argue.

Because I had to use a vase to knock my ex-fiancé unconscious.

But...I'd saved myself.

My past tried to fuck up my present, tried to steal my happiness, and I didn't let it.

Progress.

Of course, that came with a bit of assistance from Mama Bang wielding a hockey stick.

Something I'm sure that King—and Jean-Michel and Rome and Cam (and Pascal, who's now talking into his phone, looking extremely pissed off)—will find hilarious.

Eventually.

For now, though, I have other things to worry about.

Like making sure Zeus gets his medicine on time—maybe I'll make a note in King's planner—

Or maybe I won't, considering my asshole ex is the reason the pup is going to be on painkillers for a few days.

Zeus is bruised and broke a tooth biting the shit out of Phillip's leg, but otherwise he's okay.

Thank God.

But it's also why Dr. Halston is only checking me out now—after we called the police and Jean-Michel, and after I took Zeus to the vet.

I'm fine.

Way better than before.

Which...isn't going to go over well.

None of this is.

One thing.

I just want to have *one* nice thing in my life without my past creeping in and trying to ruin it.

Apparently, that's not possible.

At least I have two higher beings on my side—

My fairy godmother, er god*father*, and...

Mama Bang.

(And her hockey stick).

"Come see me in the office sometime," Dr. Halston says, handing me a card. "For a yearly exam and not"—she waves a hand at my torso—"all of this."

I chuckle. "I'll do that." I pocket the card. "Thank you for coming."

A squeeze of my shoulder. "Stay safe."

We exchange goodbyes and I see that Jean-Michel is done talking to Pascal—the security chief having disappeared somewhere. Jean-Michel nods at me before walking Dr. H. out.

But he's not gone long, striding back into the kitchen several moments later, and sinking down into the chair next to me.

Sighing.

It's exhausting being my fairy godfather.

"I know I've asked you," he says, "but are you sure you're okay?"

I nod, glad that I've taken the maximum dose of ibuprofen so that moving doesn't hurt. "I'm fine," I tell him. "I mean, I'm not because...well, how can anyone be okay with that?" I hold back my shiver. "But this means that Phillip won't be let out of jail again, right?"

Jean-Michel nods. "I'm going to make sure of that."

"Then...I'm good."

He bumps his shoulder against mine. "You and Chrissy."

My brows drag together.

"You're some of the strongest people I know."

My heart squeezes tightly. "Because you helped me get there. *No*," I add when he starts to shake his head. "I don't think you know how important you are to me. I had *no one*," I whisper. "Until you saw something in me."

"Aurora, honey—"

"You saw me and you valued me and you protected me, and there wasn't an ulterior motive—"

"Aside from free design work?" he teases, and I know it's because this is a lot and he's uncomfortable and...

I don't care.

I'm wielding vases.

I'm swimming to shore.

I'm...fuck it, I'm going to make some plans for the future —a future that includes this man and King and Chrissy and Rome and Cam.

Because I'm valuable and important—

And even if my past isn't pleasant, even if it might crop up and try to yank me down...

I don't have to let it.

I can take a hockey stick to it. Or a vase.

Or...I can live in the moment, love the people I love, and fight to make sure I have the future I want.

"He'll be pissed," Jean-Michel says quietly, probably

reading me stuck in my thoughts as worry for King. And I am worried. A lot. But also...I'm ready to fight. "I know I would be." Shadows slide across his face. "When Christina—" His eyes slide closed and I know he's thinking about Chrissy, about what she went through when she was just a teenager. "It took a long time to forgive myself for my failings."

"You didn't fail her."

"You don't see it that way." A beat. "Neither does she. But..."

"That doesn't change what's in her heart and mind," I say.

"No," he agrees. "It doesn't." His expression gentles. "But he'll see you, and he'll remember that it's not about him."

Damn.

This man.

He's pretty fucking great. Just like—

"I had a great dad," I tell him softly. "And then I had nothing. For a long time, it was...well, *nothing*. But you and Chrissy, you both gave me something huge and beautiful and—"

Be brave and kind.

"I love you and I'm so lucky that you're in my life."

He stiffens, and I know I've likely finally pushed Jean-Michel too far.

Which is why I give him an out.

My mouth hitches up. "Should I change the subject back to design work?"

He smiles, but it quickly flattens out as he turns and cups my cheeks in his hands. "If King ever hurts you, I'll take him out myself." He gathers me close, squeezes me tight, whispering in my ear. "Because I'm the lucky one." His voice drops further. "And I love you too, kiddo. "

That wound, the once-gaping crevice in my soul? It's gone.

I open my mouth—

Someone sniffs.

I lift my head from Jean-Michel's shoulder and see that Mama Bang is swiping a finger under her eyes. "Sorry," she says. "That—" A wave of her hand. "It's just...beautiful." She sniffs again.

Jean-Michel pulls back enough to meet my stare, mouth curving, expression bemused as he shakes his head. "I need to finish up with Pascal and hop on a plane." His eyes flick to the side as Stella starts yanking tissues out of the box on the counter, escape clearly in the forefront of his mind. "I'll... leave you to it."

Impending tears making the formidable businessman run.

Maybe an Achilles' heel?

I grin, but shift to the side, clearing that escape route for him. "Thank you," I say. "For everything."

He tugs a lock of my hair. "Precious girl," he murmurs.

And now I'm the one at risk of sniffing.

Something he seems to sense because he makes a quick exit.

And then it's just me and Mama Bang.

And the pie she's putting together.

King's broken hockey stick—so expertly wielded by Stella a few hours before—is on the counter because I didn't know if I should throw away the pieces or if it could be repaired. But the glass from the broken vase is swept up and my purse contents have been retrieved—though my laptop is done for.

Thankfully, my boss is cool.

Other good news? The pie is nearly done.

Carbs to make the bad news seem less...bad.

"Honey," Stella says softly.

I look up, see that she's watching me with concern—something she's done from the moment Phillip slumped to the floor.

"I'm okay," I tell her.

"*Rory*," she says, tone disapproving.

"I really *am* okay." I inhale. Exhale. "I mean, I'm not because what Phillip did should never be okay." I meet her eyes. "But also...my past isn't all rainbows and unicorns. I've—" I shake my head. "I've been through worse."

She puts down the cheese, crosses over to me and takes my hand. "Sweetheart—"

"I'm sorry you were in the crossfire of my asshole ex."

"That's not—"

"But you gave me something today, even if you don't realize it. You helped me fight. Helped me realize I don't have to stand by and take what life hands to me. I can hold tight to what I want."

She sniffs again. "Sweet girl," she murmurs. "You deserve the world."

My heart squeezes. "Don't," I order, adding lightly, "Only because I think crying will make my ribs start hurting again."

Another sniff, but this one is mixed in with a laugh, and I know we're going to be okay. "*Strong* girl." She pulls me into a gentle hug. "I'm just glad you're okay."

I carefully squeeze her back. "I'm better than I've been in a long time," I say. "Now"—I pull back, nod to the pie—"am I putting the cheese in or are you?"

She laughs and we go back to baking, the events of the morning not forgotten, but tucked away.

Being brave and kind doesn't seem like such a struggle right now.

Because I can have good things.

Because I can have *everything*.

Yes, I'm worried about King and if he's going to be upset because he wasn't here to protect me like he thinks he should.

Even though what happened wasn't on him.

If anything...

It's on me.

I picked Phillip. *I* ignored the red flags. *I* let myself become small as I was shuttled along to a future I didn't want, a life that didn't make me happy.

All because I didn't think I deserved anything better.

But I've had this time with King.

I know what love can feel like.

And now...

I'm going to fight for it.

THIRTY-SEVEN

I want a beer, a bathtub full of ice, and to use Pat's face like a punching bag again.

Alas, I've already done that and gotten the lecture from Coach, and since I'm not interested in revisiting that glorious one-on-one, I'd bitten my tongue and had taken it out on the puck instead.

Good for my slapshot.

Bad for my body.

Hence, the need for that tub full of ice.

I pull into the garage, throw the gearshift into park, cut the engine, and exhale, rolling out my shoulders.

My mom is here. And Rory. I need to not be a total grump and enjoy the time with them.

It's almost Thanksgiving and soon enough it'll be Christmas. Then January and the back half of the season, when shit gets real and the team needs to focus on scrounging each and every point we can add to our tally.

Because I haven't been working this hard for this long to let one asshole derail everything.

Especially when we're winning and gelling as a team—with the exception of Asshole Pat.

Which is why I'm going to ignore the toxic lump, let him celebrate getting pussy and the occasional goal, and focus on my own shit.

See? I'm growing.

I haven't heard the *You're not your father* ricocheting through my mind for at least a week now.

Grinning, I reach for the handle, feeling a hundred times better just being this close to seeing Rory.

Until I see the dent in the wooden frame near the lock.

Frowning, I run my fingers over the marking.

Then shrug.

Maybe Rory was bringing in dog crates and my kitchen is full of a gaggle of rescue puppies.

Yeah, I'll take that particular brand of chaos.

Because it's time that she gets everything she wants—including saving all the dogs she wants.

Grin widening, I push open the door and walk into the house.

Music echoes down the hallway and my heart squeezes, remembering other days, other songs. Knowing that I would give just about anything to keep coming home to Rory dancing in my kitchen. I hang up my bag, my jacket then move down the hall—

Only, she's not dancing.

But it's almost as good because she's sitting on the counter...

Waiting for me.

Something familiar at her side.

"Is that my old hockey stick from the garage?"

She stills, eyes lifting from the book she'd been reading—one I recommended—and connecting with mine. She sets the paperback to the side. "Yup." She slides down from the counter, leans back against it. "How was practice?"

I move toward her, cupping her face in my hands, tilting her head up and kissing her deeply. "Pat's an asshole," I say when I break the kiss, "but that's not a surprise." I tuck an unruly strand of hair behind her ear. "How was your day?"

She stills.

"What?" I ask, leaning back, staring into unfathomable green eyes. "What happened?"

"I..." She presses her lips together.

My heart starts pounding, speeding up further when her eyes close for a long moment, panic making my voice hoarse. "Princess."

She inhales, exhales, and her lids peel back.

And I know what she's about to tell me is going to change everything.

Going to destroy it.

And—

"Where's Zeus?" I ask. "He needs a walk." I spin away from her, searching the room for my mom, almost desperate for her brand of interruption right now. I'd seen her jacket on the hook, her rental at the curb. She's got to be close. "Did my mom take him out? I can go meet them, catch up and give you some time to decompress. I know you've got a lot happening with the gala and—"

"King," she whispers.

I freeze.

Because the way she says my name.

Fuck.

This is going to be bad.

"I need you to look at me," she says. "I need you to hear

me." Another breath. "And I need you to recognize that I'm here and I'm okay."

Now I'm freaked the fuck out.

She lifts her hand, extends it in my direction. "Come here, honey."

I can't deny her that, can't deny her anything, even though my pulse is thundering through my veins and my knees feel shaky and my lungs can't pull in enough air.

It's like I'm sprinting down the ice at the end of a long shift.

And it's double overtime in game seven of a series.

And I'm trying to catch a motherfucker from the other team as he bears down on my goalie.

And when I'm close enough to stop him, I catch an edge, eat shit, and slam into the boards.

While the asshole goes on to score.

And...it's all over.

Because I'm too slow. Too incapable.

You're not your father.

"King," Rory says. "Come here, baby."

I close the final few steps between us, stilling when she takes my hand, laces our fingers together. "I'm here. I'm safe. I'm fine." A squeeze. "Okay?"

I nod, but my pulse is pounding so loudly in my ears that I can barely hear her when she says,

"Phillip came to the house today."

A vice grip on my throat, my lungs. "Wh-what?" I rasp.

"He snuck into the garage—"

I pull my hand free.

She takes it back, holds it tighter.

"Then he forced his way into the house and—"

I stagger back a step, yanking out of her grip.

"*I'm* okay," she repeats. "Zeus is okay. In fact, he's a good boy who bit the hell out of Phillip's ankle—"

My head flies up.

"But he's okay too. Just a little bruised, and left part of his tooth in Phillip's ankle," she says, then adds in a rush, "I took him to the vet and he's totally fine."

"And you?" I rasp out.

"I'm fine too." Quick words. *Too* quick.

"What did he do to you?"

A wince, her eyes sliding away. Then back, as though knowing her *not* looking at me is a hundred times worse. "He likes kicking," she says softly as rage and fury and panic and...failure tangle in my stomach. "I'm bruised too," she murmurs. "But Dr. Halston checked me out and gave me a clear bill of health." She moves a little closer. "I'm *okay.*"

Okay.

She's okay.

Zeus is okay—

You're never going to be there. Not when I need you.

I'm not.

You're not your father.

I'm not that either.

"You used the stick?" I ask, trying to quiet the voices in my head, to calm the panic, to just fucking *think.*

You're. Not. Good. Enough.

"Actually," Rory says softly, her mouth turning up just barely at the edges. "It turns out that your mom has some hockey skills too. She beat the shit out of Phillip and got him to stop." Teeth pressing into her lip, those eyes sliding away and then back. "And then I hit him with a vase and knocked him unconscious."

I rasp out a laugh, gaze going to the remnants of my stick

on the counter, to the now empty spot where the flowers I'd bought for her had sat just that morning.

God. I can't do this.

My mom hit Phillip with my stick, hard enough to break it.

Fucking hell, but I *cannot* do this.

"He hit the ground like a sack of bricks," Rory says, relief in her tone. Probably mistaking my laughter for acceptance.

And I guess it is.

Acceptance that I can't be the man she needs.

A stick. A vase. A tooth from Zeus.

Kicking.

Fuck.

"—and we called the cops," she says. "They arrested him and Jean-Michel says he won't be able to get out on bail this time—"

I wasn't here.

I wasn't fucking *here.*

Not today. Not on her wedding day. Not at her house.

Three fucking strikes.

"—and Pascal's already begun to check out the security system. He'll beef it up and you won't have to worry when you're not here—"

You're not here. Not when I need you.

God, I had this beautiful moment, these beautiful weeks.

But it's still the same shit.

I'm not enough to make this work.

"—but we can meet with the security company and the detective, make sure you feel comfortable—"

That snaps me out of it.

"Make *me* feel comfortable?"

"I—" Brows drawn together, her mouth opens and closes. "I'm sorry?"

"You were assaulted again," I grind out. "And you're worried about whether or not *I'm* fucking comfortable?"

"I know this is a big trigger for you, honey," she says. "And I know that you have to go out of town." She takes another step toward me. "I just want to make sure that we both do everything we can to alleviate any concerns that might crop—"

"Stop."

She freezes. "King?"

"*Stop.*"

I can't hear my name on her tongue, can't hear her voice, not when—

You're not good enough.

Rose's is far too loud in my head.

Christ.

I'm not good enough.

And I never will be.

I turn away.

"Don't go," she whispers.

My toes dig into the floor, jaw clenching so tightly that my teeth protest.

"Just stay," she says, still whispering. "Just stay and talk to me. Tell me what's running through your head."

"I can't."

She touches my shoulder. "Try." A beat. "Fight." Another. "For me." I turn to watch her throat work, eyes glimmering with tears. "Fight for *us.*"

Rory

Be brave and kind.

"Stay," I plead. "Please."

For a second, I think he's going to.

That he'll take me in his arms and tell me he's sorry, that he loves me, that he's glad I'm okay and we'll figure this out.

But then his expression locks down.

And he takes a shaky step backward.

And another.

Then one more.

"King," I begin.

But he's in the hall now, and before I can reach for him again, he's turning away, disappearing from sight, footsteps echoing on the floor.

I move after him. "King!"

He's already twisting the handle, wrenching the door open.

"King!"

He doesn't stop.

Just walks through, pulling the door shut behind him.

And by the time I make it down the hall, manage to wrestle with the handle and open the door—my ribs protesting my jerky movements (but the ache in my heart a thousand times worse)—his car is gone.

The garage is empty.

And I'm alone.

Again.

⎯⎯

FIFTEEN MINUTES LATER, after waiting for King to come back, waiting and hoping and maybe shedding a tear or thirty, I've given up and am slowly approaching the stairs, trying to figure out what the hell my next steps should be when I hear the door slam open and collide with the wall in the mudroom.

Stella, likely, back with Zeus and hoping to find her son relaxed and calm, my plan to honestly and gently break the news to him successful.

Something that's so far from the truth, it's laughable.

And I find I can't laugh right now.

Can't think about how I clearly messed up.

How even though I'm doing the best I can, the people I love still leave me.

Every fucking time.

I can't face that right now.

I need puppy cuddles and to figure out how to move forward.

I need—

Footsteps echo toward me.

I need to lock myself in the bedroom and grasp on to a modicum of privacy before Stella sees me fall to pieces.

Faster.

I lift my foot, intending to speed run these stairs as well as I can considering my ribs.

But my toes don't make it onto the riser.

"Princess."

The rasped out word has me spinning on a gasp—

And promptly losing my balance.

I fall backward and...

My white knight saves me again—catching me, cradling me against his chest before he sinks down onto the bottom step with me in his lap. He buries his face in my throat, alternating between curses and apologies. "Fuck, princess, I'm so sorry. Fuck, I'm such an idiot. Fucking hell, I can't believe I got in my car and drove away. I'm so goddamned sorry. I didn't mean to leave. I know—I know that was fucked up. It was just like I couldn't breathe and—*fuck*, I'm sorry and—"

I press my finger to his lips. "Stop, honey." I weave my fingers into his hair, pull gently until his eyes meet mine. "Just stop for a second and breathe."

His arms tighten, but thankfully he stops talking.

And breathes.

"Good, baby."

A shaky nod. "I'm a dumbass."

"Yes," I say. "You are." I settle my forehead against his. "But you're *my* dumbass."

Thankfully that has his mouth turning up at the edges, amusement curling through blue eyes. "Knew I was going to freak the fuck out sooner or later, but I was trying not to. I didn't want—" A shake of his head. "I want to be more than that."

"I don't need you to be more." I lift my head, hold his gaze. "I just want you to be *you.*"

He looks away.

I cup his jaw. "I love every part of you."

He winces, smooths a hand down my back. "Sorry you had to be on the receiving end of my freak out."

Be brave and kind.

I stop, shake my head, try to tease out why my brain is shoving those words into the front of my mind.

Then getting it.

Fighting for us...

It's also fighting for me.

"What?" He's focused back on me.

"I was going to say it was okay," I say. "But it's not." I clear the knot from my throat, force myself to keep talking even though it feels very scary to continue. "It's not okay for you to leave me when everyone else important in my life has left me in one way or another—"

Pain ripples across his face.

But I owe this truth to him.

To myself.

He came back because he realized he fucked up.

I would be fucking up if I didn't draw this boundary.

"You left." I take a breath. "I asked you to stay and you left and that's not okay. If we really love each other, we have to find a way to talk the hard stuff through. I know this is an extreme situation, but—"

More pain, and I feel like a total jerk.

Today was bad, was triggering in so many ways for both him and I.

But...I have to keep going.

I cover his cheek with my palm, the bristles of his beard tickling my skin. "You can ask for space and take it. You can be upset that my monster of an ex did what he did. You can carry the pain of your past without me expecting you to magically be healed, but I *cannot* tolerate you walking out." My voice cracks.

Be brave and kind.

I push on. "Phillip can hurt me. My stepsisters can be their bitchy selves. My stepmom can hit me, lock me up, can use me for free labor all over again. Hell, I can lose a thousand belongings to the teeth of a naughty fluffy puppy." I drop my forehead to his. "But I cannot stand to watch you walk away from me, knowing we're both hurt and torn to pieces inside."

"Dammit," he mutters, eyes sliding closed. "I'm an asshole."

"I think we've already established that you're *my* asshole."

"I believe it was dumbass." His mouth quirks as I giggle. Then his expression flattens out and he strokes a finger down my cheek. "I won't walk out. Not when you ask me to stay. Not ever again."

I hear the truth in his voice and relax. "Thank you."

"I'm sorry."

"I know." I bury my face in his throat, hold him as tight as I'm able to with my ribs. "I'm sorry you had to come home to that."

He slides a hand into my hair, lifts my head. "Don't fucking apologize for what that man did."

"I'm not," I tell him honestly, holding his gaze when his eyes spark with fury. "But I'm okay because you're here and I fought for us, for me. I'm okay because I'm safe. Because I can make plans for the future and know they're not going to disappear."

Gentle. His expression becomes so freaking gentle that it

takes my breath away. "I love you," he whispers. "I know I'll fuck up, and probably do it far too often. I'm not my father who can navigate this stuff easily. My head is all twisted and I'm not perfect, but—" Determination fills his face. "I love you and I'm not letting you go." A beat. "Not ever."

God, I love this man.

Love that he can admit all that.

And still say *that*.

"All of that sounds perfect to me."

"And I know I'm not my father—"

"Your father's not perfect, honey."

I jump.

King jumps.

Stella's standing in the doorway, her expression worried as her eyes come to mine and hold. "I was..." She exhales, shakes her head slightly, drawing the adoring gaze of Zeus, who's sitting at her feet. "Concerned," she says. "After what happened and what you told me."

King goes still next to me.

Stella exhales again, head dropping for a second. Then her stare comes back to mine.

And I get it.

She needs to talk to her son.

I press my lips to King's. "I'm going to take Zeus for a walk."

Another walk. Not that the pooch will mind.

He frowns. "Princess—"

"I'll be back, okay?"

I wait until his gaze comes to mine and he nods, something settling in me. Not leaving. Not forcing him to stare at my back as I walk away.

Be brave and kind.

"See you soon," I murmur and then I'm pushing out of his hold, walking over to Stella, taking Zeus's leash.

He gives a little happy dance, those tiny feet tap-dancing on the hardwood floor.

We walk out the front door.

And I leave Mama Bang to work her magic.

THIRTY-NINE

King

I grind my teeth together, biting back the urge to call out to Rory.

To beg her to stay.

I just want to pretend it didn't happen, to go back to loving my woman—

Except, I haven't been doing a great job of that, have I?

Freaking out and running away when she'd been through the shit. *Again.*

Not doing anything about it. *Again.*

You're not your father.

A pain splinters through my head and I rub at the ache, trying to shove it all down...to forget, to focus on all of the good I've found despite—

"You know your father is my best friend," my mom says, sitting on the step next to me.

"I know, Mom," I mutter, starting to push up. I'll shower

or cook dinner or...fuck it, I'll go and work out in the gym until I stop feeling like an asshole.

Until I stop having these thoughts.

Except, that hasn't worked before, has it?

Her hand clamps onto my wrist. "Sit down, King."

I freeze...because Mom Tone.

It slides down my spine, locks my muscles, and my ass plunks back onto the riser before I've even processed I'm moving.

"God," I mutter, "you haven't pulled that tone with me in years."

"Probably not for a decade," she agrees, releasing my arm and bumping her shoulder against mine. "Because you always tried to be perfect, King." She sighs, voice gentling. "Do you remember the last fight we got into?"

Guilt churns in my gut.

Because, yeah, of course I do.

I was an asshole teenager who didn't appreciate being told what to do. "I should have gone to Dad's game." His last game ever playing.

And I *didn't* go because I was too busy chasing my own dreams.

We don't do selfishness in this family, Kingston Bang. Your family needs you there.

And, spoiler alert, they had.

Because my dad got hurt—bad enough that he couldn't finish the game.

And *I* wasn't there.

"I was wrong," she says. "I was wrong in pushing you to go, in expecting you to put your life on hold. You were *working*, baby. Working hard and missing out on so many fun things and I had absolutely no right to make you feel bad for not going to one game when you made an effort to be at so many others."

My throat tightens. "It wasn't enough. He could have—"

Died. My dad could have died and I would have been playing in some tiny ass Canadian town, playing in a game that meant nothing in the grand scheme of my life and—

I wouldn't have gotten to see him, to say goodbye.

"Anything can go wrong at any time," she says softly. "You know how quickly I lost Diane"—my heart pulses when her voice cracks, and I know, *know* how much losing her best friend has affected her—"but what you don't know is that it's made me understand a few things." Her hands come to my cheeks. "Life is precious and short, and"—her mouth hitches up—"as is illustrated by my terrible matchmaking attempts between you and Stacy, as well as me trying to make my relationship with Cathy something it's not..." She sighs, put out. "I'm not always right."

Something in my chest pulses, unlocks, settles. "Who dare says that?" I say lightly.

"*I* say." She straightens. "I want you all to be happy. I want you to be fulfilled. I want you to have *your* person at your side—like I have *my* person. But, honey, as much as I love your father, he's not perfect, and"—her mouth curves into a gentle smile—"you can't be either."

I take her hand, squeeze it lightly. "I know that."

"Do you?"

"You guys are both superheroes," I say quietly. "I don't know how you kept it together at home, how Dad always seems to know everything that's going on—"

She slants me a look and clarity slams into me like a two-by-four to the temple.

"It's you," I say. "Of course it's been you."

Her brows drag together.

"I don't mean that Dad hasn't been involved," I hurry to tell her. "He's always there when we need him." I bump her shoulder with mine this time. "I just...I'm thinking that's mostly because of you."

"No, baby," she says gently. "It's because your dad and I are a team. Because any problem that we've faced, we've done it together. Do I keep the mental tally of birthdays and holidays and your crazy schedules? Yes. Do I spend a bundle on Amazon every year, making sure appropriate presents arrive? Yes, I do." She smiles. "But does your dad wrap those presents because I can never make the paper look neat? Yes. And is my gas tank full and my car serviced on the regular? Are my favorite cookies always in the pantry? Does he bring me a coffee in bed every morning he's home? Yes, to all." Her hand settles on my arm. "And does he drop everything when I need him—no matter where in the world he is and what time it is and if it's something big or small? Yes, baby, he does. Because we've worked as a team to figure out the things that are important to each other. Because we love each other in a thousand small ways every day. Because he's my person."

I inhale.

"And because—" Her voice cracks and I know she's thinking of Diane again.

"—you're amazing and Dad knows he needs to bring it so you don't get smart and leave him?"

She stills, touches my cheek, eyes damp. "See, baby? You may not be perfect, but you pay attention. You're sensitive and you care and I know you can love Rory as she deserves." Her fingers flex. "The question is if you're going to have the courage to allow yourself to be loved in return. Because Rory doesn't need perfect. She just needs you."

I just want you to be you.

"I don't have to be perfect."

"No, baby."

"I—"

God, I know that. I guess. It's just...hard.

But when have I backed down from hard?

I can do the work, put the time in, just like I did to get into the league—even though I'm by far from the best player around.

I can do *this*.

I can love Rory like she deserves.

God knows, loving her is the easiest thing I've ever done.

It's the rest of it, the bullshit in my own head that's hard.

So...I start there.

"I don't have to be Dad," I murmur. "Or Jakob or anyone but me."

"Right," she says. "Because you, Kingston Bang, my favorite oldest son—"

My lips twitch.

"Are perfectly imperfect and lovable, exactly as you are." She touches my jaw. "There's give and take in every relationship, baby, and so long as you're not seeing the other person as the source of all of your problems, and you're tackling the hard stuff together then things will be okay. And I don't mean ignoring red flags if someone isn't right for you—"

I cough. "*Stacy!*"

She sighs, narrows her eyes. "—or tries to hurt you. I mean finding that right person for *you*—" A pointed look. "And occasionally doing it without any help from your well-meaning mother—"

I snort.

"I mean working through the tough stuff together—the baggage from the past, the present that tries to press in, the future that can sometimes be uncertain."

My heart squeezes.

Because Rory wants a future with me.

"You can bring the organization, can keep track of important details, can love Rory in all those small ways. And Rory brings her own wonderful parts that help you two work as a unit. *Together*. You and her against the world. That's how your father and I survived all these years—even when he thought it was a good idea to get me a vacuum for my birthday."

I freeze, incredulous. "He *what?*"

She chuckles. "Rookie mistake, right?" she says. "And in fairness to him, we were young and dumb and just starting out. We hadn't worked through a lot of the tough stuff yet. My point is that—"

"It was the two of you versus the vacuum?"

She rolls her eyes, but she's laughing too. "Yes, *that*. Not to mention the conversation that we had after I unwrapped the box..."

"Poor Dad," I say.

"Poor *me*," she says, chuckling as she bumps her shoulder against mine again. "My point is that, your dad's not perfect. He makes mistakes—we all do, right? That's the line that we're supposed to say? That mistakes are a great way to grow, and how can we learn if we don't mess up?" She sighs. "But that's also bullshit. When we mess up, it feels like the world is ending, like I'll never be able to make things right. It feels like I'm a failure as a person." Her eyes come to mine again. "The thing about kids is that they humble you—I could be the strictest most perfectionist of a mom while I was raising you guys, but toddlers are going to tantrum, siblings are going to fight, kids are still going to get hurt."

"Mom," I whisper.

"I did my best, but I still failed—still *fail*—and it's sucks and I hate it with a passion. That's the truth of it, baby. We fail. We make mistakes. And I don't have a magic wand to wave to make those feelings disappear. I've just learned to live with them, with those voices that tell me that I'm not going to be good enough—"

"Mom," I say again.

"And accept it's normal for some of us," she says. "*You're normal, baby.* There are other people with these thoughts, who struggle to let the failures go. Maybe it's not the healthiest, and maybe we both need to work on coping mechanisms together, but, baby, *you're normal. And I can't cure normal.*" Her eyes are gentle. "All we can do is acknowledge that we're having the feelings, that feelings aren't facts—"

I laugh quietly.

"What?" she asks.

"Feelings aren't facts," I say. "God, it's been *years* since I've heard that."

Her face softens. "Maybe I need to tell you that more."

I exhale, sling my arm around her shoulders, hug her tightly. "I think if there's one thing I can be certain of, Mom," I tell her, "it's that you didn't fail in this conversation."

She sniffs, hugs me back.

In fact, this conversation...it's changed my life.

And I mean that.

The gulf inside me, the one that's filled with sharply worded memories and barbed self-doubt...well, it's not magically emptied, the sides smoothed out, but—

I feel different.

Lighter.

My dad bought my mom a vacuum for her birthday.

God, that was dumb.

But they got through it. Together.

Have always gotten through the bumps in the road.

Together.

And that's the part I forgot.

Because I hadn't found the person who'd play the game of life *with* me.

Until Rory.

And even when I ran, when I fucked up, when I didn't protect her from all of the hurt and awfulness of the world... she still flowed into my arms.

She didn't yell or hold it against me or make accusations.

It really *is* Rory and I against the world.

Or it can be.

If I work at it.

And I can do that, can push away the fear of failure, of disappointment, and...

Just be me.

"Mom?"

"Yeah, baby?"

"There's something I need to tell you about Rory and my engagement."

She frowns, glances up at me, eyes filled with question.

A breath for courage. Then...I tell her the truth.

It's not perfect as I reveal that Rory and I had started off fake, that I haven't actually proposed to Rory, that it's too soon to do so.

I hate that *I'm* the reason for the disappointment on my mom's face.

Hate that *I'm* not perfect.

But I give her the messy and complicated truth.

And when I'm done explaining the why, she doesn't turn on me, doesn't do anything except draw me close, and say, "I'm sorry you felt you had to do that for me. And that you didn't feel safe to tell me that sooner."

A little more of that gulf in my belly is filled in.

My shoulders grow a little looser.

I can hate not being perfect—that's normal.

But I can still be safe *and* imperfect with the people who love me.

Because it's us.

Versus the world.

FORTY

Rory

"What do you think of this one?" Stella asks, holding a dress up for me to inspect.

It's been a couple of days since Mama Bang showed off her hockey skills, and we're shopping for a gala outfit for her while King gets ready for his game tonight.

But really, we've been messing around, cackling over dresses that are hideous, playing dress up in the pretty ones, and only recently getting down to business.

Because we have more errands to do before we head over to the arena to watch the Eagles play.

"It's gorgeous," I tell her, running my fingers over the delicate lace sleeves. Because the navy bodice with the full skirt and just a sprinkling of sparkle is indeed that.

"Good," she says with a conspiratorial smile, "because I didn't want to make my soon-to-be, *soon-to-be* daughter-in-law unhappy when I try it on regardless."

I laugh, but then a bolt of guilt slides through me.

Because this had all started as a deception.

And I'm really starting to love Stella.

She's...well, she's almost as amazing as King.

Case in point? Her reading my expression as she settles her palm on my shoulder. "Don't," she murmurs. "I understand. And you're here now. You guys are moving forward together. I'm just sorry King felt like—" She shakes her head.

I cover her hand with my own. "In fairness, it was my stupid idea. And I think—" My eyes catch on the glimmering diamond on my finger. "I think it was an excuse to spend more time with him even when I was telling myself that it was a terrible idea."

"Because in the end," Stella says quietly, "you love each other."

My heart squeezes hard. "Yes."

That hand on my shoulder tightens. "I'm happy you're part of my life, no matter how that came to be. Now"—her tone turns businesslike—"how about I try this on, we go look at jewelry for your dress, and then we hit the grocery store to fight old ladies over the last can of cranberry sauce?"

"What?" I tease. "You don't make it yourself?"

She pats my arm then starts leading the way to the changing room. "Honey, there are far more important things in life than making cranberry sauce from scratch." A beat, her smile sly. "Especially, when we have a hockey game to watch."

Why do I know that truer words have never been spoken?

STELLA'S DRESS FIT PERFECTLY.

I found a gorgeous pair of earrings to go with my gown for the gala tomorrow.

And we scored not one, but two cans of cranberry sauce.

Then watched the Eagles handily beat the Grizzlies, cheering so loudly for King that I'm surprised I still have a voice this morning.

I've been up since the sun was barely cresting the hills in the east, getting ready for my first real Thanksgiving ever.

And I'm not alone.

Chrissy's hosting, her house full to the brim with critters and people.

King's been peeling potatoes and cooking veggies.

Rome is making a sweet potato casserole.

Cam—surprisingly, since I didn't know the young forward for the Eagles liked to cook—is taking care of the turkey.

I'm working on dessert with a huge batch of Everything Cookies.

Stella is organizing—setting the table, checking timers, washing dishes, and shooing the boys away from her apple pie.

Joan of Freaking Arc—Chrissy's cranky senior cat—has spent the day on her perch in the kitchen, taking lazy, clawed swipes at everyone who gets too close.

And, finally, Jean-Michel's been keeping us in plenty of pastries from Molly's while tapping away on his laptop at the island.

Hockey's on in the background.

Kittens run this way and that. Zeus is having the time of his life reunited with his siblings, and being bossed around by his slightly older and smaller sister, Athena.

Chaos and joy. Plentiful chatter, and...it's a nice day—

The *best* day.

Full of laughter and friends and love.

But somehow, there's an ache in my heart, a pulse of something missing.

Until King wraps an arm around my middle and leads me onto the back porch. The sun is setting in the distance, turning the hills into a sea of gold. A large oak stands tall and center stage in the yard, casting a smattering of gorgeously patterned shadows on the grass.

"Look at me, princess," he says softly.

I drag my eyes from the sight of that gorgeous tree and turn to the man next to me.

"How are you doing?" he asks, gently brushing his fingers along my side, over my shirt, beneath which the bruises from Phillip that have turned a ghastly mix of purple and blue.

"I'm fine," I say softly.

"Because you look lost, princess."

"I'm—" I exhale. "I haven't had a holiday like this before."

His expression is impossibly gentle. "Like what?"

"Loud and with the scent of good food filling my nose. Chaos but somehow everyone getting along and helping and teasing each other and—" I shake my head. "It's a perfect day, and"—ugh, I can't believe that my eyes are stinging—"I guess I just...miss my dad."

It snuck up on me.

This feeling of sadness.

It's been so long since my dad's been gone that I didn't think I felt the loss any longer, not in any heavy, meaningful way. But I—

"He would love them," I whisper. "Love your mom and how beautifully she raised you. Love that crazy Zoom meeting we had with all of your siblings where everyone was talking over everyone else and no one could hear anything and...he'd love you mostly because of the way you look at me."

Now that we aren't pretending.

Now that our cards are on the table.

Because King looks at me...like I am the center of his universe.

"Princess," King murmurs, those eyes warm pools of blue seawater. "God, how did I get so lucky to find you?"

I settle my head against his shoulder. "I like to think that I was the one who ran into your arms."

He chuckles. "I think you're right."

We stand there, watching the sun set until the noise inside grows and we go back in.

It's still chaos and loud and there's a battle over yummy carbs.

But we manage to salvage a couple of Everything cookies and a slice of pie to share.

Because it's us.

Versus the world.

FOR AS WONDERFUL as yesterday was...

Today's been a shitshow.

I'm sweaty and discombobulated and have been dealing with a thousand last-minute details and crises.

All while trying to get gala glam for our event.

And fake lashes aren't cutting that.

Sighing in disgust at the glue-on that's sitting diagonally across my lid instead of rounding beautifully at my lash line, I rip it free and toss it in the trash.

Fuck it, I'm going to the gala to raise money for my pups, not to worry about perfectly curled lashes.

I touch up my lipstick, leave my hair in loose curls that flow down my back, pop in my earrings, and spend the next five minutes ignoring my ribs as I wrestle myself into my dress.

A spritz of perfume, gloss and lipstick in my purse, then I'm dousing my face in setting spray (and praying my makeup doesn't melt off when I run around like a lunatic at the winery) and slipping on my sparkling high heeled pumps that are unbelievably gorgeous, but will no doubt have me reaching for the flats I've stowed in my purse by the end of the night.

One more look in the mirror.

A deep breath.

And then...I'm ready.

Kind of.

This feels like a big moment, more than just the fundraiser, but King and I at an important event as a couple.

With no barriers between us.

No secrets.

No hidden trauma to rip us apart.

King and I...

Versus the world.

"You're good," I tell my reflection. "This is going to be good."

Exhaling, I nod then move out of the bathroom to find that King's given up on waiting for me in the bedroom. Grinning, knowing that he's been beyond patient with the whirlwind that I've been today, I make my way out into the hall, and slowly down the stairs.

King is there, standing at the bottom.

And his face, his eyes, the way he moves toward me...is like I've stepped out of the pages of a fairy tale.

"Princess," he says as he meets me at the bottom of the stairs. "You are beautiful."

"I—" I spin around. "Can you help with the last part of my zipper?"

He doesn't lean in, doesn't touch me—not for a long moment.

Then his fingers brush my skin as he tugs up my zipper, leaning in to kiss the side of my neck, murmuring in my ear, "I've never seen anything more beautiful than you in that dress."

I shiver, lean back against him. "Take a good look," I say, going for light, "because I'll likely be a sweaty mess by the end of the night."

"Newsflash"—another kiss before his hands settle on the tops of my arms and he spins me to face him—"I like it when you're sweaty too."

A wink that has my mouth curving, my body drifting toward the warmth and strength of his. "Thanks for being my hot date tonight," I say, straightening his bow tie for no reason, except that I need to touch him.

His chuckle rubs over my skin like velvet. "Anytime, princess." He tilts his head toward the garage. "Mom is in the kitchen scarfing down all of your cookies because she doesn't eat quote *fancy food*—"

"That's not true!" Stella shouts from the other room.

King grins, leans in and stage-whispers, "—so she's filling up now."

"Kingston Bang," Stella snaps, walking into the entryway —and it should be noted, doing that walking while brushing cookie crumbs from her face. "How dare you—" She freezes, eyes going wide. "Aurora, honey. My God. You're beautiful."

My throat goes tight, especially as she walks over to me and gently straightens one of my curls.

"Beautiful," she says again, squeezing my hand before

nodding at King and turning for the kitchen and the hallway leading to the garage.

Though I don't miss that she stops off for another cookie.

King takes my hand. "Your chariot awaits."

I exhale.

Because this is it.

All of the work of the last months, all of the pups we're going to be able to help over the next year, every detail I've obsessed over...it's all coming down to tonight.

A hand on my jaw.

A kiss on my forehead.

"It's going to be okay."

And somehow with his palm on my skin and his calm, confident eyes holding mine, I know that he's right.

"It's going to be great," I whisper, taking his hand and letting him lead me to the car.

The winery is beautiful.

The space is perfectly decorate.

Lots of alcohol is consumed and hardly a crumb of "fancy" food remains.

And money is flowing.

So, I decide it's safe to stop in the bathroom for a necessary pit stop.

And that's when I realize King and I were both wrong earlier.

Because I come face to face with...

"Stacy."

FORTY-ONE

King

"...and that play you made to get that puck between Sanderson's leg pads just at the buzzer"—the man in front of me is practically vibrating with excitement as he discusses our last game against the Grizzlies—"I was in the arena, man, and it was absolutely electric."

"Right," I say, scanning the crowd—and it's a crowd because the gala is sold out, and has been for weeks.

I can't see Rory in all the chaos.

Which isn't all that much of a surprise.

I haven't seen much of her since we arrived—what with her having to be everywhere at once and schmoozing all of the rich donors.

But I've caught glimpses of her in the room as she works her magic, as I've done my best to pull my weight and get people drinking and eating and spending money.

And drive up competition for the silent auction.

"...and Rome"—the man whistles—"he's smooth as hell on

the ice. I can really see how much he's grown since he left the Gold..."

"Yeah," I agree, frowning now as I've reached one end of the space and still haven't come across a glimpse of my gorgeous blond in her pale blue dress, her sparkling shoes not as bright as the light she has inside her. "Rome is great." I start to scan back the other way, searching more carefully this time.

And...not finding.

Dammit.

"And Cam Jackson," the man says. "Hell, I never thought I'd say this, but that kid has more talent in his pinky than the Great One—"

He's not wrong.

But I've now made a complete circuit of the room with my stare.

And Rory isn't here.

"His mind alone—"

"I think you were outbid on the signed jersey," I interrupt, nodding to the table full of clipboards and handwritten bids for all manner of prizes that is currently being supervised by one of Rory's volunteers.

"What?" the man asks, spinning away from me. "I need that jersey." He marches off, intent on the table and the clipboard currently housing his bid for the custom hockey sweater.

Free of the painful small talk, I make a loop of the room.

But Rory doesn't magically appear.

And there's not a crystal-dotted heel or a lost charm from her bracelet left behind to show me where to continue my search.

Fuck.

I slip from the crowded room, the air in the hallway immediately cooler, the noise dulled, then pause to think.

Kitchens to check on the cakes that should be coming out soon for the patrons to bid on.

Or bathroom to swap out those heels, take a much-needed breather.

Since that's the one that seems the most likely, I start down the hall.

Then freeze when I see a familiar face.

My mind doesn't immediately process the sight, isn't able to fit the pieces together.

Because she doesn't belong here.

She *shouldn't* be here.

And Rory's missing.

And...

I start walking faster, seeing her eyes widen as I approach, her face paling, feet skittering back.

"Stacy," I snap. "What the fuck are you doing here?"

"King," she says, and then I watch her transform, her tone becoming silky, her body coming close as she reaches for me. "I didn't know you'd be here. We should—"

I bat her hand away.

Like hell, she didn't know I was going to be here.

This was her sister's big event and she's a fucking twat and the mean glint on the edges of her expression tells me enough.

She'll do anything to compete with her sister.

And she'll do more if it means one-upping her.

Getting back at her.

Fucking with her life, with this event that's so important to Rory.

I'm not going to let that happen.

"Where is she?"

Stacy's bottom lip slides out and she reaches for me again. "Don't worry about Rory," she purrs, running a hand down my chest. "We should talk." Her mouth curves and I know she's going for sexy, for alluring, but it doesn't fucking work.

Because I can see the rotten core of her.

"I've learned some things and—"

I grab her wrist, yank her hand away from me. "*Don't.*"

That pout grows, but I just shove her arm toward her body, take a step back so that this disgusting human can't touch me again.

"Where. *The fuck.* Is Rory?"

My tone seems to finally get through to her because she doesn't try to touch me again. "I don't know," she snaps, hissy fit brewing. "And I don't care."

But her gaze darts to the side—to the closed bathroom door—and—

Fuck it.

I'm so done with this conversation.

I turn my back on Stacy, ignore the blue plastic cutout of a woman in a dress mounted there on the door, and push into the women's bathroom, not giving a fuck who I might scar on the other side, not giving a fuck when the heavy wooden panel slams into the wall.

Because then I see it.

See *her.*

And my temper boils over.

FORTY-TWO

Rory

I just wanted to use the bathroom.

Instead...

My past is being a bitch again.

Stacy comes out of the bathroom stall like she's the villain from *Scream*, appearing like a fucking murderer, silently stalking toward me.

Cathy appears on my other side, standing by the sink, eyes shrewd and body poised like she's going to strike.

And...well, I don't have time for this.

I spin for the door—

Stop when I find Dessie leaning back against the wooden panel.

And...now I'm scared.

Because the looks in their eyes, the way that Stacy is moving toward me like a mountain lion ready to pounce, Cathy's sneer, Dessie's smirk—

Right.

This isn't going to be good.

"You're going to leave him," Cathy says. "Tonight."

My brows drag together. "Leave who?"

Stacy's suddenly an inch away, winding up and I flinch back from her fist.

Only, it doesn't make contact with my face.

It flies so close to my skin that I feel the whoosh of air, one I'm still processing as it makes contact with the bodice of my dress and—

Rip!

I gasp and stumble back, my fingers clenching at the material, trying to hold my beautiful dress together. "What the hell are you doing?" I gasp.

Smack!

This time a hand is making contact with my face— *Cathy's* hand. "You're such an ungrateful little bitch!" she snaps as I stagger back, clamping my palm to my stinging cheek. "Kingston deserves better than a pathetic little orphan like you. You don't even know what the hell you're doing, what the hell you have, what kind of jumping-off point it can be, do you?" she sneers. "Of course you don't. You're not smart enough for that. Otherwise you would have married the other one who was far too good for you."

Phillip too good for me.

That's a fucking joke.

"You know that he beat me," I grind out.

Her brows lift. "I *know* that you deserved it."

"No one deserves that."

Stacy darts toward me, hands connecting with my chest, shoving me back hard into the sink, tearing my dress further. "*You* do."

"Why do you hate me so much?" I ask. "I did nothing to

you. Wanted nothing more than to have sisters, have a mother, and you've always treated me as less—"

"Because you *are* less," Cathy says. "Born from that whore of a mother, taking resources from my daughters. Your father always focused on you and—"

Be brave and kind.

My father's voice slides through my mind.

And...I stop.

Still.

Think.

Why do I have to be kind to these women who were nothing but cruel to me growing up?

"He was my only living parent," I say. "Your ex is in the picture, and he paid child support—"

"Not enough!" Stacy shouts, the words bouncing around the space.

"My babies deserve the best," Cathy says, and I see the unhinged look in her eyes, have seen it time and again.

This is the same.

Always the same.

She's never going to change, never going to understand, never going to love me.

Because she has no clue how valuable I am...and how worthy King is.

That's the part that pisses me off.

This—I wave a mental hand at the assholes from my past —I'm used to this shit.

But it's King and I. *Together.*

And that feeling of sureness prompts my next words. "King isn't a stepping stone to someone richer and more famous. He deserves better. He deserves *everything*." I clutch at the bodice of my dress, turn to the door. "Same as I deserved more from you all—more kindness and compassion and—" I take a breath. "I know you'll never see it that way." Another. "But *I* know that I deserve it."

There. It's not a grand speech reminiscent of a coming-of-age film.

It's not pummeling these women into the tile floor.

It's not an exacting punishment that will lock them up for the rest of their lives.

But...

A switch has flipped inside me.

This isn't me cutting them off because I'm too scared to interact with them, too worried about yelling and insults and hissy fits.

This is me...*done.*

They don't get it, and they never will.

And...

Maybe that's the brave and kind part.

Be brave and know when to draw a line.

Be kind to myself, knowing that I don't have to keep throwing myself into this emotional blender.

I can be done with them.

I can move on.

I can have something beautiful without them ruining it.

I turn toward Dessie, who's always been the most reasonable of the trio. "I need you to move—*ah!*"

I didn't see Stacy come close again, didn't hear or sense her. Not until she's shoving me back, sending me colliding with the line of sinks.

Pain explodes over my back, my head, and I lift a shaky hand up, feel the back of my skull, the lump that's already forming there.

Come on, universe. Throw me a lifeline.

I am *so* done with being hurt.

"You idiot," Cathy snaps at Stacy, grabbing her before she can push me again.

I glance back up at Dessie, see that she's gone pale, is shaking her head, inching toward the door. "Des—" I begin.

She slips out, the panel shutting behind her.

Great.

I struggle up to my feet, turn, and—

Stacy rips out of her mother's hold, shoves me again.

But this time, I'm ready for her bullshit, and I don't fall, just stagger back a step.

"Bring it, bitch," I mutter.

Be brave and kind?

Brave in standing up for myself.

Kind in taking notes from King and pounding my fist into my stepsister's face.

Stacy lunges for me, fingers curled, long nails like talons.

"Stop it!" Cathy growls, yanking her back. "You're making a scene and we need to be smart—"

I snort.

I can't help it.

Smart like coming here in the first place? Like confronting me in the bathroom? Like trying to kowtow me by unleashing their abuse all over again?

I'm done.

D.O.N.E. *Done.*

Cathy slowly spins her gaze toward me—and I can't lie. She's fucking terrifying. "Leave," she snaps.

"No problem, psycho," I mutter, taking another step toward the door.

"Not you," Cathy snaps at me. "*You,*" she snarls at Stacy.

Wide eyes. Begrudging expression. "But Mom—"

"*Go.*"

Stacy hesitates one more second then turns and walks out of the bathroom.

Leaving me alone with Cathy.

Who stares at me for a long, long time.

Right. Yeah, that's enough of that.

I turn for the door and—

It swings open.

Revealing King.

He takes one look at me and the murder that bleeds onto his face...

God, it shouldn't make my heart happy.

It still does though.

King and I versus the world.

"Princess?" he rasps.

"I'm okay," I tell him, rage making my hands shake. But my voice is steady when I say, "I'm done with them all."

Blue eyes on mine—searching, holding, then he nods, glances over my shoulder. "You'll gather your daughters and you'll leave." A beat. "Immediately."

Cathy's mouth opens.

"And if I see you, if my mom sees you, if I hear that annoying voice of yours for even a second, you'll regret it."

Defiance on her face, and I know King's threats aren't going to get through that stubborn skull of hers.

"I retained a lawyer," I blurt.

She stills. "You don't have any proof about Stacy—"

"Not about Stacy," I say, moving toward her, holding her gaze. "About my father's will..."

Her face goes pale.

"And how you spent my inheritance—"

"That didn't happen—"

Be brave.

I lift my brows, hold her gaze. "Didn't it?"

Brave and kind…and bullshit when necessary.

Because I don't have proof.

Because I never pursued it.

Because I didn't want to rock the boat.

But know what?

I'm diving right in and swimming to shore.

Her throat works. "You wouldn't."

I tilt my head to the side. "Wouldn't I?"

King steps next to me, takes my hand, giving me support without taking over.

God, I love this man.

"You should go," I tell her.

Cathy looks between us, hesitates, and then walks out the door.

King waits for it to shut behind her before he turns to me. "Christ, princess, do you ever not find trouble?"

"I think the question is why does trouble always find me?" I rest my forehead against his. "Are you okay?" I ask as I touch his temple. "In here?"

Because this isn't his fault.

But I know this is a trigger for him, another bit of fucked-up to add to our tally.

He tucks my hair behind my ear, leans close, sighs quietly. "You and me against the world, right?"

My throat goes tight.

God, I love this man.

"You and me against the world," I agree quietly.

Lips on my forehead before he pulls back enough to meet my eyes. "You hurt?"

And I know I can give him the truth, that no matter what, we'll sort it. *Together.*

"Nothing an ice pack and a couple of aspirin won't fix," I tell him. I glance down at the shredded bodice of my gown.

"My dress, on the other hand..." I sigh. "How the hell am I supposed to go out there with my dress like this?"

"Funny story—"

We both jump, and I turn to see Jean-Michel standing in the open door, a security guard hauling Cathy away behind him.

"—I can help with the crazy stepmother and sisters, that stolen inheritance, and"—he holds up a garment bag—"a replacement dress."

My eyes go to King's and even though it should be the last thing I'm feeling, I'm doing—

I start laughing.

King leans in, settles his hands on my face, puts his lips to my ear, murmurs,

"Fairy fucking godfather."

EPILOGUE

I push into the mudroom, hearing the sound of Christmas music drifting down the hall.

Grinning, loving that I get to come home to this, loving that Jean-Michel pulled me into his office today to tell me that Phillip's lawyer quit and because he's out of options, he's taking a deal that will put him behind bars for a long time.

Loving that Jean-Michel's news didn't end there.

He's hired a private investigator.

And they uncovered evidence of Rory's stepmother doctoring her father's will and hiding funds from the estate.

Funds that should have gone to Rory.

So, all in all, I have some great fucking news to deliver.

And, all in all, I can't wait to celebrate.

It's almost Christmas. My mom's in town for a couple of days before she goes up to hang with Jakob and the twins. The team has, dare I say, been getting along (with the exception of Pat, as always). We have a winning record. The locker room is sorted. The guys are focused.

And...I'm happy.

In love.

Not my father. Not my brothers. Not my friend.

Just...me.

And that doesn't sit like a blanket made out of barbed wire on my skin any longer.

It's right.

It's fucking perfect.

Just like Rory is—my beautiful princess, who's singing softly in the kitchen, hips swaying to the music, the pup we're fostering sprawled out near her feet.

I lean back against the opening, cross my ankles, and watch her move.

My dick twitches—like it always does when I see her.

Fucking gorgeous, especially as she slowly spins in my direction, lips parting on a gasp when she spots me.

A gasp that becomes a sweet smile the moment she realizes it's me.

A smile that melts when I take her in my arms, when I hold her close as we slowly rock to the music.

"How was practice?" she asks as the song winds down.

I press a kiss to her forehead. "Not terrible."

She grins, touches my cheek. "Considering Pat, I think *not terrible* is a victory."

I snort. "Exactly."

"Your mom is walking Zeus," she says. "And, as usual, he's abandoned me for the allure of Mama Bang. Though"—a nod to our foster, Gunner, who's barely bothered to open his eyes, the pup beyond lazy—"our guy there couldn't be tempted from his nap to join them."

"I'd prefer you didn't pair the words *tempted* and *allure* with my mom's moniker, princess."

"Why?" she asks, feigning innocence as she scratches Gunner between his ears. "Your mom is a full-blooded woman with needs and—"

I shudder. "Princess."

"Don't you mean Cactus Queen?"

God, she's fucking adorable.

And proud of herself for her sass.

And—

I draw her up against me, kiss her until we're both breathing heavy. "I fucking love you."

Soft eyes.

Her body melting against mine.

I take her hand, lift her arm so that I can clip on the newest charm I bought her—or rather *two* charms that form the number I wear for the Eagles.

One. Nine. Nineteen.

"King," she whispers, touching a finger to the crystal-studded numbers. "I'm going to run out of room."

"Then you'll need another bracelet for all the happy we make. And when *that's* full..." I brush my lips over hers. "I'll get you another." Another brush, this time over the diamond ring that's still sitting on her finger. "And another." Her forehead. Each cheek. The tip of her nose. "And another."

She sighs, melting against me. "God, I love you."

I waggle my brows. "Interested in showing me exactly how much?"

She giggles then gasps when I shift my hips and she realizes that I'm serious.

And hard.

"You're mom's just walking Zeus," she says. "She'll be back soon and we don't have time to—"

"We have time," I tell her, scooping her up, setting her on the counter. "We'll be quick—"

The front door slams open.

"Yoohoo!" my mom calls. "We're back!"

I sigh, drop my forehead against hers. "Christ."

Rory grins. "Told you."

Stealing one more kiss, I wrap my arms more tightly around her, bringing her down from the counter and setting her on her feet.

Then I dig my cell out of my pocket, start tapping at the screen, making quick work of my newly forming plan, greeting Zeus when he deigns to acknowledge my presence.

(This after my mom has rewarded him and Gunner—who's decided that treats are a worthwhile disruption to his nap—with a cookie each and he's gotten his fill of cuddles from Rory).

"Hey, bud," I mutter, getting down on my haunches and scratching him behind his floofy ears.

Then doing the same for Gunner when he joins in, resting his head on my knee.

My mom is chatting with Rory, both of them bent over my binder, discussing dinner ideas and grocery shopping for the next few days, and as much as I love making lists and planning ahead and putting together spreadsheets, I want my house back.

I want it to be just Rory and I.

I want to spend Christmas with my woman. *Alone.*

I want to fuck her on the kitchen counter without risking my mom walking in.

Which brings me back to my hastily put together plan.

"Mom," I say, tapping on my cell's screen again, sending the plane ticket I just bought to her via text.

"I think it's time for you to go visit Jakob."

Dear Diane,

Maybe I should be upset for being so unceremoniously kicked out of King's place.

But I'm not.

Young love is blooming in my eldest's house.

He and Rory need the space, and my matchmaking efforts—such as they were—are better suited elsewhere.

Jakob is so hurt, so angry.

And I get it.

I know Theresa's actions wounded him deeply.

But his boys, his beautiful, rambunctious boys need more.

And my Jakob...he deserves the world.

So, I didn't argue with King when he sent me the ticket, when he packed me off to the airport and hugged me goodbye just outside of security. I didn't argue that my trip with him and Rory was cut short.

They're happy and in love.

And I need more grandbabies.

So, old friend...

One of my kids is settled.

Now I need to make sure that the rest are as well.

Next up is Jakob.

Wish me luck—I have the feeling he's going to be a tough nut to crack.

Good thing it's Christmas time and there's no shortage of nutcrackers all around. 🙂

Love, Stella

King

"What?" Rory asks as we wave at my mom and she disappears in the direction of her gate, trusty rolling bag behind her.

"*What,* what?" I say, slinging my arm around her shoulders and tucking her close.

"Why are you smirking?" she asks.

I tug a strand of her hair then hold up my phone, showing her the texts I just sent to my brother.

And his unhappy response about Mama Bang coming early...

On a matchmaking mission.

"Your brother just might kill you," she says.

I shrug. "I can take him. Plus..."

Her hand slips into the waistband of my jeans, holding me as close as I'm holding her. "Plus, what?"

"*Plus*"—I drag her to a stop, kiss the top of her head—"a little merry matchmaking might do him some good."

THANK YOU FOR READING! I hope you enjoyed Rory and King's story as much as I did! Want to find out more about what Mama Bang has in store for Jakob? Find out in SHOW 'EM HOW. **She's all wrong for my boys and me, but tell that to my stupid heart.**

CLICK HERE TO READ SHOW 'EM HOW NOW>

IF YOU LOVED LACE 'EM UP and need more Eagles hockey boys, check out BROKEN LACES, book 1 of the Eagles Hockey series. **He's the captain...I'm the owner's daughter.**

CLICK HERE TO READ BROKEN LACES NOW>

AND IF YOU want more Jean-Michel...check out BOTTLES AND BLADES. **He's ruthless and goes after what he wants. And he's decided... That's me.**

CLICK HERE TO READ BOTTLES AND BLADES NOW>

I SO APPRECIATE your help in spreading the word about my books, including sharing with friends! Please leave a review on your favorite book site!

You can also join my Facebook group, <u>the Fabinators</u>, for exclusive giveaways and sneak peeks of future books.

If you'd like to receive emails from me for new releases and monthly giveaway sign up for my newsletter at https://www.elisefaber.com/newsletter

Meet the Bang Brothers—five hot hockey-playing brothers who are allergic to commitment.
The brothers are about to face off against their newly-retired mother...who suddenly has plenty of time to play matchmaker. Add in their baby sister and some secret dating, a single dad, an accidental pregnancy, a marriage of convenience, and a wrong bed—or two—and these siblings are not going to know what hit them!

Lace 'em Up
Show 'em How
Hit 'em Hard
Lock 'em Down
Light 'em Up
Hook 'em Hard

Broken

Boldly

Breathless

Ballsy

Bewitched

Blowout

Breathe

Blazed

Sierra Hockey Series

Over the Line

Caught from Behind

On the Fly

The Big Skate

Rush Hockey Trilogy #1

Big Puck Energy

Filthy Puckboy

So Pucking Over It

Rush Hockey Trilogy #2

Love, Pucks, and Other Stories

All's Fair in Pucks and War

No Pucks Lost Between Us

Rush Hockey Trilogy #3

Puck and Make Up

Blinded By Pucks

Match Made in Pucks

Eagles Hockey Series (all stand alone)

Broken Laces

Knotted Laces

Lace 'em Up

Sinful Bosses (all stand alone)

Ruthless Billionaire

***Billionaire's Club* (all stand alone)**

Bad Night Stand

Bad Breakup

Bad Husband

Bad Hookup

Bad Divorce

Bad Fiancé

Bad Boyfriend

Bad Blind Date

Bad Wedding

Bad Engagement

Bad Bridesmaid

Bad Swipe

Bad Girlfriend

Bad Best Friend

Bad Rebound

Bad Romance

Bad Business

Bad Billionaire's Quickies

Love, Action, Camera (all stand alone)

Dotted Line

Action Shot

Close-Up

End Scene

Meet Cute

Love After Midnight **(all stand alone)**

Rum And Notes

Virgin Daiquiri

On The Rocks

Sex On The Seats

Life Sucks Series

Train Wreck

Hot Mess

Dumpster Fire

Clusterf*@k

FUBAR

Perfect Storm

Free Fall

Lost Cause

Roosevelt Ranch Series **(all stand alone, series complete)**

Disaster at Roosevelt Ranch

Heartbreak at Roosevelt Ranch

Collision at Roosevelt Ranch

Regret at Roosevelt Ranch

Desire at Roosevelt Ranch

***Phoenix Series* (read in order)**

Phoenix Rising

Dark Phoenix

Phoenix Freed

***Phoenix: LexTal Chronicles* (rereleasing soon, stand alone, Phoenix world)**

From Ashes

In Flames

To Smoke

***KTS Series* (all stand alone, series complete)**

Riding The Edge

Crossing The Line

Leveling The Field

Scorching The Earth

Cocky Heroes World

Tattooed Troublemaker

ABOUT THE AUTHOR

USA Today bestselling author, Elise Faber, loves chocolate, Star Wars, Harry Potter, and hockey (the order depending on the day and how well her team — the Sharks! — are playing). She and her husband also play as much hockey as they can squeeze into their schedules, so much so that their typical date night is spent on the ice. Elise is the mom to two exuberant boys and lives in Northern California. Connect with her in her Facebook group, the Fabinators or find more information about her books at www.elisefaber.com.

facebook.com/elisefaberauthor

amazon.com/author/elisefaber

bookbub.com/profile/elise-faber

instagram.com/elisefaber

tiktok.com/@elisefaberauthor

goodreads.com/elisefaber